WITHOUT WARNING,
THE MEXICAN LUNGED FORWARD.

His left hand flew up to distract and his right sent the long, sharp blade of his weapon lancing in a snake-quick upthrust toward Slocum's belly.

Slocum sucked his lean gut back enough, just barely enough, to let the blade pass, and while the Comanchero was off balance and extended, Slocum flicked his own edge upward beneath the man's outthrust arm. The keen, rising edge of Slocum's knife swept along the underside of his opponent's wrist.

The Mexican looked up with stark terror in his eyes as the knife fell from his suddenly nerveless fingers.

JAKE LOGAN
HELLFIRE

PLAYBOY
PAPERBACKS

Published simultaneously in the United States and Canada by Playboy Paperbacks, New York, New York. Printed in the United States of America. Library of Congress Catalog Card Number: 80-83591. First edition.

Books are available at quantity discounts for promotional and industrial use. For further information, write to Premium Sales, Playboy Paperbacks, 747 Third Avenue, New York, New York 10017.

ISBN: 0-872-16795-X

First printing March 1981.

CHAPTER 1

Slocum pulled the leggy roan into an easy lope. Tension dragged his face into a grim set, but nothing he felt was communicated to the sweating horse. He did not want the horse to become anxious; nor, in spite of his need for haste, could he afford to wear the animal out now. John Slocum knew that in a long chase speed is not nearly as important as endurance, and he was a master at wringing the most from a tiring mount. Already he had gained a lead of twenty minutes on his pursuers—possibly more. He reached forward and felt the horse's sweat. There was no lather yet. He might have found a good mount had he had the time for a leisurely selection, but not with the bullets flying and that half-wit Dewey grabbing at his leg and yelling for him to stay. The whole screw-up was of Dewey's making, and the way Slocum saw it, the man deserved whatever grief he got. The problem was that Dewey was not the only one involved.

John Slocum snorted, causing the roan to flick an ear back toward him. For a moment the hardness of his expression twisted into an equally hard grin. He really couldn't kick. Talbot was dead, but Slocum's oft-courted luck was holding—so far. He was alive and

5

he had a horse between his knees. He knew better than to ask for more.

That morning there had been three of them: Slocum and George Talbot, who was a solid man and a good one to ride with, and Dewey Sinclair. Talbot had set it up, but he had only Dewey to side him. They had been together a long time, apparently. Even with the allowances Talbot had made for his friend, he had not been willing to go into the bank with Dewey, so the two of them had invited Slocum in for a share.

It had seemed a good plan when Talbot told him about it. Damn it, it *was* a good plan. Slocum had questioned every detail, and Talbot had had an answer to every question. Talbot had already sketched the interior of the bank, knew the lunch schedules of the employees so they would have had to handle as few people as possible, knew exactly the way it should have worked out and when.

They had needed a Thursday—before the few employers in Salt Creek pulled out cash to pay their workers and after the preceding week's payrolls had had time to return to the bank—and they had needed a day when the boy tending the town herd of milk cows and slaughter steers took the animals west of the creek to graze them. Salt Creek lay in a shallow basin. Runoff water had cut a chain of deep, sharp-sided arroyos west of the town. There was only one good crossing through that broken country, and to reach the grass beyond the crossing, all the cattle were funneled through it and allowed to spread out on the other side. By making their escape over ground so recently churned by the cattle's hooves, Talbot had reasoned that there would be no chance of anyone tracking them.

They had waited three weeks on short rations to get a Thursday when the herder would take his charges through that crossing. That morning they had saddled, leaving pack horses and extra weapons hidden near the camp. The chase—it was inevitable that there would be one—had not been expected to go anywhere near there, and a man doesn't want to burden his horse with surplus iron when he has some serious running to do. Together the three had ridden quietly into Salt Creek and left Dewey handling the horses beside the stone bank building.

Everything had been going just fine and dandy. As Slocum and Talbot arrived, the bank president and his head cashier were leaving. They had exchanged greetings as the one pair exited and the other entered. The inside of the bank had been just as Talbot had drawn it: one teller in the cage, another employee at a desk behind the wooden barrier. There was only one customer, a heavily rouged woman of middle years and abundant bosom. She looked experienced enough to take on a dozen muleskinners without breaking rhythm, and tough enough to whip them instead if that was required.

Slocum sidestepped to the right as soon as he had cleared the doorway and had dragged his iron to where it could be seen clearly. Talbot had slid off to the left and into the caged-off area.

"What we are doing here," Slocum announced calmly, "is making a sudden withdrawal. No need for fuss 'n' feathers. No need for anyone to get hurt. Ma'am?" Slocum had tipped his hat with his left hand. "Have you gotten your deposit receipt?"

She nodded.

"Then kindly shove that wad of currency over where my friend can reach it. It's the bank's to stand food for now." An almost boyish grin touched his lips. "And we need it worse than they do."

The old bawd gave him a professional looking-over. The anger—there had been no fear there—had left her face and she said, "Come spend some of it back with me and my girls, why don't you. Unless you object to the company of good honest whores."

"No objection at all, ma'am, except when I'm broke."

"Mister, you might be welcome even then if what you're hiding matches what I can see."

Slocum nodded his thanks. The exchange had been more than just so much banter. It gave the bank employees something to think about while Talbot helped himself to a sackful of currency and a few pounds of gold coin. The bulge in that canvas sack made it look like the trip had been well worthwhile, and things were going very nicely indeed. A moment more and they would be gone and no one stirred up by bloodshed. These plainsmen were funny that way. Steal their banker's cash and they wanted you, but the posse was as much an outing as it was a chase. But shoot one of their friends and they became insistent about it all. Underestimate a man with grit enough to take up a home and family life out in the raw lands and you've done a damn-fool thing.

It was going just fine, Slocum thought, and the old madam had helped and probably was sharp enough to know it. Just then he heard a shot out in the street, and quickly afterward, two more.

"Shit, George, move it."

Talbot had his gun out again now and should have had things under control, for it was beginning to sound like Slocum was needed outside the bank a whole lot more than inside. He checked on Talbot and wheeled into a crouch before darting through the doorway to the exposed sidewalk beyond. There had been no temptation about staying inside the solid bank walls, though. Any sense of sheltered protection there would have been illusory once there was a mob of townspeople howling for bank-robber blood on the other side of those walls.

There were three or four men already in the street narby with guns drawn and working. Slocum ran toward the horses. "I'm with you," he heard Talbot holler from inside the bank.

As soon as he burst into the alley where they had left Dewey and the horses, it was obvious what had happened. Christ, it couldn't have been much worse if the stupid bastard had raped the mayor's wife while he was at it.

It had been the first shot that had done the damage, and Slocum was willing to bet his hope for tomorrow —hell, he already *had* bet his hope for tomorrow—on what had happened. Dewey had been paying attention to the street, and when someone came up behind him in the alley, he had turned and fired without bothering to see who was coming at him. Jumpy nerves and a guilty conscience, and now they were all in a pickle, damn the man.

Because behind Dewey, near the pawing hooves of their three horses, lay the body of a boy, a kid who could not have been well into his teens if he was that old. At least there was not much blood showing. Maybe the kid would not die, not that it had made any difference at this point. Their fat was clearly in the fire.

Out on the street someone was shooting again, and now there was enough time for them to know where and what they were trying to hit. Directly across the street from the alleymouth someone began knocking glass out of a store window, and Slocum could see several rifle barrels being used for that purpose. It was time to move.

"Let's git," he yelled. He snapped two shots through the newly broken window in the hope that that would discourage whoever was in there. "Come runnin', George," he hollered around the stone corner of the bank.

Slocum fired his last three cartridges in an effort to give Talbot cover.

Talbot bolted through the doorway and ran toward the corner where Slocum was waiting. Talbot's boots rang hollowly against the wooden sidewalk, and his progress seemed as slow as if he had been running hip deep in blackstrap molasses.

Across the street the townspeople began firing again, and Talbot went down like a marionette with its strings cut. The heavy bag, full of the cash they had risked so much to get, hit the boardwalk and went skittering into the dirt of the street, fully exposed to the rifle fire from across the way.

"Georgie!" It was Dewey's voice, coming from the other side of the alleymouth. Slocum had forgotten about him being there. Dewey dropped his revolver, actually dropped it right down into the dust, and began running toward his friend.

"You damned fool," Slocum muttered, his eyes on Dewey but his fingers flying to punch the empties out of his cylinder and reload with fresh ammunition plucked from his belt. No time for niceties of safety now; he loaded all six chambers.

Slocum was about to reach a foot forward to trip Dewey and keep him from going out onto the sidewalk when one of the townspeople did the job for him. A bullet smashed into the man's leg and knocked him down at Slocum's feet. Slocum had no time for holding his hand at the moment. He fired twice through the now completely glassless window across from them. That seemed to be where the most effective fire was coming from, and under other circumstances Slocum probably would have admired whoever was in there doing all the thinking and all the shooting.

"Crawl for the horses, Dewey. I'll hold them a few seconds more and then we gotta go, boy. Move it!"

Instead, Dewey clutched Slocum's pantlegs and began whimpering something about not leaving his good buddy George.

"Talbot's dead, you idiot. Now move or I leave you."

Still Dewey lay there sobbing and pleading for George and then for Slocum to pick him up and carry him along, not to leave him, to do something to save them all.

Slocum had no more patience and no more time. He could hear running footsteps on the boardwalk somewhere out of his sight. He did not know for sure how many or where they were heading, but they were entirely too close for him to wait to find out.

"Let go of me, you son-of-a-bitch." Slocum kicked Dewey off of his pantleg and began retreating back toward the horses.

Slocum turned and grabbed for the bridle of his own horse, but a bullet found the animal first. The horse lunged forward in its death throes and knocked Slocum into the wall.

Slocum fired another round out of the alleymouth without bothering to aim. He just wanted the townspeople to stay afraid of him for a few seconds longer.

The horse went down and Slocum vaulted over it, grabbing for the nearest bridle on a still-living horse.

The animal—it was Talbot's—was panicked by then. Gunfire, smoke, and now the sharp, coppery scent of blood were too much for it and it shied away and ran, Dewey's scuffy pony galloping behind it with loose stirrups flopping, bucking and farting as it ran.

In the past, John Slocum had been known to indulge in select cursing and he did so again now, cussing the horses, Dewey, and those hard-shooting townsmen equally. Slocum began to race down the alley toward the backs of the Main Street buildings, desperately hoping no one had yet thought to get behind them.

"For God's sake, Slocum, don't leave me," he heard

Dewey call, and a moment later, "I give up. Don't shoot. I quit. Please!"

Terrific. That was all Slocum needed, he realized. Now that Dewey had caused the problem, he was going to compound it. Within a few minutes the good people of Salt Creek would know all about John Slocum, their hideout, where the fresh horses and spare guns were —everything Dewey could tumble past his tongue to tell them. And then they would still hang the simple-minded son-of-a-bitch. Slocum hoped so. If there had been time for it Slocum would have turned back and done a job on Dewey himself.

Behind the bank Slocum turned left: He had been running down the left side of the alley and wanted the protection of that stonework right now. In back of the line of commercial buildings was a maze of picket fences, sheds, and small stables and carriage houses. The ground was littered with enough cast-off trash to make a body think the town was much older than Slocum knew it actually to be. He angled left and for-ward toward the flimsy protection of a wooden shed. From the other end of the bank building two men burst into view with guns exposed and the glitter of a star on one's chest.

Just what I need right now, Slocum thought. He threw a shot at the sheriff or deputy or town drunk, whoever it was with the shiny target on his shirt. The bullet flew wide but it was close enough to send both men scrambling for the same stonework protection that Slocum had been hoping to enjoy.

Slocum changed direction and began pounding the ground with his boots as hard and fast as he could lay them down. Behind him he could hear shouts and shouted instructions but no more gunfire—for the moment. They would be on to him again soon enough, he knew.

He ran out onto a street parallel to Main, crossed it

at a dead run, and raced through the shrubbery in the front yard of a handsome, white-painted home in the next block. He rounded the house and came face to face with a housewife sweeping off her back stoop.

"Mornin', ma'am," he panted as he loped by at a slightly slower pace. The big .45 still filled his right hand but he used his left to make a pass at his hatbrim.

The woman—she could not have failed to hear all the shooting a block away—blanched and clutched her broom in a clublike gesture in spite of his mock courtesy. Slocum had not intended to visit with her anyway. He ran on by.

He leaped a low fence that separated the broomstick lady's yard from another to the rear of her house. A line of saplings had been planted beside a dusty driveway leading from the street back to a carriage house in that yard. He was becoming winded now and slowed still farther to a fast jog as he headed toward the street.

At the front of that house, more elegantly designed but not as carefully maintained as the first, someone had tied a saddle horse to a hitching post. Slocum thanked whatever star he was traveling under and dropped to a walk to approach the animal. He took the reins from the ornamental brass ring of the hitching post and dropped his Colt back into its holster. He swung astride the horse, finding the stirrups somewhat too short for his six-feet-plus frame. Not that he was going to stop long enough to adjust them.

The front door of the house opened with a protesting creak, and a man stepped out onto the porch. He was a well-dressed man, and Slocum was certain he had seen the fellow somewhere before. He remembered then and was almost amused. It was the bank president, to whom he had nodded on the sidewalk only a few minutes before.

"What . . . ?"

Slocum threw the man a tight-faced grin and laid the steel to the tall roan's flanks. He did not bother to wave good-bye to the loudly protesting bank president.

Now, several hours but not nearly enough miles later, both horse and man were settling into the deceptively slow pace of a long chase.

The carefully-thought-out ruse involving the cattle tracks had been no help whatsoever. Talbot had planned on an alarm being raised after they were already clear and riding, the townspeople requiring time to discover that their bank had been emptied, to decide to do something about it, and then to gather their horses and themselves into a posse. All of that would have taken time. Instead, thanks to Dewey, the gunfire had given them instant notice and equally instant intent, and they had been reaching for their horses while Slocum had been stealing his. They had followed him across the flats and through the arroyo so closely that several optimists among them had insisted on shooting while they rode. None had come close enough to be a real danger, but the idea was quite bad enough. At least, Slocum thought almost gratefully, he had been fortunate enough to steal the horse of a man rich enough to afford quality and wise enough, or lucky enough, to find an animal worth buying. The roan was turning out to be an animal with real bottom, and for that John Slocum was thankful.

He moved over the ground at a high lope, wishing without hope that he could find a lava field or some such rough and rocky place where he could lose the posse. As it was, there seemed to be only dirt and grass before him all the way to the Rocky Mountains, with no forests or badlands offering the conditions he so dearly needed. Again, forcefully, he reminded himself that he was damned lucky to be where he was and not back in Salt Creek with the dead Talbot and the soon-to-be-dead Dewey Sinclair, damn his eyes anyway.

Slocum sighed and tried to assume a stoicism he really did not feel at that moment. He tilted his hat back to let a little cooling air reach his scalp and tugged the battered Stetson back firmly into place. This promised to be a long, lonesome run and one that he had damn well better win.

CHAPTER 2

This was turning out to be a truly miserable evening, although with the posse apparently lost, finally, somewhere behind him, it should instead have been a night for celebration. The sky was clear and the breeze fresh. The stars made a blanket of purest silver over him. Unfortunately, that blanket of stars was the only blanket John Slocum happened to possess at the moment.

The Salt Creek banker quite obviously was not a man who traveled the Big Empty on this horse. When Slocum took it the roan had a saddle and bridle but no saddlebags loaded with the goodies that make a night camp a place of comfort. Worse yet, the banker had preferred a thick hair pad to protect the roan's back from saddle chafing instead of the much more common folded blanket. From Slocum's current viewpoint that was a most foolish and uncomfortable choice. Many times in the past he had wrapped himself in a sweat-soaked blanket, enduring the smell in fair swap for the warmth. But you cannot do the same with a pad, and all of his own gear had had to be abandoned back in that alley. Now he was finding the high breeze a torment instead of the clean, crisp joy it might otherwise have been.

Having nothing else to do the job with, Slocum wrapped himself in his own arms and tried to burrow a little deeper in the loose sand at the base of the cut-bank where he was huddled. He knew better than to camp in a dry wash, but at the moment he was more interested in warmth than he was worried about the unlikely danger of a flash flood. He pulled his arms even more tightly against himself.

Slocum cursed viciously under his breath. If he had been keeping track of the days properly this was the night there should have been another pair of arms wrapped around his lean, muscular frame. This was the night Anna had planned to meet him at the stage stop southeast of Salt Creek. Knowing Anna and her passionate nature he was positive she would be there, one way or another. He was also positive that Anna would have no great difficulty in finding someone to replace John Slocum in her affections when Slocum failed to make that rendezvous.

Anna. Anna Brigid Mueller. Despite the cold, despite his anger, Slocum began to get an erection from thinking about her.

John Slocum was a man to whom women came easily and often. He had known his share of them and more, but Anna had been a truly fine specimen.

Anna was an emigrant from Germany, coming to the United States as a child bride and years later retaining an accent that would have made it impossible for her to hide her origins. She was thirtyish now but no man in his right mind would have held that against her.

Most likely she was of peasant stock. Certainly she was no dainty and delicate flower so fragile it would crumble at the touch. She was a tall woman, nearly as tall as Slocum himself, and he stood inches taller than most men.

For all her size, though, Anna's body was in magnificent proportion, from her well-turned ankles to her regal, gold-crowned brow. But it was what could be found in between that first attracted Slocum's attention. Her hips were rounded and full and, Slocum had good reason to know, powerful enough to batter a man into bruised submission unless he could match her with a stallion's driving power. Her waist was girlishly slim in comparison with the rest of her, never thickened by childbearing or by the potato pancakes she made so well. And her breasts—Slocum smiled in the cold darkness—now, there was a pair that mountains might properly be named after. As perhaps some had been. Perhaps the Grand Tetons had been named in fond memory of Anna Mueller. The man who first coined the old expression about more than a mouthful being wasted had never met Anna Mueller. Yet as big as they were, they were high and firm and beautifully rose-tipped. Slocum smiled again and squeezed his hands into fists involuntarily as he thought about once again taking a double handful of Anna Mueller's tits.

Best of all, though, was that glorious, furry mound between sleek, long thighs. This was a woman who was able to milk him as completely as she was able to milk her husband's cows. John Slocum moaned aloud into the chill, moving air. He remembered quite well the first time he had seen her.

It was two weeks ago, while he and Talbot and Sinclair were waiting for the right combination of events that would allow them to hit the Salt Creek bank. It was on a Tuesday morning.

The Muellers lived on a dryland farm where Karl, twenty-three years his wife's senior, was destined to fail as a farmer, as he apparently had failed at everything else he had tried.

Slocum was on horseback, wandering the countryside around the town. His excuse was that he wanted to know the land better in case they could not use Talbot's route. The truth was that he was just plain bored with

Dewey Sinclair's company and would have found nearly anything else preferable.

Slocum had been riding for several hours and was growing a little thirsty when he saw the Mueller farmstead. He also was hoping he might be able to exchange some flattery or even a little time on the farm woodpile in return for a decent meal. Breakfast that morning had been rice and greasy gravy left over from the night before. He rode into the yard without expectation and found himself confronted by a golden-haired Valkyrie.

She was hanging clothes from a washtub onto fence rails when Slocum rode up. She was wringing them out by hand and draping each piece over the peeled wood. Her dress was not one she had made for herself, for it was too small for her, the material unable to contain the full swell of her breasts, and the hem short enough to show a good amount of ankle above her heavy shoes.

"Ma'am." Slocum reined to a halt beside her, handling his mount carefully so it would not kick dust into her laundry. He touched the brim of his hat with the customary politeness of the time and place but he had neither the desire nor the ability to ignore the poorly concealed body beneath straining cloth.

"*Ja,* step down. Step down."

He did and when he stood beside her he was both pleased and surprised to find that her eyes were nearly on a level with his own.

"You are looking for Karl? He is not here."

"No, I was hoping to find some breakfast, actually. I don't have much money, but . . ."

She waved aside whatever else he might have said. Anna Mueller knew what it was to be poor; she had never known anything else. "Come." She set her laundry aside and motioned for him to follow her into the crude shack that was her home.

Slocum removed his hat and scraped his boots before he entered the shack, and once inside he was glad he had done so. The shack for all its cramped ugliness was as tidy and as clean inside as the most elegant Denver hotel.

She had coffee on the stove and poured a cup for him at once. The coffee was strong and tasted old but it was coffee. He sat and sipped at it while the woman added wood to the firebox. When she was satisfied with her fire she set an iron griddle onto the stove and greased it with some drippings from a small crock. She took a cloth-covered bowl from a shelf near the stove and from it dipped a pale, lumpy batter onto the griddle. It was Slocum's first experience with potato pancakes. He might have been more appreciative of them if he had not been so preoccupied with wondering how the buttons on her dress managed to remain attached to the material. And with wishing they would not.

When he pushed his plate away after the best meal he had had in weeks he accepted another cup of the stout coffee and pulled a cheap rum crook from his shirt pocket. The woman lighted a pine sliver in the stove fire and leaned across the table to offer the light to Slocum. Slocum damn near choked. It just wasn't natural that mere cloth could take so much strain and not bust wide open.

The woman saw where Slocum's eyes were locked. She smiled. That, right there, was enough to set Slocum's cock to throbbing. All *right*.

John Slocum was no great respecter of the sanctity of marriage. He would happily ball any married woman who cared to spread her legs for him, with or without her husband's permission. And oddly enough, he had known one or two who had not minded giving that permission. But he did draw the line at rape. A man can, after all, maintain his own pride and personal sense of honor without going to goody-two-shoes extremes about the thing. Further, if John Slocum ever hanged—and even he conceded a strong possibility that he would—it was not going to be done by some angry farmer whose wife Slocum played an unwelcome game of grab-ass with.

But a *welcomed* game of grab-ass was just his meat, particularly when the main course was so deliciously enticing. The woman's smiling response to Slocum's stare was all the invitation he felt he needed.

"What's your name, ma'am?" he asked politely.

She told him.

"That's always a nice thing to know," he said. He motioned her a step closer and she moved near him without objection. "Why don't you slip that coffee pot over to the side of the stove, Anna, so's there will be some hot and ready when we aren't anymore?" He was smiling when he said that, his eyes languid and dark. He ran a hand down the rounded flare of her hip and onto the long, sturdy column of smooth, firm flesh that was her thigh.

Slocum was watching Anna's face as he touched her, and her reaction was all he might have hoped for. Instead of drawing away in anger or mock anger, she arched her neck under the masculine touch. Her eyelids drooped and she flicked her tongue across full lips. "I'll move the coffee pot."

There was nothing false or coquettish about this woman. She completed her minor chore at the stove, turned to face Slocum, and began shedding her clothing as rapidly as she could, no teasing or toying about it. She wanted him and she did not want to wait for it.

Slocum was slower to undress than she, and impatiently she dropped to her knees and began to work on the buttons of his fly. That suited him just fine.

She was as quick with his buttons as she had been with her own and in another moment he burst free of the confinement of his jeans, ramrod stiff and pulsingly eager. He expected that she would take him into her mouth, and he was already looking forward to the wet-hot feel of her lips and tongue, but this was not a woman to do the expected. Instead she took the time to give his rod an admiring glance, planted a brief, almost absent-minded peck of a kiss on the head of his cock, and went on with the more serious business of removing his clothing so he could do her some good.

"Come," she said, making it sound as much a German word as an English one. She rose lithely to her feet and moved unself-consciously in her nakedness to the bed. She lay on it and opened her arms and her legs to him. "Come," she repeated.

"And quit already?" If she understood Slocum's feeble joke she did not mention it.

He walked slowly to the bedside and stood over her for a moment, admiring the awesome beauty of that big, perfectly formed body. She was incredible. He lowered himself onto and into her and found that she was as wet as he was hard.

Sliding himself deep into her flesh was the same as plunging into a maelstrom. No sooner had he socketed himself into her than she exploded into a turbulent passion that was more fury than it was affection. For the first time John Slocum knew what a whore must feel like when she was used by a total stranger. Anna Mueller lay beneath him and accepted the wildest pumping he could give her and somehow made him feel as if it was he who was being ravished by their coupling.

Once, long years before in a county-fair sideshow tent in Georgia, a young John Slocum had paid twenty precious cents to see a naked dancing girl and had paid another twenty to watch a more adult performance in an even smaller adjacent tent. Among other things, the dark-haired slut had plucked a thin cigar from a drummer's mouth, shoved it into her cunt and somehow blew smoke rings with the damn thing.

Since that time Slocum had learned the foolishness of paying two dimes to look at something that you could rent all night for two dollars. But he still marveled at that old girl's ability to puff on a cigar.

Yet after feeling the way Anna Mueller could milk his balls with the talented muscles of her willing crotch he was mortally certain that she too could have performed the circus trick. Damn but she did pull it out of him.

That first time was swift and violent, but the woman seemed to come as fiercely as he did and when they were done he half expected her to fling him off her bed and order him out of the house. If she had done so he would have been too weak to protest. She did not.

Instead, sated, she turned and snuggled her lovely face into the hollow of his shoulder for a moment, running her fingertips lightly across his chest and belly for several minutes. Soon her lips began to flutter in light little butterfly kisses behind his ear, down his neck and across his chest, pausing at each nipple and again at his navel, where she began to use her tonguetip also. She bent still lower and covered his limp cock with the light kisses, lapping the droplets of spent come from him and finally engulfing him.

After the tremendous explosion that had just taken place in his groin, Slocum knew that her efforts were being wasted, however much he was enjoying them.

John Slocum was wrong.

Inside her mouth, under the heat of her tongue and the pull of her moist suction, he grew erect again. He could feel the swelling of blood pumping into his cock and as it grew he could feel his cock extend the length of her mouth and deep into her throat far past the point where even a ten-dollar Denver whore would have begun to gag, for Slocum was hung like a stallion. He grinned to himself. Well, like a Shetland stud if not a Percheron.

The grin gave way to an involuntary grunt of pleasure as she applied herself fully to the task, but gently this time. Almost tenderly.

John Slocum moaned and writhed and reached out to stroke her leg and pull her around atop him to straddle his own waiting mouth.

This, he decided, was going to be a long, lovely day.

CHAPTER 3

Slocum shivered and ached and was hard again just remembering Anna Mueller.

For a week and a half, every morning as soon as Karl Mueller had packed his dinner in a lard pail and carried it off into the distant field where he was topping beets by hand, John Slocum and Anna Mueller had romped and humped until Slocum was as limp as a cotton mecate and Anna was convinced that he was the only man who could satisfy her yearnings in the days to come. She had not, she claimed, ever reached a climax except by her own hand until she met Slocum. She was not now willing to give up her newfound pleasures.

When he told her he had work to do—without explaining precisely what that work might be—she insisted on joining him. Thwarted in that, she demanded to meet him and go with him afterward for however long and in whatever capacity he would allow.

That sounded to Slocum like an entirely sensible plan, since tame pussy of such high quality was not always available. And since he expected to be reasonably wealthy anyway . . .

Now the meeting time had been reached, but the appointed place was several hundred hard miles away and John Slocum was cold, broke, hungry, and alone instead of being lodged comfortably between Anna Mueller's long, powerful thighs.

If Anna wasn't stretching his cock out of shape, well, that posse wasn't stretching his neck out of shape either. A man should learn to recognize his pleasures.

Slocum quit worrying about it and went fitfully to sleep.

Come morning and feeling reasonably secure for the first time since he thundered out of Salt Creek on the stolen roan, Slocum shot an antelope, built a fire, and spent several hours gorging himself as thoroughly as an Indian after a buffalo surround. It was the first decent food he had had in days, and he felt much better when he pointed the roan westward and drifted steadily away from the men who might still be hunting him.

Toward sundown two days later he wandered into a fallen-down, slowly melting collection of adobe walls that looked to be a likely spot for a night's shelter.

He watered the roan in the sluggish Arkansas River and dropped a loop over a hefty chunk of driftwood to drag across the flat grass to the wall remnants, still better shelter than a grove of cottonwoods in spite of their dilapidated condition. Slocum dropped the firewood near a standing corner section of the old adobe structure, unsaddled the roan, and turned it loose after hobbling it. There was ample grass on the flat land between the ruins and the river, and he had both wood and an antelope haunch with which to make himself comfortable for the night.

Shouldering the saddle and carrying the meat, he rounded the broken end of one low wall.

A round metal cylinder stopped him there. The cylindrical object happened to be the huge, gaping muzzle of a Sharps buffalo rifle.

A startled John Slocum was at one end of that muzzle, the ring of icy steel pressed lightly against his suddenly tight throat. At the other end of the big

Sharps was a gray-haired, grizzly old character who looked like he might have stepped off the frontispiece of a James Fenimore Cooper *Leatherstocking Tale* or perhaps from Washington Irving's imaginative account of the adventures of Captain Bonneville.

The old man—he had to have left his sixties behind quite some time before—was wearing a fringed leather jacket, which was not too extraordinary at the time, but the old boy also wore a breechclout and fringed leather leggings. Slocum had never seen rigging like that on a white man and one damn seldom saw it on an Indian anymore.

Considering the time of day, the phase of the moon, and the unwavering Sharps muzzle lightly nuzzling his throat, Slocum chose to view the old gentleman with benign respect if not with gushing affection.

"If you're *that* taken with a desire for privacy I'll be plumb glad to find another spot to build my fire," Slocum offered. "Jus' tell me how far you want me to go before I light again, neighbor."

"Right there will do real nice for the time bein', sonny."

In spite of himself, Slocum had to smile. It had been one hell of a long time since anyone had called him sonny. "Whatever."

"Who are you an' who you lookin' for?" the mountain man demanded.

"I can tell you the first. John Slocum. But I'm not looking for anyone here nor for anything either except a night's sleep out of the wind." He gave the man his very best grade-A, No. 1 smile and hoped it was a charming one. At that moment he would have traded his right nut to become an Irishman with the legendary Irish gift for charm, wit, and bullshit. "I seem to have come off in a hurry and forgot to pack a blanket along. But I sure ain't choicy about where I sleep. It don't have to be here, friend."

Instead of dropping away, the muzzle of the Sharps prodded more firmly against his throat. The metal was beginning to take on some warmth from its contact with Slocum's flesh. He took absolutely no comfort from that.

"I thought I already tol' you to stay put, Mr. Slocum."

"I believe you did. I was just offering."

"My hearin's just fine, thank you."

"Sure. Would you, uh, like some fresh-killed antelope?"

Slocum started to heft the bloody haunch he still held in his left hand, but immediately the Sharps muzzle pushed harder against him.

"Jus' stay like you was, boy. I like you real fine with both hands full thataway."

"Whatever you say."

The old man nodded and leaned forward down the length of the big rifle. He might have been old but he was no weakling. Even holding the twenty pounds or so of rifle one-handed, the muzzle never wavered from its snug position. The mountain man relieved Slocum of his Colt and of the heavy Bowie at Slocum's left hip.

The old boy smiled. "There now, don't you feel lighter?"

"Uh-huh. Very kind of you, I'm sure. Thoughtful, like."

"Somehow I knew you'd take it that way." He transferred Slocum's revolver and knife into the faded red-silk sash he wore around his middle and scuttled backward into the adobe corner where Slocum had thought to spend the night. The old man sat carefully, the muzzle of the Sharps a much more comfortable distance now but still unwaveringly aimed at Slocum's body. His gut this time instead of the throat. Slocum did not view the change as much of an improvement. "Sit down, sonny. Tell me about yourself."

Slocum grunted. Very carefully, very slowly he lowered the saddle and antelope haunch to the ground and joined them there. He did not much fancy his chances if he tried to duck around the wall end and leg it toward his horse. Whoever this old fellow was, he had not survived this long by way of slow reactions or poor shooting.

"Tell you about myself, huh? Mind if I smoke?"

"Go ahead."

"You want one?"

"I wouldn't mind."

Slocum fished in his pocket. Now a smart man, he thought, would have a sleeve gun or some such dandy little hideout pistol to pop this old boy with. All Slocum had was . . . he searched again . . . one lousy cigar. He shrugged, pulled the stogie out, and broke it in half. He kept the larger of the pieces for himself and tossed the other to the gentleman with the big rifle.

"Thankee."

"You're entirely welcome, believe me." That drew a tiny softening of the features. Slocum chose to view the change as a smile.

This old bird had obviously been there and back again. Normally Slocum would have tried to palm off a lie in such circumstances, and in truth he could not claim that this was the first time he had ever faced the wrong end of a gun. The way he sometimes managed to get himself into trouble amazed even Slocum at times. Often enough he went looking for it. When he didn't the trouble usually managed to find him anyway. And lying was a good and valuable tool at such moments in a man's life. The thing was, looking into the patient old eyes he was not at all sure that a lie would serve him here. The hell with it. He shrugged and grinned and told the man the truth.

The old buzzard stared him down until Slocum felt icewater running out of his armpits, but he refused to let the old man get the better of him. Slocum stared back at him as stony and as steady as the old mountain man was doing.

The old man shifted his grip on the Sharps, hooked the massive hammer with his thumb and let it down to half cock. "You can call me Squeaks." There was a twinkle in his eye when he gave his name.

Slocum obliged him with a lifted eyebrow.

Squeaks set the rifle aside without comment and seemed to be meditating somewhere in the distant past while he licked his stub of black cigar and set the tobacco aglow. "You was askin' about how I got my name, sonny? That was a long time ago. Before you was ever born, you see."

"Hell, I come out here the first time back in the twenties, back when the Rocky Mountain Fur Company was still afloat. I knew 'em all then. All the big names folks still talk about. They was just part of the crowd then, of course. Most of 'em really was as good as the stories say they was. Some of 'em better than they've been made out to be. An' some of 'em worse.

"Take that Beckwourth fella. I remember him. Knew him real good. We wintered in parties a lot then. Had to or lose our hair, by God, an' have our cods turned into a purse for some red nigger. Folks talk today 'bout how the Indians is so honorable an' oughta get a fair shake of things. You can take it from me they're a bunch of plumb mean son-o'-bitches that oughta be grassed. Take that from me." Slocum was not necessarily in agreement with that, but he did not stir the old man up by saying so.

"Anyway, I started out to tell you about that Beckworth. He was a nigger too but the black kind. Not a drop of the red in him like some will tell you now-adays. They're also saying that ol' Beckworth was a chief of the Crows. Well, listen close to me. The onliest one that started that kind of talk was ol' Beckworth himself an' he got people to believin' it because they wasn't there at the time to know any different. Me, I was there, an' I can tell you that Jim Beckworth was for a fact the lyin'est bastard ever to cross the Missoura or steal a beaver from another man's set. Why, the sorry son-of-a-bitch wasn't even a good hand at trappin'. Never could learn to set his anchor pole right. Lost a helluva lot of traps an' good pelts that way. Stole half of what he did bring in by raidin' other fellows' sets. Wasn't worth a shit, you get right down to it.

"He was good for one thing, though. Give the devil his due, by God. That nigger Beckwourth was the horniest son-of-a-bitch I ever did see an' had a way with the squaws to match it. He'd ride into a Indian camp an' park hisself in the first teepee he come to. They was expected to be his hosts, whoever lived there. Before the night was over he'd've pronged every squaw in that family. Next night he'd go on to a fresh batch. Most times he wouldn't leave the camp 'til he'd laid every broad in that camp between the ages of bleed an' quit-bleed. Didn't care what they looked nor smelled like neither. Blind or lazy, crippled or crazy. If it was warm an' had a hole somewheres in it, ol' Beckworth would fuck it."

Slocum began to pull the makings of a fire together. For such a touchy stoneface, old Squeaks was turning out to be one hell of a talker. Better to face the old bastard's tongue than his trigger, though. And the old boy *was* a sure-enough old-time mountain man. Slocum had never met one of the breed before. Hell, there weren't many left to meet. So let him talk. He didn't

seem to mind if Slocum wanted to burn some meat
while he was rambling.

"What I started out to tell you, boy, was how I come
by my name. That was back in, oh, '38 or '39, I think
it was. Some such time as that. I'd been out a long
while by then, hadn't been back to the hard-roof country in maybe five year at the time. Long as I'd been
out, though, everybody always called me by my proper
name. Joshua that was, though I haven't hardly used
it all these years now.

"Anyhow, this was early in the season, not too long
after the rendezvous. Come to think of it, that was the
last rendezvous ever held so I reckon that would place
it in '39 if it matters, which I guess now it don't.

"This was when the Blackfoot was still snake-mean
snortin' sons-of-bitches, I know that for sure. Those
red niggers used to be pure piss an' diamondback poi-
son come to life. I swear I used to think them Blackfoot bucks never humped their women except for
exercise. When they wanted a youngun they'd catch a
rattler an' shove it in the old lady's crack an' what was
birthed from that combination would be a proper
Blackfoot brave. Later on they took sick with the pox,
near all of 'em takin' down with it and the most of 'em
dyin'. They cut their balls off for fair, it did. They
never was much of a problem afterward. But that didn't
happen 'til '40-somethin' as I recall.

"Anyhow, early this one season me an' a couple
other boys—by then the business wasn't so good that
we could make out with enough of a catch to bother with
in the big parties like we used to—we was tired of not
bein' able to make a decent catch an' we took it in our
heads that we could slip up the Marias where the
Blackfoot was so thick an' by being smarter'n God we
could make out there the whole season an' come back
out with a catch like nobody's made in half a dozen
years. We really believed it, too. 'Course we was pretty

young an' pretty dumb then compared to what a sane man ought to be.

"So's we up and drag our ponies north and get good an' deep into Blackfoot country before we set up our camp. Put out a long string of traps an' make our sets as good as anybody ever has. I'll tell you that for true. We was pretty good at what we did by then, an' we did catch us some beaver. Almost as good as it'd been back in the old days, before the cricks got trapped out so bad.

"We always worked the string together, you see. One fella workin' in the water—and don't ever let nobody tell you he knows what cold is if he hasn't worked a trap string—an' the other two up on the bank coverin' him just in case the Blackfoot ain't as dumb as we want them to be.

"Well, sonny, the Blackfoot, they wasn't as dumb as we could've hoped. This one mornin', my partner down in the water—I think his name was Ed somethin'; we all called him Longdong—he got kind of interrupted in what he was doin' when some red-nigger Blackfoot shot him in the throat with an arrow. My other partner, I guess he was as surprised as me, an' like a damn fool he went an' shot *back*. Ol' Longdong was already belly up. Couldn't do *him* any good. Didn't do Hank much good neither, because a whole bunch of them red niggers jump up with a whoop an' a holler an' proceed to have them a footrace with Hank. Far as I know the Blackfoot won it 'cause I never saw Hank again. 'Course I never found any of his parts either so I can't guarantee it one way or the other.

"Me, I wasn't quite so anxious to be squaw sport. I've always fancied my pecker as providin' pleasure for a squaw, but I never wanted none of 'em to carry it home with 'em when they was done. So what I done was to dig myself a furrow, right there on the spot, an' covered myself over with fresh leaves.

"Well, I thought it was workin' pretty good 'til this buck comes creepin' along. By rights he should've been off chasin' Hank with the rest of 'em, but this one was either too lazy or too sneaky or maybe wanted to hurry back home to prong the wife of one of 'em that was doin' all the runnin'. Whatever, he was still nosin' around lookin' to see if there was more of us, which there was. I heard him comin' right close to where I was hidin', an' I'll tell you the truth, sonny. My crotch turned wet an' warm on the spot. I'd have shit my pants except I was too scared to. He would've smelled that and found me sure if I had, and that puckered me up tight as sun-dried rawhide.

"I was plenty nervous though and must have shook some for I could hear the dry leaves rattle, an' I guess he heard it too. The sound of his walkin' changed and he come creepin' in nearer and nearer. I knew he'd heard that leaf-rattle an' I figured I was probably gone. Well, he gets down on his hands and knees and I know there's no way I can keep hid that way. So I do the only thing I can think of. You ever hear a mouse squeak?" He demonstrated. Squeaks grinned. "Pretty good, huh? Well, that Blackfoot, he bought it. Went away and I never heard more of him. I stayed right there in that hole for another day an' a half just to make sure. When I got out of there I gathered up all three of us's traps—there wasn't anythin' left at our camp, they'd gone and found it and cleaned me out— and I haven't been back to that part of the country since. Don't expect to go there again neither. Couple months later I found some of the other boys an' hooked up with 'em. I told 'em the story, of course, and I've been called Squeaks ever since."

"Uh-huh," Slocum grunted. "The meat's ready."

"Good timin', boy. Hand me over a chunk." Squeaks accepted the meat, bit into the big hunk of it Slocum gave him and used his knife to saw the bite off at lip level. Slocum had heard of the old-timers doing that but he had never seen it done before, not even by Indians. It looked like a better way to lose a lip than to eat, but it wasn't any of his nevermind. It looked like the old man had made out all right so far without John Slocum's advice and likely would keep on doing without it.

CHAPTER 4

After they ate Squeaks dragged a pipe out of one of
the pouches hanging at his waist and shoved tobacco
into it. He made no offer of his plug to Slocum, and
Slocum had no pipe to burn it in anyway, but he would
have appreciated the gesture. Besides, the old man had
taken part of Slocum's last cigar. Now he was still
smoking and Slocum was not. If Squeaks noticed his
companion's mood, though, he did not mention it.

Squeaks leaned back against the crumbling adobe
in apparent contentment. "Yes, sir, sonny, it's been a
long time ago those things happened. Long time since
I been by here too but not quite *that* long. I never
come down this far south until the beaver played out
up north, though of course I wintered a few times in
Bayou Salade. Good country that used to be. They call
it South Park now but it's still the Bayou Salade to me
an' my kind."

"You know this place then?"

"Hell yes, don't you?"

Slocum shook his head, and the old man looked at
him as if he were a schoolboy who had asked a stupid
question with an obvious answer to it.

"Boy, this place was *some* when there wasn't no
such place as Denver nor Cheyenne nor much of anythin' out this far except Taos an' Santa Fe, an' neither

36

of 'em had hardly any white people in 'em. This is what's left of Bent's Fort, boy. Bent's Fort. Surely you heard of the Bents and St. Vrain. Surely you have."

"I guess I must have." And maybe Slocum was not lying, maybe he really had. If he ever did, though, it had been nothing important enough to bother remembering.

The old trapper grunted loudly. "Hell, boy, you don't know a thing about this country. Not like me, I can tell you sure. Why, this here was *the* tradin' place for a while, for down this part of the country anyhow. The Bent brothers built her about the time I come out this side of the big river. One of 'em, there was two, had had him a post farther upstream a ways but he closed that down an' him and his brother opened this place. You seen those wagon ruts when you was ridin' in?"

Slocum nodded.

"Those ruts is all that's left of the Santa Fe Trail. Now I *know* you heard about that."

He waited for Slocum's agreement before he went on.

"Yeah, well, they put this place here so they could get some business off the freighters an' get their own freight hauled and do business with the Indians too. All at the same time. A man could come here an' raise him some hell without havin' to go down into greaser country, see. Indians come here, trappers, white men, ever' damn body.

"In those days it was a whole damn fort. A real one, not like the Army builds nowadays. Those new forts is just so many shacks that happen to have bluebellies livin' in them. This here place was *big* I tell you, an' it had 'dobe walls eight foot thick and twice that tall. Never did have no kind of Army garrison, just trappers an' traders, but for a few dragoons that passed through on their way down to make Santa Fe an' that country safe for white men to trade in.

"Word for a time was that Bill Bent built the whole shebang with the idea of sellin' it to the gov'mint when they went to war with Mexico, but of course that didn't work out. The greasers down to Santa Fe rolled over an' played dead soon as there was stars an' stripes in sight of the city, and Billy's fort wasn't needed by anybody but him and his partners."

Squeaks shook his head and smiled. "Lord, but those was good times, boy. There was still beaver up in the mountains then. A man could make a fortune each an' every season and have himself two fortunes worth of fun when he took his pay for it. I know I never had so much fun as back in those summers when I was gettin' rid of my past year's work. Fight an' fuck an' likker up an' just háve a helluva time from eye-open to pass-out.

" 'Course then the beaver played out an' the market for 'em at about the same time. They said the fops an' fancy queers over across the ocean changed the kind of hats they wás wearin' and that dried the beaver market all to hell and gone. Wouldn't think a silly thing like that would affect a red heathen nigger out here a thousand miles past the nearest church, would you, boy? But it happened, surer'n hell it did. After that the Bents kept on here anyhow. They had their own piece of the Santa Fe trade an' they had business from the other freight outfits. Had them one hell of a smithy set up here they did." He waved vaguely past Slocum's left shoulder. "Right over there, it was. I remember it real well.

"They still had the Indian trade, too, of course. 'Cept they had to convince the red niggers—I think they was mostly tradin' with Utes and Cheyennes and Arapahoes—to bring in buffalo hides instead of beaver. All that time they'd been gettin' the Indians to trap beaver an' now all of a sudden it was buffalo they wanted.

Which was all right with the Indians anyhow. Takin'
beaver was a nuisance for them since you don't get so
much meat off a beaver."

He paused and squinted at Slocum. "You ever tasted
beaver tail, boy?"

Slocum shook his head patiently.

"You damn sure missed somethin' then. Man
shouldn't have to die without he gets a taste of broiled
beaver tail first. That an' roast buff'lo hump and if he's
lucky a saddle of painter cat."

Slocum cocked an eyebrow. "Painter?"

"Sure. Big cats. Mountain lion, some call them. Next
one you kill, roast you some of it. It might even beat
beaver tail for pure good."

Slocum smiled politely and nodded his head. It would
be an awfully hungry day before he ate a mountain
lion for his dinner.

"Yeah, well anyhow, there was some people back
East as was findin' out that buffalo robes are awful
warm on a winter's night and that the leather makes
tougher harness an' such than just about anythin' else
you can buy. Awful fine stuff. And some of 'em asked
the Bents to get it for 'em.

"You know, boy, I guess in a way you could say
that ol' William Bent—he's years dead now, of course
—is the one that started this whole thing about buff'lo
hides. Why, nowadays the plains is covered with hunters like fleas on a coyote's back or lice on a Piegan
squaw's pussy. Thick they are, an' when I first crossed
'em you wouldn't see a white man from the time you
left the fort here 'til you pulled into Missoura. That's
the truth. An' don't let anybody tell you different, boy.
Most of the time you could make the whole ride and
never see a hostile neither, Comanche, Kiowa, Apache,
nor Navajo. They just wasn't so many of 'em roamin'
around, though sure God did you see one he'd take
your hair or die tryin'."

"Navajo? I always thought they were a peaceable bunch."

"Huh. Don't you believe that, sonny. I remember when the Navajo was about as bad a bunch of boys as there was. Fighters? God, I mean to tell you they was. Tough and smart too. Apaches, they're just mean. So is the Kiowa. Comanche, now he's a mean son-of-a-bitch and has some brains to go with it. But I swear the Navajo was better'n any of 'em when they took the notion for it. Some reason I never could hate them as good as I could the others. Them an' the Nez Perce. Them I have to admit it. I'd take their word if they gave it an' I'd back off from fightin' with either of 'em if I could. They was that tough. The Navajo now, they quit the warpath back in the fifties or maybe sixties. Not that long ago, anyway. Carson bottled them up in a canyon down southwest of here an' across a mountain chain or two. Caught 'em cold an' give 'em a choice: Quit or go under. They said they'd quit and they did, and I don't guess they'll be on the fight ever again now that they've said they wouldn't. Most Indians I wouldn't say that about, but the Navajo I guess I would. They're a different kind of Indian."

Squeaks rubbed his jaw. "Come to think of it, maybe them not bein' so needful of the buffalo has somethin' to do with that too. The Plains tribes, now they live an' die by the buffalo an' with so many hide hunters out on the grass these days they may be figurin' they'll starve it they don't fight."

The old hunter grinned. "Ain't that a lovely thought? All them Indians up an' dyin', spread out over the ground just a-clutchin' their bellies an' goin' under. Yes, sir, I'd like to live to see that day come. I would for a fact."

"You're a sweet and a gentle soul, aren't you?" Slocum teased.

The old man went into a fit of cackling. The laughter

ended in a fit of coughs. Finally he spat into the fire and wiped his fingers on his leggings, adding a fresh layer to the grease that was already there.

"There's somethin' I expect I oughta do," he said. He pulled Slocum's Colt and big knife from his sash and tossed them across the fire to the younger man. "I don't calculate that I'll be needin' these." He grinned. "If I do it's my own damn fault for givin' 'em back."

Slocum felt better with the .45 and knife back where they belonged. "You said the buffalo hunting is going good now. That where you're headed?" He nodded toward the huge Sharps beside the old man.

"I thought some about it. Reckon I likely will. Trappin' and huntin's all I know. I been a railroad meat hunter an' ranch-country wolfer the last few years. Paid all right, really. Hell, I don't need much. A little powder and lead, a bottle from time to time. A woman when one's handy." He bared his teeth again. "I ain't so old that I'd wanta give *that* up. Don't have to neither. Takes a little longer than it used to but it feels jus' as good as ever, boy. Take that from me. Don't let no silly son-of-a-bitch tell you different. Keep it well greased an' use it often. They don't wear out from overuse."

"Thanks. I'll remember that." Not that Slocum thought he would ever live to an age to be concerned about that anyway. He had long since accepted the idea that he would die young and die hard. Well, maybe he was already too old to think he would die all *that* young. But he wasn't making any long-range plans.

Squeaks hefted his big rifle, admired it fondly for a moment and, surprisingly, handed it to Slocum.

"You ever see one of these, boy?"

"Time to time." Actually Slocum had owned—by one means or another—several Sharps rifles very much like this one. This was a particularly fine rifle, though. The lock had been engraved in a floral pattern too meticulously done for it to have been factory work, and the cheekpiece was inlaid with an elongated, eight-pointed hunter's-star emblem of German silver. "Never one as good as this," Slocum offered.

Squeaks beamed at the compliment. The words of praise might have been directed at the owner instead of the gun. "You likely never will again neither. That engraving? I did that myself three winters ago. Took near the whole winter season. That star? Cut, shaped, and inlet it myself. Nobody does that kind of work anymore."

"You sure don't see any that good, it's true."

"I used to be apprenticed to a gunsmith back . . . back East. Liked the work. Couldn't stand the man. That's when I took off and come West to see if all those tales I'd been hearin' were lies. They weren't. But I never forgot what the old bastard had taught me."

"You learned it well." Slocum turned the rifle over. There were more inlays on the underside of the forearm, these in the shape of fishes.

Squeaks saw what he was looking at. "That helps to make a gun shoot true. I know, you don't have to tell me. Don't be scoffin' in my face, son. It's superstition. They all say that. But it works, b'God. It works. Almost as good as takin' a new barrel an' cleanin' it out the right way by unpluggin' the breech—'course, you don't hafta do that with these cartridge loaders, you know—an' settin' it down in a fast-runnin', clear crick. Mind that you always put the muzzle end up-stream, though. It won't work otherwise."

"It really works, huh?"

"Absolutely."

The old man was batty as hell, Slocum decided. Squeaks sure sounded like he believed all that crap, though. Slocum went back to admiring the big Sharps, which turned out to be not nearly as old as Slocum would have expected. He flicked the finger lever to drop the heavy, machined-steel breechblock. The bore of the weapon was factory fresh and much smaller than Slocum would have guessed. "What is it?" he asked.

Squeaks nodded happily. "You like it, don't you? Well, you ought to. It's a fine gun. Not one of them slow damn .56s neither. That right there, John" (the use of Slocum's first name did not go unnoticed) "is a .50-110-550. New out from Sharps last year. They call it an express loadin'. I call it the best damn cartridge I ever in my life fired."

He cocked his head and winked at Slocum with the twinkle back in his eye. "You expected me to be some kind of stuck-in-the-mud old fuddy-duddy, didn't you, John? Admit it, I won't mind."

"It crossed my mind."

" 'Course it did. You wouldn't be a normal human person if it didn't. Well, I'll tell you somethin', John, the onliest old ways I stick with are the good ones. When a man comes along with a better idea I'll lay my money down mighy quick for the privilege of joinin' him in his good idea. Which is exactly what I did the first time I heard about this new Sharps model. I never knew a gun, 'specially a big gun like this one is, to shoot so flat an' hit so hard and yet be accurate all at the same time. This here gun, John, is a huntin' man's dream, an' that's the truth."

"If it's all that good, Squeaks, maybe I should just keep it now that I have it in my hands." He said it as a joke. More or less. John Slocum was a man who was tempted easily and tempted often, which may have accounted at least in part for why he kept finding himself in troubled waters.

The old man grinned at him. He looked perhaps even happier than when Slocum had complimented his rifle. "B'God, John, if you'd care to try that, why, I'm all for it. I ain't had a good scrap in three, four days now. Haven't killed a man in longer than that."

"You're beginning to sound downright serious," Slocum said.

"I am." He said it with a very sincere and very convincing simplicity.

Slocum gave him an indulgent smile and glanced down. Slocum held the now empty Sharps in his own hands. At Slocum's belt was the only handgun anywhere in evidence. It was not at all likely that an old mountain man like Squeaks would be carrying a hideout gun in his sleeve. "Friend, we have just been jawing here, but I do want to ask you something. Do you seriously think you could take me when I'm the only one that's armed of the two of us?"

"You're the only one with a gun, sonny. You ain't the only one armed." Slocum quickly caught the change back from John to sonny.

"I guess I'm willing to believe that you believe it, anyhow?"

Squeaks smiled. "However you want to take it. It don't make me any difference until you say you're takin' my rifle. Or tryin' to."

Slocum shook his head. "I don't steal from my friends." He reloaded the Sharps with the long, fat cartridge he had taken from it a moment earlier and handed it back, butt first and trigger handy, to its owner. "Thanks for letting me look it over. I take that as a kindly thing for you to do."

"That's the way I intended it." Squeaks laid the rifle aside tenderly. Without looking toward Slocum again he chuckled. "You don't hardly believe it, though."

Slocum shrugged.

The old trapper's hand twitched. Slocum would have sworn on a stack of Bibles or on a fifty-pound sack of cathouse tokens that the man's hand no more than twitched.

It was a little hard for Slocum to accept then that a slim-bladed Arkansas toothpick had suddenly made an appearance in a chunk of wood beside his right boot. The movement had been that quick. The knife was not there and then it was, just that fast, with only a solid thump to announce its arrival.

Slocum reached out and pulled the blade free. He had to give it a second sharp tug to get it loose, it was buried so deeply into the wood. He held it by the blade and tossed it gently back to Squeaks. "It's nice that you and I are friends, my friend."

"Ain't it just."

The two men, one a living page from a history book who had roamed the mountains wild and free before there were enough white men who had *seen* the Rocky Mountains, much less walked them, to put together a decent-sized gang-bang; the other a lean, dark man, part Indian, part what remained of a proud and handsome and deadly efficient Confederate cavalry officer —the two men sat in the firelight on a chill Plains night and began truly to like each other.

CHAPTER 5

A boot thudded into Slocum's side, yanking him from sleep into instant, painful wakefulness. The fire was burned nearly out but there was light enough for him to make out a pair of legs, one of them drawn back to plant another kick.

Slocum's hand shot without thought toward the holster that always lay beside his head when he slept but his fingers brushed against another boot toe instead of the comforting walnut grip of his .45. The boot thumped into his ribs again. It felt like a heated lance being driven into him there but he was past caring. His lips pulled tight over his teeth in a wolfish grimace that in no way could ever have been mistaken for a grin, and a fire-red haze of anger swept through his brain, wiping out pain and rational thought alike. He was not interested now in reasoning but in reacting, and his reactions were automatic.

Denied the revolver, Slocum snatched his knife from its sheath and swept it in a glistening, snake-quick arc to slice through leather and deep into the leg of the man who had kicked him. He felt the keen edge touch bone and grate across it, and fresh blood warmed his hand. The dark silence of the night was shattered by a piercing cry from the man standing over Slocum.

The sweep of the blade ended permaturely as someone else grabbed Slocum's arm at the end of his swing. The second fighter dropped onto Slocum's extended arm and began trying to wrestle the big Bowie from his grip. Slocum brought his left hand up and clamped it around the man's throat, determined to crush the fragile tube there through which air must pass to reach the lungs. A few more seconds and the man was as good as dead. Slocum did not have those seconds. From behind someone smashed a rifle barrel across his skull, splitting the scalp open and sending John Slocum into a gray half sleep. He felt himself being kicked again and then for a time felt no more.

The next thing he was aware of, he was propped against the adobe wall near where he had been sleeping—his saddle and the meager pad he had been trying to use for a small measure of comfort were still there where he had placed them—and his hands were securely tied.

"Who the hell is this?" someone was demanding loudly.

"Another damn thief," someone answered.

"I already tried to . . ." There was a flat, dull sound of flesh striking flesh and Squeaks was cut off. "Goddamn it, will you quit that. You already got me trussed up like a shoat ready for its throat to be cut. You figure I c'n *talk* you to death? If you wanta know who that boy is, shut up an' I'll tell you."

"You expect us to take the word of a horse thief?" It was the first voice again.

"You know plenty about me, Arnold Johnson, an' one of the things you know is that I don't lie. Not about nothin'. If I'm man enough to do it, or damn fool enough, then by God I'm man enough or fool enough to own up to it."

Johnson grunted. "I'll give you that much, old man. I never yet heard you tell a lie."

"You just bet you never have, nor never will neither. Nowthens, you was askin' about that fellow there. His name's John an' he come onto my camp here last night. We shared a fire an' a piece of meat he was carryin', an' that's the extent of it. I never seen him before last night and he never seen me before. As you should damn well know if you've seen any tracks I left at all."

Johnson—he had a shiny badge pinned to his breast pocket—shifted his eyes briefly away from the old man.

Squeaks cackled. "Haw, b'God, you never did find any tracks. Did you, Arnold? Answer me, damnit."

The sheriff shook his head reluctantly.

"That makes an ol' man feel *some* better, anyhow. I thought maybe I was gettin' senile or somethin'. So how the hell did you find me?"

"We knew what way you were headed. We just guessed you might come here. You know. It being a trapper hangout back in the old days." Johnson shrugged. "We got lucky."

"Shit. Too late now to worry about bein' outguessed, though. At least I ain't lost my touch. I'm pure glad about that. Depended on it often enough before to save my hair from bein' hung on a lodgepole."

"Sure, Squeaks. You never lost your touch for dodging, all right." The sheriff sounded almost respectful. "You swear to me, Squeaks, that this John fellow wasn't with you?"

"I swear it, Arnold. I never seen him before dusk yestiddy."

"You could ask the John fellow," Slocum said drily. His head hurt like hell and with his hands bound the way they were he could not reach it to inspect the wound.

"I thought you were still out," Johnson said. "Your name's John?"

"It is."

"What's the rest of it?"

"That's a damned personal question."

"Uh-huh, it is for a fact, but there's going to be a hanging around here pretty soon. We're trying to figure out how many ropes to prepare."

"Am I supposed to be impressed?"

"Hell, John, I don't care if I impress you or not. Come to think of it, I don't much care if I hang you or not."

"The last name's Burton," Slocum said. It was the first name that popped into his mind. A sheriff, wherever he might be from, could well have gotten a flyer on John Slocum. The moment did not seem appropriate for the pushing of one's luck, he decided. Squeaks, of course, knew the rest of his name, but Slocum did not for a minute think the old trapper would be making any corrections.

"John Burton, huh. I never heard of you."

"I would not go to hurt your feelings here, Sheriff, not for anything I wouldn't, so please forgive me for the admission . . . but I've never heard of you neither."

"All right."

"Now that we've been introduced proper, why don't you kindly untie my hands, Sheriff."

"Not quite yet, Mr. Burton. There is a small matter of assaulting a deputy you need to answer to."

"Deputy?"

"You sliced Harry Powell's leg open, John, like you was fixing to cut some chops off and have them for breakfast."

"Goddamnit, Sheriff, when some fool comes up to me in my bed and goes to kicking me he damn well better expect me to wake up swinging. If I could've got my hands onto my gun I would've blown his fool head apart like a green punkin on the Fourth of July. I suppose then you'd have been calling it murder too instead of self-defense. Mister, I got to say it. You have strange ways in this part of the country if a man can't defend himself without first inspecting the other fellow for badges or certified writs of authority."

The sheriff smiled briefly and dug a fingernail into his ear. He scratched vigorously. "Some sort of fungus, the doc said. Itches."

"Maybe it reached your brain," Slocum suggested.

"Mr. Burton, it is possible that we owe you an apology. But don't push me too far, hear?"

"I hear. I'll be a whole helluva lot more agreeable when you cut me loose."

"I want to think on that a while first. Being tied up won't kill you."

"No but it might cause me a laundry bill. Unless one of your boys wants to take it out for me and give me a fair shake when it's done. I got to piss, Sheriff."

"Your pants will dry before midmorning, I'll bet."

Slocum shrugged. It had been worth a try. The request had only been an excuse to get his hands free anyway.

"Squeaks," the sheriff said, "I swear I don't like this. You're a likable old son-of-a-gun, but I don't see how I can get around having to hang you this time. I've warned you till you're as tired of hearing it as I am of saying it. You *knew* I'd have to catch you at it one of these times."

"Hell, Arnold, I don't hold it against you none."

"Are you comfortable there? You aren't tied too tight?"

"I'm fine. I would like to smoke, though."

Several other possemen were drifting back into the camp now, apparently having gone out to bring their horses in closer and to haul in more firewood. One of the men began rebuilding the fire while another produced a coffee pot and river water. The sheriff could have asked one of them to help Squeaks but he knelt himself and prepared the old man's pipe, lighting it for him and placing it carefully between the remaining teeth in the old hunter's jaws.

"Thanks, Arnold. You got a cigar for my friend?"

"I have the makings of a cigarette."

"I'd be glad to save you the trouble of rolling it," Slocum offered.

"I can manage."

The dry, light smoke of the cigarette was a poor substitute for the rich flavor of a good cigar, but something is usually better than nothing and Slocum did not complain.

"We'll wait for dawn, Squeaks. That should give you time to make your peace or whatever."

"We could find a tree in the dark, Sheriff," one of the deputies said. "Two of them, for that matter."

"Shut up, Bernard. A man has a right to see the sun rise a last time. We ain't in that big a hurry."

"Whatever you say."

"Thankee, Arnold. I do have a couple last requests."

"Name them."

"All that I stole was that studhorse." Squeaks grinned and shook his head. "B'God, he was mine for a little while there, wasn't he. Fine stallion. Finest I've seen in a lot of years. Medicine Hat horse, Arnold. You don't know what that means, but an Indian would, same as I do. A man rides a horse like that, why, he just naturally feels like a king. No, better than some fancy king would ever know how to feel. On a horse like that he feels like he's part of the wind, an' all the sons and daughters of a Medicine Hat horse will make him feel the same. So I reckon it was worth the try." He sighed.

"Anyhow, Arnold, everythin' else I own is mine,

b'God. Paid for legal and mine to do with what I want. 'Specially that Sharps an' all my reloadin' gear an' powder an' lead. Saddle, bridle . . . everythin'. It's mine."

The sheriff nodded.

"Right. Well, what I want to do is to give it away. I got seventeen dollars cash money and all my truck over there. I want my good friend John there to have it all as he's down on his luck a mite these days. All of it, Arnold. Except for this bearclaw foofarah I wear around my neck. I kilt every animal that contributed to this neckpiece an' it's been rattled and sung over by three different medicine men. You ought to know that about it. Anyways, I want you to have it. You'd best take it off now, though, lest you mess it up catchin' it in the noose."

Johnson looked embarrassed but it was just as plain he did not want to refuse the old man's generosity. "For such a sorry old fart you're a pretty good man, Squeaks. I just wish to hell you weren't a thief too. Or at least that I could hate you the way a man ought to when he has to do a thing like this."

"No, Arnold. That's another thing I learnt from the Indians. They're a bunch of damned red niggers, but they know a thing or two too. Enemy or food, either one, when you kill somethin' it should be with respect, Arnold. Not so many white men learn that. They think you got to kill from hate to keep your gut from churnin' and turnin' sour afterward, but it don't work. Them as think so has to drown the sourness in whiskey an' that don't work either. Whiskey's for bringin' on fun. It won't do worth a shit for hidin' sorrows. No, the onliest way to kill and not have it turn back in on you is to do it with respect for the thing that's doin' the dyin'. Knowin' that you feel the way you do, why, that's the reason I can feel that noose come over my neck an' still go out likin' you, Arnold. Same as you have respect for an old man that's lived five times as long as he ever thought he would."

Squeaks stopped for a moment and shifted his eyes to Slocum. "John, I hope you was listenin' to what I was sayin' there. A man has a right to be listened to when it's his last words."

"I was listening, Squeaks. And I thank you for the kindness."

Squeaks laughed. "Sonny boy, I sure God wouldn't give you a lick or a spittle 'cept I won't have a damn bit of use for that stuff where I'm goin'."

"I'll thank you just the same," Slocum said.

"You're quite welcome. Under the circumstances, which I would damn sure change if I could."

"Is there anything I can do for you?" Slocum asked.

"I can't think of ary thing—unless, that is, you can think of a way to get us both out of here."

"I can't do that. But I could maybe carve you a marker afterward. Would you like that?"

The old man's eyes lit up. "By God, John, I would. I always expected to end up in a coyote's belly and my bones gone to powder. I'd sure like a marker, John. I would."

He could not have been more pleased if Slocum had guaranteed him salvation. And in a way perhaps Slocum had offered him immortality, more of it than he had ever dared hope for.

"What would you like on it?"

"I . . . it's a lot of work."

"I don't mind."

"My full name. Would that be all right?"

Slocum nodded.

"Then carve it for Joshua Lewis Clark Meriwether." He chuckled. "It's been a hell of a time since I've used all that."

The sheriff looked curious, and Slocum was too for that matter.

"You wouldn't happen to be kin to . . . ?" the sheriff began.

"Distant. Just distant. My mama, rest her soul, was kinda proud of that. I came along not long after we heard news of them gettin' back to the States. But my mama was a woman of the Word too an' she just couldn't stand not to give me a name from it. That's why I got so many of them."

The sheriff shook his head.

"I'll carve it," Slocum promised. "I'll find a flat slab of rock and scratch it in as deep as I'm able."

"That's good of you, John." He sat up straighter, "Hey, now, it's comin' close to sunrise an' I ain't had my breakfast yet. A man shouldn't ought to die without his belly full. What say we finish that piece of antelope you dragged in las' night, John. It ain't quite as fine as buff'lo, but it will do. And John, I think maybe you should go down in the Canadian River country an' put in some work down there huntin'. You don't see so many people there, but a man can make out all right at it." He gave Slocum a sly wink. Advice from a man caught to a man yet on the run.

"I'll do that. Thanks to you."

Squeaks—Joshua L. C. Meriwether—laughed and said, "Anytime you see me I'll be glad to do as much for you again."

They had their breakfast and they watched the sun come up out of the distant plains, and they hanged the old man from a sturdy cottonwood branch after the redness had gone out of the newly risen sun.

"You hanged him with respect," Slocum said after the body had been cut down and Slocum was finally released and allowed to help dig the grave that the sheriff insisted be done before the posse left.

"He was a good man, Mr. Burton." The sheriff wiped sweat from his forehead although the morning was still far from being hot or even warm. "I'll tell you something else. Until the moment that old man went I was scared to death of one thing. I was scared he was going to ask me to let him go if he'd promise to stay out of my part of the country or something. If he had, I swear to God I don't know how I could've said yes and I don't know how I could've said no to him. I was really scared of that."

"He wouldn't have asked you that. It would have been too much like begging. I don't reckon that old man ever once begged, his whole life long."

"Yeah." The sheriff sighed. His expression hardened. "You weren't lying to him about . . ." Slocum's eyes flashed green ice shards and his face might have turned to cold steel. "No," the sheriff answered himself. "I guess you were being straight with him, Mr. Burton."

"A man ought to stay straight with his friends, Sheriff."

"Yes, well . . ." Whatever he might have said tailed lamely away into silence. He moved his hand as if to offer it, thought better of that and shuffled his feet awkwardly for a moment. Finally he turned and shouted, much louder than necessary as the others were all near, "Get the lead out, you horny bastards. We've all been four days away from home and we got some catching up to do. Let's get out of here. Now!"

They got. None of them seemed anxious now to hang around where old Squeaks had so recently hung around. Within a minute or two Slocum was left alone with a deep hole, a dead friend, and a promise that had to be kept before he could pick up the big Sharps and move on.

Slocum didn't really mind. He had seen dead men before, several of them even, and at least this was a dead man that he liked. He talked to the old gentleman while he worked and afterward he spent the remainder of the day finding a flat slab of rock that met his approval and carving the promised words with Meriwether's quickly ruined knife.

CHAPTER 6

The vast High Plains were not exactly the way Slocum had expected to find them. The country must once have been given only to grass and heat, a seemingly limitless herd of shaggy buffalo, and an occasional band of traveling Comanches. No longer. Now the hard, sun-baked earth was scored by the iron rims of hide-laden wagons, and the great Southern Herd had been broken into scattered bunches of the huge animals. Their numbers were still in the tens of thousands but now they ate and moved and bellowed and fornicated in groups of hundreds rather than masses of a hundred thousand or more.

For all the great number of people who were engaged in hunting the buffalo, though, Slocum had little fear that he would be recognized here or hounded by the law, for this was country where a man with a badge would fare poorly and probably for very little time. The hunters were a law unto themselves. And that suited John Slocum just fine.

At least he did have an outfit now. Meriwether's bedroll and equipment were as good as those Slocum had been forced to leave behind. Meriwether's seventeen dollars provided him with coffee and flour and a sack of dried fruit. Meriwether's saddle and bridle he swapped for a pack mule. Slocum was riding loose and free again, and the feeling was a good one.

He made his camp on the south bank of the Canadian and spent a lazy day becoming acquainted with the long-barreled Sharps that Meriwether had left him. There seemed to be no other people in the immediate vicinity, which was all right. There were no women about, but Slocum had had to do without before and likely would have to again in the future. And with no women it seemed logical that there were no men. That part of it Slocum could put up with quite nicely. He was not in a social mood at the moment in any case.

The big rifle was a pleasure to shoot. The stock was well designed and set the impact of 110 grains of black powder a solid but not at all uncomfortable shove into his shoulder, sending the thumb-sized slug out of the heavy barrel with pinpoint accuracy out to nearly 600 yards, and with a reasonable degree of accuracy even farther. This was a gun to hang onto no matter what the future temptations of a battle and a bawd might be.

He tested the gun to its limits, burning up old Meriwether's supply of ammunition, and that evening he built a fire to melt lead for a new supply of bullets to reload the fat, brass cartridges.

Keeping a fire going after dark turned out to be a mistake.

If a man had foresight as good as his hindsight, we'd all be rich.

They came out of the shadows, making no attempt to muffle the sounds of their horses' arrival, and that at least was a good sign, even if Slocum did not particularly want company. From the looks of them they were buffalo hunters and they had been out in the grass for a good long time.

There were nine of them who approached Slocum's fire without invitation, a group of men as shaggy as the animals they hunted and smelling somewhat worse even though there was ample water in the shallow Canadian that they could have bathed if they had damn well pleased. Slocum had been known to take on an odor like ripe cheese himself a time or two in the past but not when he had any choice in the matter. He wrinkled his nose but offered no objections. It was their business.

"Good evening, gents. Is there anything I can do for you?"

"Is there anything he can do for us," one of them repeated loudly. "Now, that's a pretty good one, ain't it, boys?"

Slocum found no particular humor in the simple question, but then maybe this crowd was about as intelligent as they were sweet-smelling. "I'm a regular card, I am," he muttered.

Still without waiting for the customary invitation, the man who had spoken flopped onto the ground at Slocum's side. The bastard at least could have taken a spot downwind, Slocum thought.

The man shoved a hand out. "I'm Pete Hutchison, neighbor. Hutch to my friends, an' I reckon you'll be wanting to call me Hutch. That over there is Big. He prob'ly has another name but nobody I've ever knowed has heard it." Big was rather well named. "An' my dark-skinned friend there is Carlos Jesus Francisco Onate, otherwise known as Cisco." Slocum was not much given to calling a Mexican a greaser, but in Cisco's case he might be tempted. The man looked just plain greasy. "The rest of my boys are . . ." he rattled off a half dozen more names that Slocum was not really much interested in hearing. They all smelled bad as far as he could tell, though with a crowd like that it would have been hard to sniff a rose out from among the general muck.

"That's mighty nice to learn," Slocum said when Hutch got done with his round of introductions. "I have a little coffee on there, but I don't know as there's enough for everybody."

"Oh, we wouldn't want to cut that deep into your outfit. No, sir, we wouldn't. You'll be needing all you got before you go back to the bright lights an' the whores, neighbor. And, uh, your name would be . . . ?" Hutch left the question hanging in the rank air between them.

"Burton," Slocum said. "John Burton." The name had served him well enough lately, he might as well hang onto it for a while. Just in case.

"It's a sure enough genuine pleasure to make your acquaintance, Mr. Burton. Sure is." Hutch handed Slocum a cigar, a good cigar at that, and waited patiently for Slocum to snip the twisted end from it and lick it to his satisfaction. When Slocum was ready it was Hutch who spent a match to light it for him before he lit his own. Hutch rocked back on his heels and exhaled the thick, bluish smoke. "Nothin, better than a good cigar, don't you agree?"

"Nope."

The buffalo hunter raised an eyebrow.

"Fourth best maybe. Behind a tight pussy, a full bottle and a good horse. No, make that fifth. I'll take a straight-shooting gun ahead of it too."

Hutch laughed. "I like you, Burton. Damned if I don't."

"And I think you're a generous man, Hutch. Which if you don't mind me saying so kinda raises a question in my mind."

Hutch grinned at him. "I was fixing to get to that, John. Uh-huh. I surely was. Wasn't I, boys?"

A murmur of agreement came from the others. It would have been difficult for Slocum not to notice that their voices came from a tight semicircle behind him. Big and Cisco slid around front to flank Hutch.

"I think we are, John." Hutch grinned even wider and puffed happily on his cigar. "Yes, sir, I do like a good cigar. It pleasures my soul when I can afford the best. Always go for the best in life, John, because life can be so short. You know?"

"So I've heard."

"It's true, too."

Slocum was tempted to remind his generous new friend that there was always a question of for *whom* the shortening might occur. But on second thought he glanced around at the men who were with Hutch and decided he already knew the answer to that. The deck was very nicely stacked in Hutch's favor. This time.

"Tell me more about what you have in mind," he invited.

"See, John. I knew I liked you for more than one reason. You're a sensible man. That's one of the things I like about you. What I was coming to, you see, is that my partners and I are one of the few groups working out here—I daresay the only group working out here—that is large enough and well enough equipped to offer assistance to our friends in times of need. A man will run out of primers from time to time or lead or salt or such. An' the Injuns, they get bad whenever they figure they can get away with it. Well, the way it is, John, times like that you just come to us, just run to any one of us, an' we'll help take care of the problem, no matter what it is. We believe in helping our friends, you see."

"Any little problem at all, huh."

"That's right, John. We feel real strong about wanting to help our friends."

"And your friends in turn, they maybe try to help you out sometimes?"

Hutch's smile became very warm indeed. "That's right, John. My oh my, but you are a bright fella an' that's a fact. Out friends help us just like we help them. But in their case—your case, for instance—the help we get is in the form of a little something to keep our costs from getting too high."

"A little something?"

"That's right, John. A little something like . . . one hide in every four, say."

"Twenty-five percent. That's quite a little something, all right."

"Oh, it isn't so bad. Nobody objects much. Not very often, anyhow."

"I don't suppose I could think it over before I let you know."

Hutch shook his head. "John, John, have I figured you wrong after all? Are you not so bright as I thought you was? You maybe didn't understand me. It wasn't exactly a question, you see. It was more in the way of a polite explanation. You know?"

"I know."

"Fine." Hutch slapped his hands together and just beamed. "That's real fine, John. I just *knew* we wouldn't have any problems that a little pleasant conversation wouldn't take care of." He sighed. "I surely am glad, too. I just don't like trouble. I'm a very easy-goin' fellow, you understand. Just like my friends here."

Cisco's smile was even broader than Hutch's. Big looked like he was not smart enough to have figured out yet what they were talking about—maybe not smart enough to have learned yet how to control his facial muscles so that he *could* smile when someone wanted him to. The others were behind Slocum where he could not see them, and he did not care in any event what they might be thinking or looking like. He was sure they had their hands close to their gunbutts, and that was really all he needed to know at the moment. The skin at the back of his neck felt cold and crawly just from knowing they were back there.

Impatience has killed as many cats as curiosity ever did, boy, so set still and shut up. Tomorrow only comes for those that are alive to see it.

Slocum jammed his cigar into the corner of his jaw and tried to look just as happy as Hutch did. "I'll keep that in mind, Hutch. After all, a man likes to know who his friends are. An' how he ought to act when he's in somebody else's territory."

"That's fine, John. Just fine."

They stood and Hutch offered his hand. "It's been a pleasure meeting you, John. And since you haven't had time to do any hunting since you got here we brung you a chunk of hump meat. To seal the friendship, so to speak."

One of the men who had been behind Slocum stepped forward and laid a good ten pounds of meat down. It was a beautiful piece of meat but it was not that fine a gift under the circumstances. Tons of the stuff were left to rot on the ground each and every day.

"Mighty thoughtful of you boys," Slocum said.

The interesting thing about it was not that they had brought it but that they had known he had not yet shot any of his own meat. Now that he did find interesting.

Hutch and his party said a round of courteous good nights and drifted back into the darkness.

Slocum puffed on his cigar—the damn thing was entirely too good to throw away—and cussed some to himself. At least 125 miles from the nearest town and damned if Slocum hadn't found some bothersome neighbors. Now that he was here, though, he was not about to give them the satisfaction of moving. Or of paying them a 25 percent cut of his hunt.

Sometimes Slocum got the impression that the world was 90 percent bastards and 9 percent fools. At the moment he was not sure which percentage group he might fall into.

CHAPTER 7

The big Sharps rocked solidly against his shoulder and
the bellowing crash of the shot outdid the best the
buffalo bulls could offer in competition. Two hundred
yards away a cow, neatly heart-shot high behind the
shoulder, coughed and dropped to her knees. None
of the others in the bunch paid any attention. So far
Slocum had knocked down seven of the dark beasts
without disturbing the others. The way they stood
patient and stupid while they were cut down one by
one was an amazement to him.

He slipped another stubby cartridge into the chamber
and felt the thick barrel. It was far from hot still. The
rifle cracked again but just as his finger drew gently
back on the trigger the young bull he was aiming at
swiveled its head to a fresh patch of dry bunchgrass
and shifted its massive bulk. The change was just
enough to send his bullet into the bull's shoulder. The
animal bawled out its pain and broke into a lumbering,
three-legged run. Slocum jumped to his feet—the stand
was blown now anyway—and crammed another cartridge into place. He brought the bull down with a second shot but by that time the rest of the small herd
was racing away. They dropped out of sight behind a
swell in the ground, and Slocum cursed himself mildly

at the error. Not that it was any great problem. There were plenty of buffalo to choose from.

He used a wiping rod and a splash of water from his canteen to swab the bore out and reloaded the big rifle before he picked up his gear and his empty shells and moved toward the eight buffalo crumpled on the ground before him.

One by one he laboriously skinned the huge animals and packed their hides, thick and awkwardly heavy things when green, back to his base camp beside the river. He had thought about shifting to a new location, but Hutch and his men seemed to keep a close eye on whatever happened on this patch of the Great Plains. And in any event it was not Slocum's way to step aside for any man.

He spent the afternoon staking and scraping the hides into a saleable condition. It was heavy work for a man alone. Most hunters went out in crews with hunters, hide tenders, and teamsters operating together and sharing the profits. Even as slow as the one-man operation was going to be, though, it was clear that a man could make a healthy income with a rifle here. At a dollar and a half per hide he had already earned twelve times the normal day wage. If he could get his take to market.

It was good work and it was work John Slocum, onetime sharpshooter for the Confederate States of America, was well suited to. Happily enough the rifle he had used then, late in the war, was another, earlier version of the same Sharps rifle he inherited from Joshua Meriwether, although that captured Yankee Sharps had been a percussion model using packaged powder and ball and the old high-hat percussion caps. The rifle, in fact, had been where the name sharpshooter came from, for even then the Sharps had a reputation for quality and accuracy unmatched by any other rifle in the world.

The only thing Slocum regretted about the occupation was not the hard work, for he was not a lazy man, but the incredible waste of fine meat that was associated with the slaughter. Many of the buffalo would dress out to a carcass weight of a thousand pounds. Eight animals on the ground—just Slocum's measly take of eight buffalo—meant four tons of meat left to rot or be consumed by the wolves and coyotes and vultures that followed the hide wagons like faithful companions.

Slocum did not like the waste but there was no way to prevent it without also preventing the taking of the hides, for there was no way known to get the meat to market without spoilage. Oh, there were some few of the big outfits, he knew, that picked up a few extra bucks by saving the choicer pieces like the tongues, pickling them in brine, and shipping them back East as delicacies for the fancy carriage-trade houses in New York and Boston and such foreign places. But it takes a hell of a lot of dead buffalo to provide enough barrels full of pickled tongues to make that worth the trouble of packing them. Most of the smaller wagons just left it all as carrion.

By the time he was done with his day's work Slocum was a caked mass of mingled sweat and blood and the slimy, sticky glop that coated the inside of the hides. He felt and probably smelled as bad as Hutch and his crew had the night before. It was no wonder, he decided, that whores in the buffalo country camps were the oldest and the ugliest bawds in the profession and still were able to charge two bucks for a quickie when anywhere civilized they would have been spreading their legs for a dollar at the most or a half buck even likelier. Even a whore has a sense of smell.

The temptations of running water were just too much to let go by, and Slocum shucked his clothes and washed them as well as he could, then slid into the water, tepid in its shallow run but still infinitely refreshing. Damn but that felt good, he thought.

He lay back against the sand-and-gravel bottom of the Canadian and let the moving water cleanse the filth from his body. He ducked his head beneath the surface and reveled in the sensations.

When he sat upright again he tossed his head and splashed droplets of water in a circle ten feet around him.

"Feels good after a long day, don't it?"

What Slocum felt then was naked. Far more naked than a lack of clothing could ever make him. His .45 was in its holster a half dozen feet away on the riverbank. He wiped the water from his eyes and looked. "Shit," he muttered under his breath. The speaker was the Mexican called Cisco. Shit, he thought; twice and with 6 percent interest.

"So? You were not expecting us?"

"You boys figure to come collecting from everybody every day? That must keep you awful busy."

"Not everyone. Not every day, no. Las' night, though, you did not say you agree to our arrangement. Not with so many words, you do not. We want to make sure, eh? No-no, Mr. Burton. Stay where you are, please. If I make a mistake, maybe think you are moving closer to that fine gun, I might shoot you. It would be a regrettable accident. An' anyway, you see, I am not alone."

Slocum sat back down. The moving water no longer felt good on his skin. He just felt wet and the river bottom grated harshly against his ass. Triple shit, with chocolate sprinkles.

"You have eight hides, I see. Two of them are ours, yes?"

"No."

Cisco got an even uglier look about him, and he was not a good-looking man to start with. He managed to look eager as well as nasty, as if he would enjoy being able to enforce the homemade laws laid down by Hutch and his crew.

"A quarter isn't near as good as a third," Slocum went on calmly. "What I had in mind was something else. A business agreement, you might say."

Cisco did not immediately look agreeable, but he did not begin shooting either. He waited.

"What I had in mind was this. Hides are worth a dollar fifty. That's delivered to a buying point. As it happens, I don't own a wagon. I'll have this problem with transportation anyway, which you boys don't seem to have trouble with. So what I'll do is sell you *all* my hides at a buck apiece, meaning you get a third of the value just for haulage. It solves a problem for me and gives you a one-third profit too. Much better than a quarter any old time."

Cisco grinned, and for a moment Slocum thought he had gone for it. That thought was short-lived. "I think mebe Hutchinson would do this for you. He is, after all, a good friend an' a generous man. But I think he would do this for the six hides that are yours. We do not have to buy the other two. They already belong to us. It is foolish for a man to pay for what he already owns, yes?"

"Let me consider it." Slocum stood. The water dripping off his skin turned chill in the rising evening breeze. He had never felt so naked as he did now. His gun and his knife were out of reach, and he did not even have his boots to get in some serious kicking. All he had was bone and sinew, and he seriously doubted that those would be enough. Still, he had to try it. And he had only Cisco's word that there were more of them handy. If they tried to keep such a good watch on everything that went on hereabouts they had to be spreading themselves pretty thin.

Slocum smiled and shrugged and launched himself at Cisco as hard and as fast as he could.

Slocum wanted and fully intended to end the fight with the same punch that began it. He closed his hand into a sharp, rock-hard slab with the finger joints extended instead of in a fist and aimed his blow toward the tender area below Cisco's Adam's apple. A hard punch there can crush the fragile cartilage that allows air to flow into the lungs and within minutes the victim will be on the ground writhing the last of his death throes. With Cisco that would have been a particular pleasure to watch. The deep-purple skin tone of strangulation would have looked good on him.

The Mexican tried to duck away from the blow, though, and Slocum felt his hand instead strike the hard plane of Cisco's cheekbone. Slocum could feel his own skin tear open at the impact but at least he had the satisfaction of seeing Cisco's cheek split and a flow of bright blood flood the man's neck and collar.

He followed with a left to the gut, but Cisco was in too hard a condition for body blows to have any immediate effect. The man was no slouch with his hands either. Slocum took a quick tattoo of rapid-fire punches in the belly and heart area.

They separated almost as quickly as they had come together, neither now having an advantage of surprise, and both crouched like cats as they circled each other.

"*Cabron,*" the Mexican hissed.

Slocum grinned. "*Su madre es puta.*"

"*Sí,*" Cisco agreed. "In the cribs of Juarez."

"I'll bet she even gives you a cut rate, don't she."

"No such luck, but for you, *señor,* she would cut your balls off. As I will do for her when I am done with you here today."

Cisco feinted with a looping right that Slocum easily ducked under, but he tagged Slocum hard with another left over the heart. Well-placed shots like that could get old in a big hurry, Slocum thought.

They were close now, though, and Slocum was no slouch himself. As a boy in Arkansas he had been no stranger to the rough and tumble and his life since then had done nothing to make him any more mellow.

Slocum feinted with his left and quickly, without the right-hand follow that Cisco might have expected, unloaded the same left hand into Cisco's jaw. Slocum came in behind that with a crossing right hand and slapped the Mexican's head back around again from the travel Slocum's first punch had given it. Slocum lowered his head and began to work hard on Cisco's belly and came up almost as soon as he had begun with a head butt into the Mexican's face. Slocum thought he could feel Cisco's nose give and he knew he would feel the heat of the other man's blood mat his own hair.

The white heat of the fight was upon him now and he probably would not have felt pain if Cisco had taken a sword and slashed him in half. In a fight Slocum tended at times to go berserk and he did so now. He began raining his fists onto Cisco anywhere and everywhere he could reach the man, no longer planning his blows, no longer attacking cautiously or with any thought to self-defense.

He knew he was taking punishment in return but the knowledge was dim, coming from some distant corner of his mind that was of no concern to him and of almost as little interest. He was aware of being hit mostly because some of the blows changed the direction of his own punches and caused them to miss, and the whole focus of Slocum's existence at that moment was in his desire to strike the Mexican in any way and anywhere that might become possible.

Slocum's fury, the almost crazed furor of his attack, drove Cisco back away from the riverbank and sent him sprawling.

Forgetting that he was barefoot and naked, Slocum tried to destroy the man's ribcage with kicks but soon the pain coming up from his own foot reminded him that he was accomplishing little. With a deep sound of anger rising unnoticed from his throat, a sound very close to that of a growling wolf, Slocum dropped onto the Mexican and took hold of his throat. Slocum had every intention of tearing Cisco's throat out with his own bare hands.

Cisco, fear reaching his eyes for the first time as he realized he was no longer merely fighting another human being but being attacked by a virtual madman, bucked violently beneath Slocum. Cisco smashed a knee into Slocum's unprotected crotch but even that could not lessen the hold on his throat. Cisco tried again to knee Slocum, tried to thumb his eyes out, but nothing seemed to do any good. The Mexican could feel himself slipping away, could see a film of furry red haze forming between himself and the twisted face of his opponent. Cisco would have uttered a prayer, the first he wanted to say since he was seven years old and had had to help his mother service a particularly lecherous fat man with enough money to be able to indulge his peculiar and widely varied tastes, but by then Carlos Jesus Francisco Onate had not breath left to deliver a final prayer. He felt himself dying.

"Helluva fight, wasn't it?" Hutch asked mildly. He poured another hatful of water onto Cisco's face and upper body and laughed when Cisco was unable to speak in return.

Cisco sat up. By then he had forgotten that he had expected to be able to sit again or to see the sunshine or feel the wind on his face. All he remembered of the fight now was a consuming hatred for the tall, lean, dark-faced man who was stretched out unconscious at Big's feet.

"Still can't talk about it, huh?" Hutch chuckled. "You looked a damn pretty sight there, you did. Sprawled out on the ground with your face all red an' a naked feller laying across your bones. Looked like one of you was getting him some buggering. For a fact it did. Woulda been funny if he hadn't been so close to killing you." Hutch shook his head. "I sure never thought I'd see the day when you was on the short end of a fight, Cisco. It makes me wonder if you're losing your touch, *amigo.*"

Cisco got his voice back to answer that one. In a rasping, throaty whisper he hissed, "I show you my touch in just one minute now. I will cut that bastard's balls from their sack and stuff them in his asshole. I will cut off his cock an' ram it down his throat. And *then* I will kill him. Not before, my friend."

"Like hell you will."

"Like hell I will not."

"Goddamnit, Cisco, I said you won't and you won't. You know my policy. These are a bunch of rough bastards we're dealing with out here. Nearly ever last one of them has to be beat half to death before he's going to see it our way. If they weren't tough enough to stand up to us they wouldn't be out here to start with. And the few that might get here by mistake wouldn't be worth a shit when it comes to shooting a buff stand. We need this Burton just the same as we need the rest of them before him an' the ones that will come after. Now, that's my *rules* and I don't want you forgetting them. They ain't changed lately. But maybe you have."

"I have changed, my friend," Cisco said. He was speaking a little easier now. "I have the good hate for this son-of-a-bitch gringo Burton. That will not change. This one I must kill."

"This one you might have to kill. If he still won't come across the way he ought to. But you won't kill him if there's any chance we can make a profit off him.

That's final, Cisco. An' you damn well better know I mean it."

"I cannot rest until I see this one dead at my feet and his *cojones* placed as I have said. This you should know, my friend."

"I'll go this far with you, Cisco. If we have to kill him, he's yours."

"It is not enough."

"When he decides to quit the country and stop shooting here, you may have him, Cisco. But not before. Not as long as he's bringing in the cash for us."

Cisco continued to look dissatisfied.

"That's as far as I go for you, Cisco. I like you, boy, but you nor nobody else is gonna get in the way of my making money. Now, you know that to be a fact. If you think any different, before I tell you it's okay for you to beef this John Burton or any other son-of-a-bitch I say, I'll sic Big on you. You know what that'd mean."

Cisco's glance moved involuntarily to the man they called Big. The Mexican licked his lips. Of a sudden they felt dry to him. He could argue no farther.

Big used to be the one to do their work of convincing reluctant buffalo hunters that they should participate in Hutchison's assistance program, but no longer. The huge man had killed several hunters by mistake, simply because when he hit them he had no concept of how fragile the human body can be in comparison with his own awesome strength. And the human body is amazingly durable.

The last time, the time that convinced Hutch he could no longer let Big do that sort of work for him, Big took on two buffalo hunters, each of whom was at least as large and as burly as Big was himself. But an ordinary man, even a large man such as these two were, could not hope to match Big's power.

The two of them had not taken Big seriously. Working together as a well-practiced team, they had flanked Hutchison's man and closed in on him at the same time. Big had not tried to avoid them. He merely stood waiting for them and when they were near enough reached out to grab whatever was nearest. One of the men he caught by the upper arm, the other by a fist that had been directed toward Big's face. Big stood quietly and smiled at them. With his right hand he squeezed until the other's fist crumpled with a dull crackle of breaking bones. The man screamed and passed out cold. The first hunter was not so lucky. Big swung the man around and met him with a clubbed fist that left a soft, mushy indentation in the side of the hunter's skull. When that one went down it was forever. Big swore to Hutchison afterward that he had not intended to do it; he had only wanted to tap the fellow and knock him out the way he had the man's friend. Big was truly sorry and would never, ever do it again.

Hutchison believed him. Big had never been known to tell a lie to Hutch or to anyone else. Big was not bright enough or devious enough to lie. The big man simply did whatever he was told to do and seemed to have no thoughts of feelings or ambitions beyond that. No, he would not have lied about it.

But Hutchison could not afford to lose prospective contributors to his purse, either. One of those hunters was dead and the other would never be able to hold a rifle again in the twisted claw that Big had left at the end of his wrist. Two hunters rendered useless wastefully, by accident. No, that would not do at all.

Hutch did not bother to tell Big about the demotion. Hutch was sure the big man would never notice the difference, or care if somehow he did. Even Hutchison did not understand what faint images or impressions might wobble around inside of Big's head, but as long as he had the man's loyalty—and he did—he did not care.

Neither Cisco nor any other member of the bunch was ever apt to cross him so long as he had Big on his leash, and Hutchison knew that Cisco would not dream of doing so now. Hutchison could use Burton as long as he liked or until the man decided to quit. Then Cisco could have him for his own enjoyment. For that matter, it might work out very well that way. He could let this Burton complete a fine hunt and then turn Cisco loose on him. Cisco could have Burton. And Alvin Peter Hutchison could have Burton's entire take of hides, minus 25 percent, of course, which he would already own.

Hutch smiled. "Be patient, my fine Mexican friend. Your time will come soon enough. That is a promise I make to you."

Cisco looked at least a little bit mollified.

"If it will make you feel any better, Cisco, when he wakes up you can kick him around a little. Enough to put a good hurting in him for three or four days, say, but no more than that. All right?"

"*Sí*. Four days. An' maybe some ribs, *sí?*"

"Four days. No more." Hutch smiled. "He has work to do. Here. Dip yourself some water and wake him up. I want to get back to camp for supper before it gets too late."

Cisco jumped to his feet, winced, and went to get the water to splash onto Slocum. Cisco was looking forward to this.

CHAPTER 8

When Slocum was fully conscious again he was surprised almost to the point of being disappointed. First, he was alive. That was no disappointment but it was certainly a surprise.

He remembered the fight with the Mexican and that Slocum had been winning it until somone bashed him from behind. He vaguely remembered too that he had come groping up toward consciousness once before and found Cisco very much alive and very much angry. He remembered being too groggy to care or very much to feel as Cisco put his boots into Slocum's body time and time again. That time Slocum had been certain he would die. He was prepared for death; he had been for a long time. Now he was awake again, although he hurt so badly he was not entirely sure the other would not have been preferable. Jeez, but those pointy-toe boots could put a hurting into a man's ribs, he thought.

The real amazement, though, was when he sat up and looked around. His camp was intact. Not a thing had been touched, including the fine Sharps rifle, his clothing piled beside the river, and his holstered Colt lying on that pile. His food, saddle, picketed roan horse . . . everything appeared to be exactly the way he left it.

No, he told himself. Almost but not quite everything was as it had been. There were his buffalo hides neatly staked and scraped the way he had left them. Six buffalo hides. Only six. The other two had been carted off by that Cisco or some other one of Hutchison's crowd. They had helped themselves to what they considered to be their share and had left the rest strictly alone.

Nice of them, Slocum thought. More'n likely they thought that left them as decent and honorable men. Well, maybe not that far, but they probably thought the whole thing was just fine. The punishment no doubt had been a warning.

Slocum moved and found that the pain ran very deep indeed. Tending camp was going to be no joy until this went away, and he did not even have a bottle to smooth the rougher edges of what the next day or two were going to be like.

Grimly he began the long crawl to retrieve his clothing.

"I'll help you with that if you like," someone offered.

"This is one damn well public camp I've got here," Slocum said without expending the energy and paying the price in increased pain to look around so he could see who was speaking. "Or are you one of Hutchison's crowd?"

The voice responded with a laugh. Obviously he was not feeling Slocum's pain for him. "Just what I thought it was. One of Hutch's gentle warnings. You only get one, you know. Or did they tell you that already?"

"They didn't bother. When they left I wasn't in much shape to do any listening anyhow."

"I don't wonder, judging from the way you look. You never did answer my question about whether you want some help."

"Hell, yes I want some help. Any kind you got to give, man, including a jug if you got one handy."

"Sorry. I don't use the stuff myself." Slocum could hear the creak of saddle leather as the man dismounted. "I can help you become decent again, though, and perhaps pour some food into your belly."

"Mister, you're twenty-some years too damn late to help me get decent. But I reckon I wouldn't mind getting dressed again. As for the food, anything easier to chew than a handful of rocks would be real nice just now."

The man got Slocum's gunbelt and clothing from the riverbank and brought them to him. The fellow was perhaps a little below average height—it was hard for Slocum to judge while lying flat on his belly—and stockily built. He wore a spade beard and lace-up boots of the kind seen more on loggers than on the hunters and freighters and cowhands who might have business out on the big grass.

"In case you are wondering," he said as he helped Slocum carefully into his clothing, "my name is Charles Fortson. Charles to my friends, if you please. I loathe the nickname Chuck and detest Charlie even worse. Can't much abide any nicknames, actually. My friends call me Charles. It is Mr. Fortson to all others."

"And Hutch? What does he call you?"

"Mr. Hutchison calls me Mr. Fortson. We reached an understanding about that."

"I kinda thought he was a hard man to reach an agreement with," Slocum said.

"Not at all. Unless, of course, pride begins to stand in the way of practicality. I try not to let that happen. I came here with the intention of making a great deal of money, not of becoming involved in silly disputes with others. I particularly do not want to become involved in disputes requiring the use of firearms to settle them. I am an excellent shot, sir, but I have no desire to prove that with another human being as my target. I have quite enough regrets without adding more to the list."

"That's an interesting philosophy, Mr. Fortson . . . Charles."

"One you do not share, I take it."

"No, I reckon I don't. But I'll make a deal with you. I won't ask you to take up my way of thinking if you don't ask me to adopt yours."

"Done," Fortson said. He smiled and extended his hand. Under the circumstances, Slocum was delighted to be able to accept it. "Would my curiosity be out of line if I were to ask your name?"

"Huh? Oh, no. 'Course not. It's John Burton."

"Very good, John." They shook again. "Let me help you over against the bank there so you can be a little more upright . . . there, better?"

Slocum nodded.

"Good. Wait here then and I shall put a meal together." He grinned. "Will buffalo hump be good enough? It isn't too expensive this time of year here."

"Huh. I'm beginning to think it can be awful damned expensive. But by all means fix us a batch of the stuff. In fact, if you don't wanta bother cooking I'll just chew it down raw. I'm that hungry for red meat."

"Red meat it will be, then. Nothing better to rebuild strength after a mishap."

They ate, Slocum wolfing down the half-raw meat until his gut threatened to burst, while Fortson ate as tidily as if he had been seated at an elegantly laid table in K.C.'s most elegant eatery.

"I have a suggestion, Mr. Burton," he offered when they were both done.

"Try me."

"Is your shooting as good as your rifle would indicate, sir?"

"At least that good, Charles. Maybe better."

"Excellent. My recent partner chose to dissolve our union after a minor, uh, disagreement between us. I have a respectable crew for skinning, scraping, and hauling, you see, but I really need another gun at work to get the most out of my help. Would you consider entering into a working relationship with me?"

"Partnership?"

"Something like that."

"You pay Hutch his quarter of your take?"

"I pay Hutchison, yes. He believes it to be a quarter of my hunt, that is true also. Actually it works out to something closer to 15 percent."

"Points the same either way. You pay."

"I believe I mentioned before, John, I am a practical man. I have been in business before. In Philadelphia I paid rent to a landlord, taxes to a city, and protection—I believe they preferred to call it insurance—to a gang of petty toughs. That was all part of the cost of doing business in Philadelphia. Paying Hutchison a portion of my take in buffalo skins is a part of doing business here."

"Somehow I don't think I'd do so good as a Philadelphia businessman, Charles. I think before a week was out I'd end up trying to shove somebody's head up his own asshole."

Fortson gave him a wry grin. "As you have just finished doing here, John?"

In spite of himself Slocum grinned back at the man. "I s'pose I earned that shot, didn't I?"

"I suppose you did, John."

"I don't know as I'd want a quarter of the hides I took going to Pete Hutchison," Slocum said.

"Then I shall buy your hides in the field, as it were, and make my own arrangements with Hutchison,"

Fortson suggested. "I really do need another gun, you see."

"But you'd be paying me full price and then paying Hutchison out of that too."

Fortson smiled. "But I only intend to pay you a dollar per hide for what you provide, John. I *am* a businessman, you see."

Slocum had to laugh out loud in spite of the pain the deep laughter caused him. That was precisely the deal he had offered to Hutchison. Hutch had refused it and Fortson was proposing it.

"Could I ask what you find so funny about that, John? Personally I thought it quite fair, considering."

"Oh, so do I, Charles. So do I." He explained.

"You accept, then?"

"Yes, Charles, I reckon I do accept. It sure hell beats lying here too stiff an' sore to move for a spell and maybe ending up starved and broke at one an' the same time. So yeah, I reckon I do accept."

"Good. Consider the agreement struck."

It took Slocum three full days of sacking out in one of Fortson's camp wagons, being tended to by the cook and by Fortson himself, before Slocum felt up to straddling a horse again, and even then he did not feel worth a damn. It was another week before he felt like himself.

He was able to get in some shooting from the fourth day on, though, and by the end of a week of hunting —gunning, really, for it had little to do with hunting as Slocum had always thought of that term—Slocum was becoming adept at the business of exterminating buffalo cleanly and efficiently. The seventh day of his hunting he was able to knock down fifty-two animals out of a single stand of the beasts, and he was quite frankly proud of himself when he returned to the base wagon that night.

"It is good," Fortson said. "Especially so soon. I don't believe I've ever seen a man so deadly with any kind of firearm as you are, John. But if you think you have yourself a record of some sort, I must disappoint you."

"Close?"

"Not even halfway there," Fortson told him. "Why, I am no great hand at the business myself. Not yet at any rate, and I personally have taken 84 from one stand and 79 from another. I am told that Billy Dixon took 143 from a single stand last year and Rafe Furst 131 several weeks before him. So you do have quite a distance to go."

"Oh, well," Slocum said. "It ain't exactly the sort of record I care about anyhow." Which was mostly true. Slocum did not really care that much one way or another about the killing of buffalo. But the money certainly was good. And he was, after all, a fairly competitive man, whether the subject was poker or getting a woman into bed or shooting down buffalo. Whatever the subject, Slocum would rather be on top than No. 2.

By that time Slocum was feeling well enough that one of those competitive instincts was becoming uncomfortable. He had not had a woman since before that Salt Creek holdup and that was weeks in the past now. It was getting so he crawled into his bedroll at night with a hard-on, slept with his blanket poked high toward the night sky, and woke up so hard he ached.

The others in the buffalo camp, from the greasy-skinned slob who did their cooking to the Mexican skinners—who each bathed on a daily basis despite the Anglo insistence on calling them greasers, Slocum noticed—apparently were having the same sort of trouble.

The camp conversations came more and more often to the subject of women, particularly whores and willing dancehall girls, and once they arrived on that topic lingered there the longer as more time passed without a break from the womanless monotony of the work. The only ones who seemed to have little problem with the subject were the freight-wagon drivers, who spent most of their time hauling hides from Fortson's camp to a buying point and then back again to pick up the skins that had been taken while they were on the road. With Slocum shooting too, Fortson had no trouble keeping his two freight wagons busy. And the freighters had no trouble incurring the envy of the men who could not reach a whorehouse every two weeks or so for a fresh ass hauling. The freighters tended to lord that little side benefit over their less fortunate coworkers, and every time one of the wagons pulled out with a fresh load of hides there was a renewed round of groaning and pup-pulling among those left behind.

Even Fortson, who usually managed to maintain his dignity in spite of sweat, gore, lice, and high odors, seemed to become affected by it eventually.

Slocum and Fortson had fallen into a habit after supper of letting the other men take to their bedrolls or build a separate fire beside a spread blanket for some low-stakes gaming while the two hunters took possession of the main campfire so they could melt lead for the constantly needed supply of fresh bullets.

Reloading is a time-consuming chore but essentially a boring one. Molding the bullets and patching them with a wrap of paper, repriming the many-times-fired case, dumping in the powder charge and sealing the newly made bullets. They were routine tasks, the kinds of things that can be done by habit-directed fingers while the mind wanders and the tongue wags. The two got into the habit of talking and drinking coffee far into the night while they did their loading.

On one of those evenings the subject turned to the pressures of doing without.

"Are you as frustrated as I've been getting lately, John?"

Slocum thought he understood what Fortson meant. From any of the other men in the camp he would have been sure of it. But Fortson always seemed such a proper and reserved sort, almost a prude, that when the words were coming from him Slocum was not so sure. As a matter of fact, Slocum realized, he had never once heard Fortson discuss women in any way before.

"Are you talking about what I think you are, Charles? Like, not getting any pussy?"

Fortson blushed. It had been an awfully long time since John Slocum had seen a grown man blush. Come to think of it, he decided, he wasn't sure he ever *had* seen a grown man blush before. Of course, Fortson was a bit of a prig. Maybe even a bit of a wimp too. Still there was no damned doubt. The man was sitting there with a lap full of unprimed brass cartridge cases and a definite bulge in his britches splitting the brass into two piles.

"Yeah, I guess you are at that," Slocum went on. "Sure I'm horny. Who the hell wouldn't be after so long?"

"Of course you are. It is only natural after so long without . . . uh . . . companionship. Especially a man as physically attractive and obviously virile as you are, John."

"Big words, Charles, an' I don't know that I could agree. Hell, I ain't no pretty boy. Mostly, I reckon, I look mean as hell. Women seem to take to that, though. Bless 'em. For some reason they seem to like finding a man they think can fuck 'em until their eyeballs bulge and they have to quit the screwing and go to sucking if they wanta keep things going."

Fortson's already red face darkened even further. But he was not willing to drop the subject. "And, uh, are you . . . a man who can do that?"

"You bet your butt I can, Charles. I expect to the next chance I get too. Count on it." Slocum grinned.

Fortson muttered something too low for Slocum to hear.

"What?"

"Oh, I . . . nothing. Really, John, I . . . Gawd!" Fortson groaned aloud.

"Hey, are you all right?" Slocum leaned forward and put a hand on Fortson's shoulder. Instead of the offered support giving him comfort, though, it seemed to make Fortson groan all the worse and all the louder.

"John, please . . ."

Without warning—without warning that Slocum had taken as such, at any rate—the stocky Philadelphia businessman grabbed Slocum's hand and turned it palm up. He kissed Slocum's palm and began to lick Slocum's hand with a disgustingly wet tongue.

Without stopping to think about it, Slocum balled his free hand into a fist and smashed it into Fortson's face, sending the smaller man rocking backward into the dirt and spraying the immediate area with a shower of cartridge cases that flashed like so much gold in the firelight.

"John, I'm sorry. Oh, God, I am so awfully, awfully sorry," Fortson blubbered.

"Sit up, you sorry son-of-a-bitch, before the other men notice. I don't think any of them noticed yet. Now sit up, damnit. *Now.*"

"Yes." Fortson did so. He wiped hastily at his face with a dirt-fouled hand. "John . . . truly . . . I am so very . . ."

"Will you shut your damned face for a minute. Now looka here, if I'd had a little warning maybe I wouldn't of punched you like that, Charles, but you damn sure earned it anyhow. Silly son-of-a-bitchin' thing to do, Charles. You could get your gut sliced open that way sometime or a bullet in your brainless damn head. You know that, don't you?"

Fortson nodded. His expression was a study in misery. Total, pure, abject misery. "I know that. I have known better for as long as I can remember, but . . ."

"Jee-zus, Charles, don't go giving me any explanations or stinking sob stories. I don't want to hear them. You understand that?"

"Yes. Completely."

"Thank goodness for small favors, anyhow. Now I want you to listen to me, Charles, because we're gonna get something straight here an' it ain't gonna be your pecker that gets straightened out. I won't tell you this but the one time. After that, you do it again it'll be me doing the cutting or the shooting you're going to get anyhow someday if you keep on this way. You follow me?"

Fortson nodded unhappily. He sat with his head down, his fingers knotting together in his lap, and his hands twisting in his misery.

"Right. So listen, Charles. I ain't one of those guys that gets all worried that having a queer in the same bar with him or the same camp with him is going to rub off and make him one too. I know it don't work that way, and I've worked and lived and fought side by side with a lot of queers before. A man can't pull time in the Army nor in jail nor on hardly any other job without it. I've played poker many a night with old Bill Hickok and he was about as flaming a fag as ever swished down the pink pike, Charles, and none of him nor of those other boys ever rubbed off on me. They knew enough to leave me alone an' so they weren't any threat to me. I reckon you won't rub off on me either,

Charles. As a matter of fact, I'm willing to state right here and now that you won't rub off on me. Nor get it off anywheres near me. Understand that?"

"Uh-huh."

"You damn sure better, Charles, because if you once forget it again I'll likely take it as a personal thing and not just the little mistake I'm willing to let this time go as. So my advice to you is for you to do the same thing I do, and that is when it gets so bad you just can't stand it anymore you tuck yourself up to your chin in blankets an' whack off. Just the same as the rest of us. Hear?"

"Yes, but I . . ."

"Goddamnit, Charles, I told you already. Don't give me no explanations or stories. I've heard them all already anyhow, how at least I don't have to spend my time looking at women an' not being able to touch an' how you're just as needful of pussy or whatever you call it as the next man. I've heard all that stuff before, Charles. It don't cut shit with me. That's a fact. Do you go to playing with my knee again you'll pull back a wet, red stump instead of the hand you started out with. Now gather up your brass. We still got a lot of cartridges to load tonight or we won't be getting much shooting done tomorrow."

Fortson nodded and began to pick up the empties he had dropped.

After a few minutes of painful silence, Fortson said, "Did you hear Enrique say today that the camp just west of us took 170-some hides today?"

"No. How many shooters?"

"Three, I think."

"Damn good. Maybe we can outgun them tomorrow, eh, Charles?"

Fortson gave him a small smile. "Yes. Perhaps we can, John."

Slocum finished repriming his brass and reached for the big can of coarse powder and the scoop he had sized to give him the load he most liked in old Meriwether's Sharps rifle. He sighed. "This loading gets to be a bore, don't it, partner."

CHAPTER 9

Three days later none of them cared at all if they had
not seen a woman for a month or if they might have
just crawled off one wet and sticky and satiated. Three
days later as the sun was breasting the horizon the
horsemen came, sweeping out of the east with the new
sun at their backs and long shadows racing ahead of
them, reaching almost as far ahead as their wild, ululat-
ing screeches and war whoops.

They came naked, themselves stripped of clothing
and their horses stripped of the crude saddles and
apishamores they normally used. Their bodies and their
mounts were painted gaudily to terrify their enemies
and to beseech their spirit-world guardians. Their faces
were hideously marked and only some of those marks
had been artificially applied. Others, a good many
others, were the badges of victory they wore from past
encounters. Their lances bore streamers made of feathers and soft leather. And human hair.

"Kiowa," one of the freighters cried.

"For God's sake, don't move," Fortson commanded.
His voice was not loud but it was pitched to carry
throughout the camp and he spoke the words with the
sure authority of command. Slocum recognized the tone
—he had used it often enough himself when he wore

gray and gold instead of Levi's and a flannel shirt—
and he approved.

"Don't any one of you move or try to run away.
Stand firm and above all don't let them see any fear
here. They're testing us. They'll sweep through a time
or two before they talk. If any one of us fires a gun or
tries to get away we have to fight for sure. Otherwise
we have a chance. So *don't* show any fear."

"Too late, boss," the freighter drawled. "I already
pissed my pants."

Slocum looked. The man had for a fact fouled himself. There was a dark stain spreading at his crotch. He
showed none of his fear in his face, though, merely
pulled a plug of tobacco from his pocket and gnawed
a generous chew from it. Slocum caught his eye and
gave him a thumbs-up sign. The freighter nodded sol-
emnly.

"Here they come, boys. Firm now," Fortson told
them all.

The man was a queer but he was no coward, Slocum acknowledged. Fortson moved into the center of
their camp and stood empty-handed to face the oncoming Kiowa, his back straight and his chin high. He
stared them down as they came.

The Kiowa were as fearsome as any people on the
face of the earth, and their reputation was one they had
earned. They carved it out of living flesh and colored it
with the hot, pumping blood of their enemies. And nearly all men who walked the face of the earth were their
enemies, the few exceptions being the Comanches and,
from time to time by tenuous truce, the Comancheros
who came up out of Mexico with oxcarts laden with trade
goods and went back South again with loads of goods
the Kiowa brought to them, goods up to and often including captives who could be used or sold or ransomed
for handsome profits.

There were several dozen in this painted group, and

there might be ten times that number more hidden in the swales and wallows within a half mile of the camp.

It took no great powers of logic to see that these warriors were ready to fight. Their paint, their defiant screams, their brandished lances told their mood clearly.

They thundered into the camp and through it, brushing past Fortson as if he were a rock placed in the middle of the camp, and like a rock he stood there as they raced by. Exen when one of the younger Kiowa, a youth with few symbols on his lance and with little paint on his face, seemed bent on running him down, Fortson did not move but stared into the hatred streaming out of the Kiowa's eyes. At the last possible instant the Kiowa brave swerved his horse, jostling it into the flank of another warrior's mount and spitting guttural insults at Fortson as he charged by. Within seconds after their arrival the camp was a mass of churned dust through which it was almost impossible to see, but still Fortson stood without moving.

The Kiowa hauled their sweating warhorses to a stop within a few yards of the camp, and the few among them who had guns fired them recklessly into the air. They wheeled and heeled the horses into another mad charge through the hunters' camp.

Fortson, Slocum saw, still had not moved. He stood facing east in the same pose he had first taken as the Indians approached, and even the sound of the second charge coming down on his unprotected back was not enough to make him move or to look around to see if one of the Kiowa might be dipping a lance point toward the small of his back.

That, Slocum thought, took more guts than any one man alive was entitled to have. The back of Fortson's shirt was drenched with sweat, and Slocum knew that that would be icy-cold sweat, the sweat of raw fear, but still the man's position held and he did not so much as flinch when a tall, ugly Kiowa with streaks of gray in his hair and a torso crisscrossed with old scars leaned down from his running pony to touch Fortson lightly on the shoulder with a coup stick.

That feathered and medicine-decorated coup stick was proof enough of the Indian's importance. While most warriors who carried a coup stick instead of a weapon—and they were few enough as it was—would have carried a stick as long as a staff and stout enough to serve as a club, this man carried a stick no longer than a quirt and no heavier than a slip of young willow. The weight of several medicine pouches was enough to bend the stick. Except for that slight wand and the power of his spirit-given medicine, the Kiowa carried no weapons.

He touched Fortson with his coup stick and while he watched the white man closely for a reaction—and got none—he howled a cry of great victory in his elation. The coup he had just counted was a powerful one and a deed that would bring him much honor, for this was an enemy of courage he had touched.

Again the Kiowa cruelly yanked their ponies to sliding stops and wheeled to face the camp.

The tall Kiowa who had counted coup on Fortson jammed his heels into his horse's sides and drew back on his single rein at the same time, sending the already excited and nervous animal dancing sideways. Skillfully the tall Indian moved the animal forward until he faced Fortson from a distance of only a few feet. For a long minute the two men faced each other that way, the haughty Indian staring coldly down from the advantage of horseback and the white man just as stern and rock-faced staring up at the man who would probably try to kill him.

Without taking his eyes from the Kiowa, Fortson said, "John, bring that big Sharps of yours and stroll over here beside me, please."

"Will do."

Slocum agreed with Fortson's choice. It would show the Kiowa that they were not afraid—which would be the damnedest, God-awful lie ever perpetrated on an Indian by a white man—and would also show them that these white men were armed with the big guns that shoot far and kill so well. It would remind the tall one that he and his friends were vulnerable. And while an Indian loves war he hates dying in one and seems to have no concept of sustained combat. He lacks the white's bulldog tenacity in war and when he thinks he has taken too many casualties he will stop and ride away to wait for a better day to die. That was a fact. The question now was whether this Kiowa and his friends knew it too.

Slocum eased the heavy Sharps up across his shoulder in what he hoped was a casual position. With all the false bravado he could muster he sauntered out to join Fortson at the center of attention. Slocum's skin crawled and he could feel the sweat rolling out of his armpits and down his sides, but he was too old a hand at the poker tables to let any of it show on his face.

"What do you need, old cock?" he asked when he got there. It was an expression he had heard some Englishmen using in a Cheyenne cathouse, but Fortson seemed to take it another way.

Incredibly, Fortson smiled at him, and the smile was one of genuine amusement. "This is not the time for pornographic references, John. Nor for accepting old propositions."

"Silly bastard. Except for that one thing you're just a helluva fellow."

"Except for one thing, so are you, John."

Slocum grinned at him, and damned if it wasn't real. He surprised himself with that.

The Kiowa seemed to be getting impatient. The man said something that Slocum could not understand. The words were just so much growling noise to him. The

Kiowa spoke as well in the universal sign language of the Plains, but Slocum could catch only a fraction from the rapid shifting of the man's hands. He caught the sign for dead. That one was all too clear. He saw the sign for buffalo. Most of the rest was just a jumble of movement.

"Did you understand him?" Fortson asked. Fortson's eyes still had not left the Indian's.

"No."

"Is there anyone here who knows what this man is saying?" Fortson asked in a louder tone.

Slocum could hear some foot shuffling behind them and a few coughs. After a moment one of the men said, *"Sí."* He came forward, the Mexican skinner they called Tonio.

Tonio joined them. He looked a little nervous but gained control of himself soon enough. He and the Kiowa went into conversation, most of it through the sign language but some spoken as well. Their talk went on for some time.

"They are unhappy," Tonio said finally. "Very unhappy, yes. They, their people, depend on the buffalo for their lives, yes. From the buffalo they take their food, their homes, their clothing."

Jeez, Slocum thought, a fucking schoolhouse lecture in the middle of the Plains. And delivered by a painted savage at that. Slocum had a bit of Indian blood himself. More than a bit, actually. But right at this moment the Kiowa and all his kin and cousins were a bunch of painted savages. Another time, without that paint on themselves and their horses, they might be grand fellows to have a feast with. But right now they were painted savages.

Tonio went on in that vein for quite a while, occasionally checking back with the Kiowa to get a point clarified or—Slocum was almost sure from what little he had been able to catch—asking if he could throw something else in that was his own idea.

That, Slocum thought, is called brown-nosing. Queer or not, Fortson surely had never sucked ass as hard as Tonio was trying to do right then.

The lecture ran on for a while until finally the two of them, the Kiowa and Tonio, who Slocum was almost certain by now had once worked with the Comancheros because several times Slocum had caught the sign for oxcarts, got down to the meat of things.

"This," Tonio said, "is Two Trees Walking. He is a great war chief of the Kiowa nation."

By then Slocum was bored enough to think briefly that a name like that must have had an interesting origin. As for the rest of it, it was awfully rare for a white man to be introduced to a fighting Indian of any tribe who did not label himself a great war chief.

War chief, of course, meant anybody who had ever suggested a raid on somebody else's horse herd, household, or pumpkin patch, and really did not mean all it was cracked up to be.

"Two Trees Walking had a vision," Tonio said. "He is a dream seeker, and among his people that is a great thing. As great a thing as being a war chief, yes. Two Trees Walking placed himself in a sweat lodge to purify himself. Afterward he took with him the magic buttons of the Yaqui people and for three days and three nights he sat on a high place and sought his dream."

Peyote, Slocum thought. The poor man's opium. That stuff would make a blind man see green and purple elephants or convince a legless man he could fly instead. Slocum knew; he had tried it once himself. A couple times, maybe. Anyway, it was no wonder the great war chief and dreamer Two Trees Walking had himself a vision if he was using that for a crutch when he went looking for glory.

"This dream," Tonio said, "took him out of his

Kiowa body and into the world of the Little People. The Little People swept him under the ground and through their secret places, and he saw there many wonders that man has never known. When again they came above the surface of the great mother the earth Two Trees Walking was no longer in the land of his people in the Wichitas but was here, on this land of grass and much sky. These Little People brought Two Trees Walking to a council where Buffalo and Wolf and Coyote sat in the circle and the great chief of the Little People sat at the north." Tonio paused to wipe his forehead. He was getting as involved in the story as if it were his own. As if it were real even.

"Buffalo told Two Trees Walking that he was sad. Very sad, yes. The white men in this country were killing him. Wolf said without Buffalo his people could not live either. Coyote said without Buffalo his people must surely die as well. All agreed that Two Trees Walking should put a stop to this. They gave him powerful medicine so he could drive the white men from his country. Two Trees Walking gave them his oath and in return they promised to him that he could not die until the last white man had been killed or driven from the Plains and Buffalo and Wolf and Coyote left to the old ways of all the ages."

"If I was him," Slocum said drily, "I'd damn sure take to selling town lots all the way from the Canadian down to the Rio Bravo then an' make sure I wouldn't never die. Keep us white folks coming for all I was worth."

Tonio looked positively stricken. Slocum was beginning to think *he* believed all this crap as much as the Kiowa did. Probably more. The Indian would know it was full of shit even if Tonio believed it.

"Two Trees Walking," Tonio said, "has come here with all the warriors of his people to sweep the whites from the country of Buffalo and Wolf and Coyote as he promised the Little People he would do."

Now, that one just *had* to be a lie, Slocum thought. You couldn't get *all* the Indians of any tribe to agree that the sun came up in the east every day. They were a notional crowd if there ever was one, medicine or no medicine, and whatever one claimed to have dreamed another would dream the opposite. Their downright ornery independence was one of the reasons Slocum liked them. Most of the time.

"Two Trees Walking," Tonio persisted, "says you are brave men and he will allow one of you to live so you can carry his message and the power of his medicine to all the other whites of this country. You are to determine which one by the strength of your courage and the power of your arms. You may have until first light tomorrow to do this, because that is what Buffalo and Wolf and Coyote have told him to have you do. Tomorrow morning he will return to counsel the one who remains. Those are the words of Two Trees Walking."

For the first time since he had taken his stand before the rushing crowd of Kiowas, Charles Fortson turned his eyes away from his enemy. He looked at Tonio and said, "There's something I noticed in that speech you just delivered for our guest, Tonio. You're white. And you're a hell of a lot littler than me. You start any fighting here I figure to whittle my initials on your neck the first thing I do."

Tonio blanched.

"Unless, of course, you figure to ride out with them Kiowa. Do you?"

Tonio began to talk to the tall Kiowa again. Rapidly and with growing agitation. The answer he got did not need translation.

"I believe you are staying with us, friend Tonio?"

Tonio spat. "But of course, *señor* bossman. Do you think I would go with this dirty son-of-a-whore sow and leave my friends behind?"

"Only if you were invited, Tonio. Only if you were invited."

Slocum shrugged. "At least we can get in a long nap today. We might be glad of that come morning." He smiled at Two Trees Walking and bowed to him as formally as a Spanish grandee being presented to French royalty—which he had seen one time in New Orleans—and said in a pleasant tone, "May your balls provide a meal for ten thousand ants this very evening, great war chief Two Trees Walking."

Fortson, chuckling, gave his own best imitation of a proper bow and told the tall Kiowa, "Your medicine pouches would make an excellent cork for the rectum beneath your nose, great farter in the wind." To Tonio he added, "Tell the red bastard something nice and send him on his way now. We have some preparing to do."

"That will not be needed, white man who shits in his own soup pot," Two Trees Walking said. "I think this is a fine day for one of us to die."

"Well, hell," Slocum said. "I sure was looking forward to a nap."

"You will have a long rest and a cold one when your hair is decorating my lance, ball eater."

"You got the wrong boy on that subject," Slocum said. "Not that it matters right now, I don't reckon."

Two Trees Walking looked puzzled but not diverted. "Yes, a good day for you to die." With a shriek and a wild brandishing of his lance he wheeled his pony and raced away. The rest of the Kiowa set up their yammering again and streaked across the grass after him and quickly out of sight.

"Goddamn, Charles, those fellows have spoiled my appetite for breakfast."

"For Chrissake, John, this is not the time to get all ballsy and brave. Let's get busy throwing up some barriers to hide behind, boy. This next time they'll be getting serious."

CHAPTER 10

"What about the water barrel?" Fortson asked.

"Wrapped with hides and protected as well as we'll be able to," Slocum answered.

"The men are settled in their positions, Enrique? They are ready with their weapons?"

"As you said for them to do," the skinner assured him.

"Then I suppose we wait for our callers."

"Me, I'm beginning to wonder about them already. They've should've been here practically right away. Leastways the way I would've figured it any other time with any other Indian. That boy Two Trees is a caution," Slocum said. The Kiowa had been out of sight for nearly forty-five minutes now.

"I always heard the Kiowa were an impulsive tribe. Do you think they might have seen our firepower and given it up?" Fortson asked.

"No bloody way," Slocum said. "You heard all that crap Tonio was telling us. He ain't bright enough to've made it up himself. Two Trees said it an' he probably believes at least a piece of it. Enough that those painted bastards are across a hill somewhere working them up one powerful batch of medicine. When they come after us—and they damn sure will come after us, Charles— they're going to be hard to handle because they'll each

101

and every one believe, *absolutely* believe that they can't lose. That's why they're taking so long. Ol' Two Trees is no dummy. He won't turn loose of them until he has the whole crowd exactly as riled as he wants them to be."

Fortson sighed. "One can continue to hope, in any event."

"Hope all you please, but keep your rifle in your hands," Slocum said.

"Yes, well, I think we should take our positions now. Everything seems ready enough except for a severe lack of targets. John, I'll take this side. You place your rifle opposite me and facing out the other way if you would, please."

Slocum nodded. Fortson had taken for himself the direction Kiowa had first charged from—the direction they probably would come from again when they came seeking blood. No, the man was anything but a coward.

The nest Slocum prepared for himself was an above-ground rifle pit of sorts, three stacks of hastily piled buffalo hides placed in a triangle with a shoulder-deep gap in the center of them where Slocum could sit in reasonable protection while he fired.

He had a total of 143 cartridges for the big .50-110-550 Sharps. Meriwether had had 150 of them, but repeated use had split 7 of the cases since Slocum got them. All of these Slocum placed on a clean cloth beneath his right hand. His Colt and .45 ammo were always handy. For that he never needed advance preparation.

The sun by now was high enough to begin pouring dry heat onto the land, and inside the close confinement of the rifle pit Slocum began to sweat. At least his sweat was from the increasing heat, though, and not from fear. The first of that had worn off through sheer boredom. Later there would be no time for fear, unless it became too late, and then it would no longer matter if he died afraid or not because by then there would be no one left to care.

Slocum took a short swallow from his canteen and hefted the flat wooden container to make sure it was nearly full still. He was satisfied. In a firefight a man will often become thirsty, so much so that the Canadian in flood could not carry enough water to satisfy his thirst, and the Mexican skinners did not own canteens to have at their sides. Slocum considered himself lucky.

The time dragged. An hour and a half had passed since any Kiowa were last seen, then two hours. The men began to mutter and shift restlessly from position to position.

"What do you think, John?" Fortson called over his shoulder.

"I think they haven't come yet."

"There is no hope that they won't?"

"There's always hope, Charles. But damn little likelihood. They'll come, all right, in their own good time. We ain't going anywhere that they have to worry about us getting away. The show is theirs to run when and how they please, and they know it."

"It would be nice to find you proven wrong, John."

"I surely do agree, Charles."

After several minutes more of silence Fortson said, "One thing I am beginning to regret about my rules of camp behavior."

"What's that, Charles?"

"No booze."

Slocum was about to agree with that regret when he heard a rising cry from somewhere in the distance. "I think we're done waiting, boys."

"Look to your guns, gentlemen," Fortson said calmly.

The Kiowa came the same way they had first appeared and from the same direction, bursting into view already at a dead run, shrieking hatred for their white enemy, charms and decorations streaming out behind them in the wind of their own speed. This time, though, the lances were held low for thrusting into the bellies of the waiting white men and there was a grimness in the way they rode that had not been there on that first mock attack earlier.

They rode roughly fifty abreast, in a line more than wide enough to engulf the small buffalo camp, and there were three waves of them spaced one after the other and about a hundred yards between waves.

Call it about 150 warriors, Slocum thought. Hell and damnation, he told himself, an' me with only 143 shells.

The Indians came nearer and the shrill yammer of their howls grew all the more fierce. If they expected to break the nerve of the waiting hunters, though, they were disappointed, for the men waited quietly in whatever shelter they had found for themselves—if only because there was no place to run to, nowhere to hide. It was fight or die now and no choice about it.

The first wave reached the camp and broke around the wagon that had been rolled into place near the hide stacks, sweeping around the camp like water breaking against a rock set firm in a riverbed.

The hunters on that side of the camp began a steady fire, fire that was returned with a rain of arrows and short spears and an occasional gunshot.

The Kiowa swept around the camp again, flowing like water, and Slocum added the heavy boom of his big Sharps to the confused din of combat.

He got off four shots before the first wave had spun swiftly away, leaving spent arrows and a thick stir of dust behind them, but the shooting had had no more effect than its emotional lift to Slocum's spirits. So far the big gun had been no more than a noisemaker, for as they circled around the entrenched camp the Indians rode with a knee hooked over the withers of their horses but their bodies protected behind the sturdy flesh of their mounts.

Shit, Slocum thought, this won't cut it.

The second wave reached the camp and burst upon it in a flurry of noise and dust and deadly arrows as the first had done. One of the camp tenders screamed as an arrow found him. He died a moment later, drowning in his own blood and lengthening the odds all the more for the remaining whites.

Again Slocum accomplished nothing but the waste of three more shots as the Indians swept around the camp and dashed away untouched so far as Slocum could see.

"¿Enrique?" Slocum called to the man nearest him. "¿Si?"

"This ain't gonna cut it. We can't hit 'em when they ride down low like that. I got an idea, though, if you're a good enough shot."

"I am good enough, Señor Burton."

"Good. Get your butt in here beside me before the next bunch . . . oops. We'll do it in a minute."

The third wave came, and again the big Sharps roared, if without effect, and the living, fighting, yelling Indians raced away once again.

"Hop over here, Enrique."

The Mexican scrambled into Slocum's pit. It was a close fit for two men but it was big enough.

Enrique carried a Spencer carbine and a sack of loading tubes, each tube holding seven of the stubby .52-caliber rimfire shells ready for dumping into the built-in magazine in the butt of the short, heavy little carbine. The Spencer was underpowered for the weight of its slug and not nearly so fast to fire as the more popular Winchester, but military surplus Spencers could be had for a dollar apiece and they were as ruggedly durable as any gun ever made. And that thick, heavy slug had tremendous impact at close range.

"What we're gonna do, Enrique, is for you to knock the horses down, an' I'll pop the rider as he comes off his animal."

Enrique grinned. "I like."

"So do I. My barrel's longer, so I'll sit up here behind you an' follow over your shoulder. I'll point wherever you do so we don't have to waste time talkin' about which one to pick out, okay?"

"Okay, *sí*. I like."

"Squat down there, pal. I think we've got our chance to try it."

The Kiowa had regrouped and were coming again. From this direction they would not be in sight so long before they reached the camp and there was no way to tell yet if they were still forming in waves the way they had for the first series of attacks, but there were still about fifty in the line as they came over a slight rise and thundered down on the camp straight into Slocum's position.

Slocum sat on the rearmost of his three stacks of hides. He was exposed to fire here, but he had more freedom to swing his heavy rifle for the snapshooting that would be required when or if Enrique was able to spill some Kiowa horses. At the moment that seemed more important than the increased danger, for if the Kiowa did not soon take some losses—heavy losses at that—they would *really* believe the bullshit Two Trees Walking had been feeding them, and then they would be totally impossible to discourage.

Slocum had almost forgotten the tall Kiowa leader, had forgotten about him in the first pass although he had been at their center. If Slocum saw him this time he would have to try to take him. Everyone said if a war chief is killed his tribe will call it a day. This seemed a fine time to test that opinion.

They came again at a full run and as they reached

effective rifle range split into two groups, the riders in each group dropping to the side of his horse away from the white men's guns.

Enrique bent over the sights of his Spencer and went to work, Slocum bending over Enrique and lining the Sharps barrel with that of the Spencer.

Enrique fired and a stocky little sorrel took a slug in its head. The horse flipped ass over eartips, and its rider leaped free at the last possible second. The Kiowa —he was painted to resemble an owl, complete with black and yellow feathers on his chest and upper arms —was too heavily disguised with gaudy decoration to tell if he was old or young, bounced immediately to his feet, and reached up to another Indian racing down on him to pick him up and carry him away to safety. Slocum's bullet reached the Kiowa before the other warrior could, and the thumb-sized Sharps slug smashed into the brave's head. The high speed impact of so heavy a bullet turned the air around the Kiowa's head red with a wet mist that the other Indian rode through while his buddy was still falling toward the ground.

Enrique looked over his shoulder at Slocum and grinned. "I like."

"Me too, partner. There. Quick, damnit, that's the chief."

Two Trees Walking was in the middle of the leading wave again, placing himself in the worst of the danger as before.

Even so, Slocum thought, he wasn't trusting his damned heathen medicine so far that he'd ride straight up on the horse where we could get a shot at him. He was down as low as any of them. Slocum was positive, though, that that was Two Trees's horse. He remembered the animal well.

"That one. Quick now."

Enrique nodded and aimed his Spencer where Slocum pointed.

Slocum cursed. Another Indian's horse had come between them and Two Trees Walking, and it was that horse that Enrique was aiming at.

The horse dropped, and Slocum had no choice but to beef its rider before he could get away. Better to be sure of that one than to take a chance on Two Trees Walking.

By then the lead wave was gone again and Two Trees with it.

Slocum might have taken that as an opportunity to relax but there was no time for that. This time the second wave was almost on the heels of the first, and the third immediately behind the second.

"Shoot, Enrique. Goddamnit, shoot."

Shoot Enrique did and again and again after that, dropping horses so efficiently that Slocum's single-shot Sharps could not keep up with the deadly effectiveness of the Spencer and several Kiowa warriors tumbled into the grass only to be picked up and swept to safety by the others riding close behind them.

At the tail end of the last wave Enrique dropped another before Slocum was ready with the slower Sharps, but this time there was no one coming behind to pick up the sprawling brave.

The Kiowa, his face and body hidden under a layer of white clay and ocher stain, saw his predicament but he made no attempt to squirm to safety in the short grass. He leaped up at once and grabbed a hand ax from a thong at his waist. With only that for a weapon he screamed and spat and on foot charged the waiting whites. Someone shot him down before Slocum could finish the job of reloading his Sharps.

"We've been getting some of them," Fortson yelled excitedly. "We're hurting them."

"Enrique an' me worked out a system," Slocum called. He explained what they had been doing.

"Pair up," Fortson called. "Everyone pair up before

they come back. If we hurt them badly enough they may give up."

The men reshuffled themselves into pairs, but there were not so many pairing now as there could have been at the start of the fight. Two of the hunting crew were already dead and another wounded so badly he could not use his right arm to fire a weapon. He did hold a pistol awkwardly in his left hand, but no one wanted to pair with him.

"Hurry, gentlemen. They won't delay long," Fortson urged. He was right, too. The Indians took only moments to regroup and come again for their third assault on the makeshift fortress of wagons and hides and, now, dead mules.

"Ready, Enrique?"

"But of course."

"Damn good thing you are, 'cause so are they."

CHAPTER 11

They came in a mass this time, no more of the succes-
sive waves, which seemed to have lost their effectiveness. The Kiowa came in a screaming, fearsome mass
of color and noise and hate, and the mere sight of them
would have been enough to prompt surrender in a
"civilized" war like the Civil War. But with the Kiowa
surrender was another word for death and so the whites
had no choice but to fight.

Death might still be the result. It most likely would
be, Slocum knew. But at least they still had the choice
to die as men and not as quitters.

Enrique shot horses until the barrel of his Spencer
was overheated, and Slocum knocked down Kiowa
warriors nearly as often, and still the Kiowa continued
their mad, classic circle, moving ever closer to the
small knot of desperate whites.

The other hunters were using Slocum's technique
now too and the toll on the Kiowa was worse than
Slocum had ever heard of Indians taking without dropping the fight until a better time.

The whipped-up hatred and religious intensity held
in the warriors' attack until Slocum thought the camp
must surely be overrun, and still the Indians howled
and sent their arrows slicing into the makeshift fortress

with that peculiar hissing sizzle that was so awesomely frightening to have to hear.

The stacks of buffalo hides looked like a huge pin-cushion designed for the storage of an entire tribe's supply of arrows, and few of the hunters escaped the gaping, bloody wounds those arrows could cause.

Enrique had taken one shaft along his ribs and another in his thigh but he continued to fight as he did not yet realize they were there.

Slocum's upper arm was laid open by a grazing hit and another sliced against the side of his head. He could hear the arrowhead grate on bone as it passed along his skull and he could feel the hot flow of blood afterward, but in the heat of the combat he was not aware of feeling any pain. His vitals, at least, were protected by Enrique's upper body as he sat behind the Mexican to follow the other man's rifle aim.

There was no time for Slocum to look around to check the others but he knew they had to be getting chewed up too. There was no way to avoid it under such a constant, vicious assault as the Kiowa continued to press.

"There!" Slocum shouted into the din once, but he was too late. Two Trees Walking disappeared into the dust of the melee again before Enrique could bring down the spectacularly colored stallion the tall Kiowa was riding.

Slocum saw Enrique duck as a Kiowa brave came racing toward them out of the dust cloud with a hand ax raised and a high-pitched scream streaming out of his throat.

Enrique's Spencer was empty and Slocum had just fired the single round that the big Sharps held.

Slocum palmed his .45 and pumped two fast shots into the Kiowa, the first taking the man high in the chest and the next bursting his throat open in a spray of blood.

"Thank you," he thought he heard Enrique politely say, but in the midst of so much noise he could not be sure.

The Indians came on and on until it seemed the fight had been going on for days already and still they would not quit.

They were so near now that Enrique shot a horse and the falling animal collapsed onto the front of their hide barricade and for a moment kept Slocum from bringing the Sharps to bear on his target.

The Kiowa kept his feet as his horse dropped out from under him and he leaped off the stricken animal and onto a pile of salt sacks that two others of the hunters were using for protection. Slocum shot the brave but not before he had buried a knife into the belly of a hide scraper named Julio. Both men died there, their blood mingling on the ground to form a thick red mud as they lay together in a twisted huddle behind the bags of salt.

Slocum reloaded his Sharps feverishly and raised it again to follow Enrique's lead, but this time there was no fresh target. This time the ring of dust that encircled the camp was empty of living horses and empty of living men, although there were several dozen lifeless carcasses on the ground around them and almost as many dead Kiowa as well.

"Gawd," someone said wonderingly, "they're gone."

"We beat 'em. We *beat* them," another voice exclaimed.

"Maybe," Slocum said drily.

"Who do we still have here?" Fortson asked. He stood up from the bed of one of the two wagons that had been at the camp ready for loading when the Indians came. Slocum had thought the Philadelphian was dead.

Slowly, almost timidly, the living rose from their cramped, crouched places of almost-concealment.

Slocum and Enrique both still lived. Fortson was alive, although his left arm dangled uselessly at his side. Tonio was alive and as far as Slocum could see untouched. There were only two others, both wounded, a freighter named Hank and a wagon swamper or harness tender called Beanass in honor of the trumpeting volume that came from his bedroll at night.

Six men, Slocum thought, to stand off the whole damned Kiowa nation.

At least they seemed like the entire nation. If they chose to come again he did not see how they could possibly keep them off again.

Slocum reached for his canteen. It seemed impossible that any one human being could be so thirsty. He took two swallows, forced himself to wait, and took one more. It was only the sternest brand of self-discipline that enabled him to recap the wooden canteen and lay it down with water still inside. He might as well save the water, he knew, because his thirst had little to do with any need for water, and neither that canteen nor the entire camp's supply of water by the barrelful would slake the dryness that was in him now. Later he might really need the water, so he would save it until then.

It took the six men a long time before they began to move again or to speak above a whisper. The silence and the emptiness around them seemed somehow unnatural after the loud confusion of the battle.

Slocum glanced at the sky, looked away, and did a double take, unable to force himself not to look again, unable to make himself believe the truth of what he saw there without confirmation.

"Jesus Christ, boys, it ain't even noon yet," he said. It seemed like the fight must have been going on for days. Instad the sun had not yet peaked in its travel across the clear sky.

"I figured they quit 'cause it was gettin' close to dark," Beanass said.

"Indians won't fight after dark, you know," Hank said. There was an optimistic note in his voice even though it was still so early in the day.

"Don't believe that crap," Slocum told them. "I was handling an eight-up Studebaker rig down in Arizona one time. Forty wagons, most of us with trailers, two tenders, and a driver to each rig. That's a helluva-sized camp every night. And some Apaches came in in the dead of night and damn near wiped us out before there was ever the first shot fired to wake the rest of us. If I'd been sleeping down at the other end of the train I reckon I'd have been worm food long ago, boys. And you couldn't have had a blacker night than that was."

Fortson coughed deliberately into his remaining good hand. "I think, considering the time of day, that nightfall is one of the least of our concerns at the moment, gentlemen. I think we need to do somthing constructive here. Consolidate our positions somewhat, since there are so few of us."

"I can't argue with that, Charles," Slocum said.

"Your idea about the paired firing was good, John. Do you have any more ideas?"

Slocum looked around him. The place was a mess. It never ceased to amaze him how quickly a tidy camp where men lived could become a littered charnelhouse once a brisk firefight took place. It had been the same during the war.

"That wagonbed could be lifted down off the running gear," he suggested. "Its sides are high and pretty stout, and we might need some moving-around room if more of us go down. The box should be big enough for that and small enough to defend. Move hides around all four sides of the thing to give us more protection. There aren't many guns in that crowd out there but a few can be too many if they shoot them often enough. Put the water barrel inside and something to eat. I don't know about you boys, but I'm hungry enough to start at the tail end of that mule lying over there and eat my way to his ears. Gather up all the ammunition on the ones that haven't made it this far. And hope for the best."

"Are you a praying man, John?"

"Nope."

"Pity. Neither am I."

"I will pray for us all, *señor,*" Tonio volunteered.

"You?" Fortson returned. "I'll do without, you chickenshit little son-of-a-bitch. I saw you bellied down behind those hides with your gun cold on the ground beside you and your hands over your ears. If your prayers are my ticket to heaven, I'll book passage to hell instead."

Tonio reddened but he said nothing.

"He won't be doing that again, boss," Beanass offered. "This time he's my shootin' partner, an' if he tries to dog it I'll save the Kiowa the bother of killin' him."

"Thank you," Fortson said seriously. "I appreciate that."

Tonio did not look quite so appreciative but still he said nothing.

"Hell, if nobody else is gonna start moving I s'pose I will," Hank said. Wearily he dragged himself over to the wagon Fortson still stood inside and began unbolting the heavy bed.

They worked until noon and for several hours past, moving slowly with the total fatigue that came after the fight, and still there was no further sign of the Indians.

By midafternoon they were settled within their miniature fort and had nothing more to do except to worry.

"I'm thinking they might be done," Beanass said.

"They lost an awful lot of braves. We might've took the fight clean out of them."

"That don't make sense," Hank argued. "They could see easy enough how few there was of us. It's more sensible to think they'll want to finish us off now. They must know they can do it easy enough. They lost a lot but not *that* many."

"I have heard that Indians won't accept casualties," Fortson said.

Tonio was still being silent and Enrique had not said a word to anyone in more than an hour.

Slocum wiped sweat from his forehead and briefly lifted his hat and resettled it so that a touch of fresh, relatively cool air could reach his scalp. "There's only one damn thing you can count on with Indians an' especially with Kiowa. You don't know what they might do. A wild Indian, not the blanket variety now but one of these wild bucks like this bare-ass crowd, they're as notional as the wind itself. They could ride in here and raise all our scalps or they might decide to ride in slow and ask for the loan of some tobacco. Hell, they might've already gone home to swap lice with their squaws or they might camp on our tails another six weeks an' *then* decide to kill us. There's just no way in the world to figure them out until you see them do it. An' then they may be fooling you somehow. It all makes sense to them but not to a white man."

"Forgive me for saying so, John, but with your dark coloring and high cheekbones you almost look like an Indian yourself," Fortson said.

"Part of me is though I guess this ain't a good time to brag on it," Slocum answered without embarrassment.

"Can you . . . ?" Beanass began. "No, I reckon not."

"No, I reckon not too or I already would have figured them out. These Kiowa, they're not my tribe, white man. Besides, I'm civilized." Slocum gave the man a taut, tough grin that had no humor in it whatsoever. At that moment he looked anything *but* civilized.

"No offense, Burton. Really," Beanass said quickly.

"None taken."

They slumped back against the rough boards of the wagonbox sides and waited and sweated—there was no air movement at all inside the box that might become their common coffin—and expected at any moment to hear the renewed yammer of Kiowa on the attack.

The long day turned to twilight and finally into darkness and still the Kiowa had not returned.

"We should keep a watch through the night," Fortson said. "You never know. . . ."

"I'll take the last watch if you like," Slocum offered. "We all better be up and ready before the first peep of sunlight, though."

"I agree," Fortson said. "I can take the middle watch." That was the one that would most disrupt a man's rest, Slocum knew. Fortson was not one for passing burdens off onto others.

"Enrique," Fortson went on, "you can take the first watch. Enrique? He is asleep already, I guess. Wake him up, Tonio. He can get this over with quickly and get back to sleep."

Tonio shook Enrique by the shoulder. There was no response so Tonio shook him harder. Enrique's head flopped loosely. Tonio shrugged.

"I never even noticed he was dead," Slocum said.

Slocum and Tonio lifted Enrique's body and toppled it outside their barrier.

No one seemed particularly distressed, though. After so many, one more could make little difference. Any one more.

"I think, then, you can take the first watch, Hank. Then Beanass, Tonio, myself, and John," Fortson continued. "Are there any complaints with that?"

There were none.

"Good. Then I suggest we all make ourselves as comfortable as possible and get some rest. One way or another, I think tomorrow is going to be a very tiring day."

One way or another, Slocum thought. Fighting or walking, either one could wear a man down. If he had to guess, though, he would say they would be fighting.

Slocum slipped easily into sleep. Being able to sleep any time an opportunity was presented was something he had learned well enough in the Army to retain the knowledge now. If any of the others tossed uncomfortably he was not awake to know it.

First light, Slocum thought. There was something vaguely wrong about that. Something . . .

He came bolt upright, his heartbeat thumping and his throat tight. He was supposed to have been awake and on watch several hours ago. They were *all* supposed to be awake and manning their rifles now.

"Get up! Everybody up, goddamnit. Somebody screwed up here. It's comin' daylight." He kicked Beanass awake and saw that Hank and Fortson's eyes were opening too. Tonio . . .

Tonio was not there.

"Where's that chickenshit little Mex?" Slocum demanded.

Beanass rubbed his eyes. "I woke him up when I thought it was time. I seen him get up an' get his rifle."

Hank stood and peered over the sides of the wagon-box. "Do you think one of them Kiowa slipped in here while he was on guard and sliced him?"

"I think he deserted the sinking ship," Fortson said.

"Reckon you're right, Charles. There's a bag of jerky gone and so is my canteen," Slocum said. "If I get to make a wish it's that the Kiowa caught him."

"Yes, well, now is not the time to worry about that. I think. . . ."

Whatever Fortson might have wished he did not say, for he was interrupted by the shrill yap of a hundred voices and the rolling thunder of four hundred pounding hooves.

"Let's be gettin' busy, boys. I think we've got a problem here," Slocum said.

He began firing at once. The range was still long, but what the hell. He still had a pocketfull of shells and probably wouldn't have time to shoot half of them anyway before the Kiowa put him down.

No matter how long a man knows for certain that he is going to go down hard and hurting sooner or later, he still would prefer the later to the sooner. But the Indians had a phrase for it. It's a good day to die.

CHAPTER 12

Slocum could feel a violent pounding in his head. There seemed to be a violent pounding going on somewhere outside his head too, although he could not be so sure of that. He was sure of practically nothing at all at that moment. His own thoughts seemed to be fuzzy and viewed from a distance.

The ache in his head seemed to correspond to his heartbeat. That, he decided after some effort, was not a bad thing. It meant that he still had a heartbeat. In that case the fact that it hurt was well worth the pain of it. That was just fine.

The pounding outside . . . he listened closely. It was noise, sounds of some dull, regular kind. With a great intensity of effort he fought to bring his mind under control and identify what should have been a completely routine scrap of knowledge. Of course. Drums. He had heard them often enough before. As friendly sounds and as ominous ones. At the moment he could not remember which these might be.

Slocum stirred and thought he heard himself groan. He might have been mistaken about that. He really did not care anyway.

Having gained that much, he began to regain more. He was beginning to remember things now. The fight, the Kiowa coming at them out of the bright yellow-red slice of sun that showed above the horizon, the wagon-box itself and the four lonely whites waiting to defend it, the sudden noise and renewed dust and the mingled sweet flavors of blood and fear in his mouth.

He remembered the Indians coming so close so soon and dropping the heavy, single-shot Sharps because it was too slow to reload. Oh, he remembered it very well now.

The day before the hunters had been able to stand the Kiowa off because of their circling attack. They had been able to drop first the horses and then the men who had been behind them. That Slocum remembered very well, and it had worked.

This time the Kiowa had come straight on, not swerving, not even thinking in terms of a circle. They intended not to wear down the defenders but to over-whelm them despite any number of casualties they might have to take in the process. And they had done it well.

They came out of the sun and broke not around but directly onto the wagonbox fortress and simply swarmed over and into it.

Slocum remembered it now. He remembered seeing a steel-tipped lance shaft being driven into Hank's chest and a brightly feathered arrow—oddly, he remembered now that the colors of the feathers and shaft had been very pretty in the early-morning light—protruding from the hollow of Beanass's throat.

He remembered his Colt clicking empty and ducking down to retrieve the heavy Sharps. He had intended to use it as a club, since there was no time to think about loading and firing. Not when the Kiowa were already leaping into the wagonbox with the whites. He remem-bered that . . . and nothing more. The rest of it, what-ever else might have happened, was gone. He had the faintest impression of a snarling Indian face, possibly

Two Trees Walking, but that was more feeling than memory.

Now—he tried to move—he seemed to be still alive. That, his ability to think and feel and breathe, was the great surprise of the whole thing. He fully expected to die. He had not. That part of it made the least sense of all.

Slocum opened his eyes. He had difficulty making them focus but he worked at it. He had nothing else, after all, to do.

He seemed to be in a lodge. The light was poor—or his eyes were—but he could make out two slender poles rising to meet in their neat, precise pattern at the top. He could see the overlapped hides that formed the walls, dropped now to the ground although it did not seem to be cold. There was a firepit in the center of the lodge but no fire now and apparently no live coals. The smoke hole at the top was closed at the moment and so was the flap that served as a door. With no ventilation the inside of the lodge was musty and the odors of old hides and spilled food were strong.

Slocum did not like it inside the lodge. He decided to go somewhere else.

Easier decided than accomplished. His hands and feet were securely bound. Funny that he had not noticed that before, he thought.

Not so funny after all. He still was far from being able to think clearly. Individual sensations tended to blur and to mix themselves together. He was not at all certain he had seen the shape of the lodge or felt it or possibly even smelled it. And his sense of color seemed to be distorted. His memory of color, like that of the arrow that had killed Beanass, was sharp and clear and vivid. But now everything seemed to be seen in shades of gray. Very strange, he decided. He did not like it.

On second thought, he liked it just fine. Seeing anything at all was better than being supper for the buzzards and the mice that undoubtedly by now were having themselves a feast at what was left of the camp.

Slocum heard another sound, very close to him, and he felt a chill shaft of sudden fear run through him.

"Did you move just then or was it my imagination?"

"I moved," Slocum said. He knew he should remember that voice but he did not.

"Fancy that," the man said. "I've been talking to you for several hours. Trying to keep myself occupied, as it were. This is the first time you've talked back."

"Who . . . ? Oh, hell. Charles. Charles Fortson."

"Were you speaking to me or to yourself?" Fortson asked.

"Hell, I dunno."

"You sound a bit hazy, John. It is a silly question, I admit, but are you all right?"

"I dunno that either. I think I got hit in the head. Feels like it anyhow. Could I, uh, could I ask you a silly question Charles?"

"Of course."

"My name. You said it was John. What's the rest of it?" Slocum remembered that he had given Fortson some sort of name that was not his own but he could not begin to remember what it was.

"Burton. John Burton. I say, you really *did* get a rap then, didn't you."

"Don't ask me. I'm not at all sure I was there at the time."

"Yes, I understand completely. Actually it was that Two Trees Walking fellow who saved us. Preserved, I believe is a more accurate way to put it. I don't think he did it out of any sense of kindness whatsoever. I saw you go down with the rest although I did not see from what cause and there were several of them at my throat, one with a long and rather ugly butcher knife that he seemed bent on using to whack my head off. It was Two Trees Walking who stepped in to put a stop to it all. Or a delay, I suspect. I don't at all understand the language but facial expressions and tone of voice seem to change very little from culture to culture. Judging from what I saw on Two Trees's face I would say that he was saving us for a bit of sport."

"Jesus Christ! I wish to hell he'd beefed us on the spot if you're right about that."

"Do you mean that, John?"

"Well, almost. I mean, a man always hopes but . . ."

"Uh-huh. I've had similar thoughts myself these last few hours."

"Hours, huh? How long have we been here, anyway?"

"The attack was at dawn. It is early evening now. Is that significant?"

"Damned if I know. I don't know very much about Kiowas. The little I do know is all bad. Ornery bastards, from what I've heard. And what I've seen lately too."

"Since we have nothing better to do, John, why don't we try to escape?"

"You're kind of a cool bastard yourself, Charles. You almost sound like an Englishman."

"I took some of my education in England, if that makes any difference."

"It don't except for making things seem more sensible, sort of."

"Yes, well, both of us seem to be rather securely trussed, but I think if we were to lie back to back—not my style, but advisable under the circumstances—one of us might be able to tug the other's bands loose."

"We can give it a whirl anyhow, Charles."

They shifted nearer, and at the cost of considerable pain Slocum was able to turn onto his side with Fortson behind him. After being tied so long there was hardly any feeling in Slocum's fingers, which he had not noticed before but which he found now to be immensely frustrating.

"I can't hardly feel a damn thing, Charles."

"Nor can I, but I see no reason to quit trying."

Trying to unravel the tight, Kiowa-tied knots with his hands in such condition was like trying to pluck a frozen-in coin from a sheet of ice with his elbows.

"Rest your hands a while, John, and let me try. Try to flex your fingers while you're waiting. It may do some good."

They shifted position slightly and Fortson began to make some sort of unsuccessful effort in his turn. Slocum did keep his fingers moving, clenching and unclenching his fists repeatedly, but all he seemed to be accomplishing was to cause his hands to hurt like hell.

Their efforts were interrupted—not exactly mercifully—by four Kiowa entering the lodge.

The light inside the lodge was even poorer now than it had been when they started, but with the door flap pulled open enough firelight was admitted that Slocum could get a good look at the braves.

None of them looked familiar, although almost certainly they had been among the party that was in the attack. It was unlikely that Slocum would have recognized even Two Trees Walking now, for the hideous designs of their Kiowa warpaint were gone now.

"Great," Slocum said bitterly. "No paint. Shit!"

"Is that bad?" Fortson asked.

"I think so. No paint, the way I understand it, means they aren't keeping us for any kind of special ceremony. I mean, we aren't gonna be offered as some sacrifice. Which might at least be quick and clean. What I think this bare-faced business is about is that we've been brought home as playtoys for the good folks back at the village. Sort of like bringing a bone to a puppy. Fun for the pup but kinda hard on the bone."

"Bones last quite a while generally," Fortson observed calmly.

"So will we if I'm guessing right."

"Is it important to put up a good front? Die bravely and all that?"

"It is with some. The Apache, the Yaqui. I don't know about these boys."

Fortson opened his mouth to speak again but the nearest Kiowa silenced him by kicking him in the jaw. It was downright effective, Slocum saw.

The four Kiowa picked up the two white men, lifting them by the arms and dragging them outside the lodge.

The cool evening air felt good to John Slocum, but the sight of the Kiowa village was hardly refreshing. They were roughly in the middle of an encampment that must have contained a hundred lodges. The occupants of those lodges, men and women and children alike, were all gathered in a mass of humanity at the center of the village. The people, even the smallest of them, were ghostly silent. They seemed to be waiting for something. Slocum had too good an idea of what that might be.

There were, surprisingly, not large fires, though. That puzzled Slocum until he realized that they must be some distance from the Canadian now. The river would be the only likely source of firewood, so these Indians must be making do with dried buffalo chips for their fires. Chips give good heat but little flame and would not likely be wasted on a minor amusement.

The four Kiowa hauled both Slocum and Fortson into the center of the gathered people, and a great cheering went up.

"Ain't it nice to make people happy," Slocum said. He got an elbow in the face for his troubles. He did not fault Fortson for not answering him under the circumstances.

"It is indeed nice to make an entire people happy," one of the Indians standing near a small fire said.

Slocum had been wrong earlier. He had no trouble at all recognizing Two Trees Walking. Without the warpaint the Kiowa was a tall and even a handsome man. Even considering the cruel twist at his lips he was a handsome man, his dark face and high cheekbones much like Slocum's, his torso hard and roped with slabs of muscle.

Slocum decided that the prudent thing to do would be to remain silent. He was not so hung up on ballsy pride that he would pay for it by risking the loss of the source of that pride. And he was quite sure that Two Trees Walking was fully capable of cutting a smart-alec's balls off on a whim.

Fortson apparently was not so prudent. Or perhaps he felt he had more to prove in the way of his manhood.

"I hope you will understand if we would prefer to see a little less happiness around us at the moment," he said.

"I try, but I just can't please everyone," Two Trees Walking said.

"Your English is excellent, you know," Fortson told him.

"I know."

"Actually that was a form of a question," Fortson persisted. Slocum wished he would shut his damned mouth.

"Was it really?" the Kiowa mocked. "Fancy that. I suppose you want to know my background, hear all about my education at the Shawnee Mission School, share my past misery and commiserate with me, understand all about my previously misunderstood brilliance . . . become fine, fast friends even?"

"The thought crossed my mind," Fortson said cheerfully.

The man was a total idiot at times, Slocum decided. But he sure in hell was a brave idiot.

"Your thoughts would also include the theory, then, that once friends, companions of a sort on a man-to-man basis, I would not then be able to turn you over to the unkind attentions of my people."

"Naturally," Fortson admitted.

Two Trees's face twisted a little farther. "Then listen to me, you white cocksucker. I will *lead* my people in stripping the flesh from your bones before you die."

"How . . . ?"

"Jesus, Charles." The game was up anyhow. And Slocum just couldn't stand the stoic silence any longer. "You don't have to be such a damn fool. It was only an *expression,* for God's sake. He didn't mean anything personal about it."

Two Trees Walking turned sharply on Slocum and a glint of understanding appeared in Two Trees's dark eyes. "Do you mean to tell me that this one, this *macho* son-of-a-whore here, really *is* one who likes the brown-holed boys?" He laughed loudly and with apparent great pleasure. "Oh, now, this is going to be a thing of interest as well as one of much pleasure, cocksucker."

Two Trees Walking patted Fortson gently on the shoulder. "My manly, marvelous *joto* friend. You are going to be much joy. Much joy indeed while I learn whether your *cojones* are real."

Slocum did not know it at the time, but he had just given himself a short renewal of his lease on life.

CHAPTER 13

Two Trees Walking said something in the hard-to-follow tongue of the Kiowa, and a group of Indian women came forward out of the crowd. The women ranged from early puberty to doddering senility but they had one thing in common and that was the fierce eagerness in their expressions as they looked at their play pretties, living dolls that could be torn apart and examined inside and out however they pleased.

Slocum watched them come. He had faced warfare and the blaze of guns for half his life. He had stood up to injuries and freezing cold and waterless deserts, lynch mobs and irate husbands. But never had his blood run so cold as it did when he saw those Kiowa women.

He steeled himself for the worst and still knew that they were capable of more than his imagination could ever hope to conjure.

The women gleefully stripped the clothing from both men. The scrape of their fingers, work-hardened and dry, brushing against his skin made Slocum cringe, and he did not need to know the language to understand at least some of the comments the women were making about him. He was an exceptionally well-hung man, although that fact was of small comfort now. It was likely to give them an extra and highly painful, for him, incentive when the women began their work of joyous destruction of human flesh.

Damnation, Slocum thought, he had taken enough pleasure from that particular tool over the years past. It looked now like he was going to have to take an equivalent amount of pain from it now, and all of it at once.

Fortson caught Slocum's eye and somehow managed a sickly grin. "My, my, old fellow. It really is a shame you aren't that way, you know?" Fortson was not nearly as well hung as Slocum, and the women were making that obvious comparison.

One of the Kiowa squaws, an old dried-up prune of a thing, reached out with clawlike fingers and stroked Slocum's limp member. She cackled and said something to him.

"She says she is very apologetic about what the younger ones wish to do, white one," Two Trees translated for him. "She says her husband's bed has been cold for many years but not for so many that her memory cannot recall what a proper stallion is like."

Two Trees Walking said something to her in the Kiowa language, apparently telling her that he had told Slocum what she said.

The old woman cackled again and pointed to an elderly man standing on the fringe of the close-pressing crowd. She said something more and the crowd, including the old man, broke into laughter.

"She offers to make an exchange, dried jerky for a succulent roast, if you will warm her bed, white one," Two Trees said.

"You can tell the lovely lady for me then that I'll be glad to do just that. Beautiful as she is I won't have no trouble at all keeping it up all night long. Satisfaction guaranteed or I'll go away an' never bother her again."

Two Trees Walking translated that into Kiowa and received another, even louder round of laughter.

When Two Trees Walking returned his gaze to Slocum there was no laughter reaching his eyes, though. "You amuse my people, white one. That is fine. But it buys you nothing. When we are done with the man who is not a man we will have our fun with you too. You should know that, white one. I do not lie to you. A true man does not need lies to smooth his path. He takes whatever trail he finds before him."

Slocum nodded. He figured it was time to shut his mouth again.

Two Trees motioned to the warriors who were still holding Slocum by the arms. They hauled him to a pole that had been planted firmly in the ground and tied him there at the throat. That was just fine, Slocum thought. As soon as they were not paying attention he could—if he had the strength of purpose—hang himself by the rawhide thongs and deny them their sport.

Two Trees Walking spoke again and the Kiowa guards nodded. They lashed Slocum to the pole at the waist and knees as well. Tied that way he could slump only enough to make himself uncomfortable but not enough to do himself any damage. The tall Kiowa was no fool. Not that Slocum had really thought he was, just hoped that the man would be unobservant on that one subject.

The two men who had been guarding Fortson slipped away to join the crowd, and the women slowly moved in around him. They remained directly in front of Slocum, where he could not possibly avoid seeing what they were doing. That was, no doubt, a deliberate little extra on their part. By making Slocum anticipate what was to come they would make it that much worse for him.

Fortson stood upright and unbending before them. He smiled at their leering faces as they reached forward to pinch him tentatively. They pinched harder and Fortson's smile became broader.

Over the women's heads Fortson called to Two Trees Walking, "Ask them to take their time if you would, please. We sent for help last night, you see, and I'd like to still be alive when the other boys get here."

Two Trees Walking laughed. "A very nice try, man with a cock at each end. But they will not be so kind as to kill you quickly. You speak of my good friend and translator Antonio, of course. We watched him leave your camp and some of us called him wise and others of us called him cowardly. When we asked him about this he proved to us that the ones who believed him a coward were correct. He was not a brave man, but with care we were able to see that he survived long enough to live through several long and painful lifetimes last night. So if we are very tired and cross tonight it is because we have had so little sleep."

"I would be glad to make this a short night for you," Fortson offered.

Two Trees Walking had had enough conversation for a while, though, for he stood there stonily and watched as the women renewed their slow and at first almost gentle assault on Charles Fortson's cold flesh.

The women seemed to be taking turns, Slocum saw. First one approaching and then another in an order that seemed to have nothing to do with age. Perhaps, he thought, they received their opportunities based on their husbands' status in the tribe or perhaps on some basis that he could never guess without himself being a Kiowa. Whatever the case they seemed to know who was to go next and to stand for no argument if another seemed about to step in ahead of her rightful place.

With no more tools than their fingers and fingernails and an occasional flake of sharp rock, the Kiowa women slowly reduced Charles Fortson to a bright red statue covered with a sticky ooze of blood and dust mixed together on what had been his skin.

Still the man did not cry out although his jaws looked like they were clamped so firmly they might have turned to stone. Slocum did not think Fortson could have spoken now if he had wanted to. How he remained on his feet throughout all that was more than Slocum could understand.

Eventually the pain and shock and loss of blood forced the sturdy Philadelphian off his feet. When he fell it was like a lodgepole pine being dropped by a lumberjack. He went face forward, his knees locked as firmly as his jaw and his hands lashed behind his back so that he could not have caught himself if he had tried. As far as Slocum could see Fortson made no effort to catch himself and might not have been aware that he was falling.

The squaws were angry that he had fallen face down so they could not reach his crotch and the tender, enormously sensitive parts there that they lavished so much time and attention on. By then Slocum doubted that it made that much difference anyway. There was practically nothing left between Fortson's legs except a damp red patch of matted hair. He was bleeding heavily there and Slocum hoped that he would soon die of the blood loss.

On the other hand, Slocum was not exactly anxious for Fortson to die, since Two Trees Walking had said that Slocum was next in line for the fun.

Slocum need not have worried so soon. The squaws were not about to let their plaything get away so easily as he already had. One of them scooped a ladle of coals from the buffalo-chip fire while others rolled the unconscious Fortson onto his side. The first squaw held the ladle to what was left of the man's cods.

The heat had two effects, both of which the Kiowa women seemed to approve. It cauterized the wounds they had inflicted and so stopped the blood loss that threatened to kill Fortson. It also was so excruciatingly painful that the feeling reached down deep and touched him even though he was unconscious and brought him screamingly awake.

That was the first time Fortson had uttered a sound, and the squaws were ecstatic with delight. They yipped and howled and danced in their glee, and the squaw with the ladle applied the coals to Fortson's shredded cock again.

Again the man screamed, and the women squealed their delight. This was what they had been waiting for. This was what they wanted. It had taken more than an hour, but at last they had broken this strong, proud man. Now they could really have their fun.

If it would not have been taken as a sign of weakness—and called attention to him instead of to Charles Fortson—Slocum would have puked at what they did to the man once they got their second wind about it.

And once the breach had been made, once that first sound had escaped Fortson's mangled lips, his agony was constantly reflected in the tortured sounds being torn from his throat.

Slocum could keep from looking at what they were doing now but there was no way he could close his ears as well. The sound of Fortson's screams seemed to beat through his skull in time with the still painful beating of Slocum's own heart as it pumped blood through the torn section of his scalp.

At one point a smiling Two Trees Walking sidled over near Slocum and pointed to the disgusting scene the squaws were staging.

"Just think, white one. Soon that will be you who receives so much attention. I wonder if you will be as brave as your friend the man who loves men."

Slocum shrugged and kept his eyes carefully ahead, toward the living, screaming pulp that used to be Charles Fortson.

"You try to fool me, white one. Your eyes. I can see your eyes. They are far now, not near where your friend is. You try to make me think you are watching while you do not. You try to make me think you are braver than you are. No matter. I will know soon enough how brave you are. It may be that the one who is not a man at all is more a man than you."

Slocum said nothing, kept his unfocused eyes staring out into the night. Eventually Two Trees Walking tired of looking at Slocum. After all, Fortson was much more interesting to watch at the moment. The tall Indian walked contentedly away.

As soon as Two Trees Walking had gone Slocum tried again to hang himself by the rawhide that bound his neck to the pole. He tried his best to make his knees bend. Just a little would have been enough to give the rawhide a decent bite and make it strangle him, but try as he might he could not flex them enough, could not take enough weight off his legs to let him kill himself. He could not do it.

Somehow, incredibly, Fortson continued to hang onto life. His screams were hoarse now and falling in volume. His throat must have been as raw from the screaming as his body was from all the things the squaws had been doing to him, but still he clung to some faint vestige of life and still he screamed hoarsely into the night.

The Kiowa had to keep bringing fresh supplies of buffalo chips to the fire that dimly lighted the events, and Slocum realized that it was growing late.

A few of the Kiowa, the very oldest and the very youngest at first and soon more following, began to slip away from the crush of people who encircled the busy squaws. As Fortson's screaming died in volume some of the smaller children curled up in the dust at their mothers' feet and went to sleep. The children's casual disregard of the sights before their eyes was as appalling to Slocum as anything the women were doing to Fortson. And that they planned to do to him.

The time dragged on and the incessant pain continued and finally Fortson's cries had faded to a prolonged, whimpering moan.

By then at least half the crowd had dispersed to their lodges. After all, they had seen one white man die late into the previous night and now another. It was too much of a good thing.

Two Trees Walking stepped into the circle of squaws and spoke to them.

One, a dumpy woman whose nicely tailored calico blouse—Slocum could not help wondering how she had come by such a garment—was smeared with drying, red-brown blood, gave the war chief some backtalk. That was easy enough to tell without knowing the language, for she looked and acted and had a tone of voice that any man from any culture and speaking any tongue could have identified at once. She spoke shrilly and wagged a finger at him and gave him a sneer over her shoulder that was obviously intended to put this mere male into his place.

Two Trees Walking seemed to be in no mood to take badgering from a woman. He gave her a backhanded slap that would have rattled a grown man's brains. The woman clamped her mouth shut, ducked, and slid quietly away from the group.

With the loud protester gone the other women listened respectfully as Two Trees Walking spoke to them again, and reluctantly but without argument, the women dispersed.

Fortson—what little remained of him—was left lying on the ground where he had fallen. Thin, keening sounds continued to whistle from his throat but Slocum doubted that he had heard or felt anything in quite some time now. No one could have.

Two Trees left him there unattended while the last of the Kiowa people drifted sleepily back toward their quarters. To Slocum he said, "It is late so you may have more time, white one, to think about what you face tomorrow. You will end up like this one. This I promise." He smiled, a friendly, civilized expression that took Slocum by surprise. "Good night, white one. Rest well on your pole so that you can entertain us tomorrow. Wait." Two Trees pulled a knife from the sheath at his waist. "I will make this a medicine pole to help give you strength."

Casually Two Trees Walking bent over Fortson's still living form. He sliced into the creature's throat with practiced ease and with a second slice of the long blade and a deft twist of his wrist removed Fortson's scalp.

Two Trees Walking hunted in his pouch until he found a strand of horsehair and used that to tie the still-dripping scalp to the pole directly over Slocum's head.

"There, white one. That is much better." Again the friendly smile. "Sleep well."

"Thank you," Slocum said. He watched the Kiowa walk away into the darkness. Slocum was proud of himself. He had not been sure that he could get any words out. He felt weak. And very much afraid.

CHAPTER 14

John Slocum was dreaming. This was a God-awful time to be dreaming but that was what he seemed to be doing. Actually, he decided with detached disinterest, it must be a sort of daydream because he could not possibly be asleep while he was lashed to that pole. He was in a stupor of some sort. That had to be the explanation.

But how could he possibly be horny at a time like this? He liked sex, sure, but this was ridiculous. Yet in his dream he could feel a light touch toying with him, running up and down the unusual length of him, playing with him and bringing him erect. That part was damn sure no dream. He had a hard-on for real and it was almost like he could feel a soft mouth engulf him there.

"Ow!"

Dreams don't hurt, at least none he had ever experienced before, and this had hurt. He opened his eyes and came fully awake. It was hard to look down with his neck tied like that but he could see enough to make out a dark shape in the darkness of the night.

"Shhhhhssss." That was no dream either.

The shape moved, rose to chin height beside him. It was too dark for him to tell much about the person who had been playing with him but it seemed to be a woman of some sort, with very long, very dark hair falling around her face. Her form was a blur in the night but she looked to be small.

At the moment Slocum cared nothing at all about who she was or what she might look like. His first reaction was fear, considering what Kiowa women liked to do with white men, even very-well-hung white men apparently. But his second thought was that she had not been handling him in any remotely threatening manner so far.

"Cut me loose and we'll find a way to give you the rest of that," he whispered.

The woman shook her head.

Great, Slocum thought. She doesn't speak English and I don't speak Kiowa, and between the two of us we're going to get me killed.

The woman leaned closer and held a finger to her lips in a universally accepted gesture for silence.

Slocum nodded his head eagerly. Hell, yes. Anything the lady wants. And marvel of marvels, when she got that close to him she even smelled good. No rancid grease or ancient sweat on this one. She had bathed not too long ago.

He wanted desperately to be able to talk to her, to tell her she should cut the rawhide that bound him. He did not need to. From somewhere she produced a knife and held it to his throat.

If she was wanting to cut his throat he would not have minded all that much under the circumstances. Even that would beat waiting for the squaws to take up where they had left off the night before. She did not, though. Instead she sliced expertly at the rawhide thong, and the iron-hard scrap of rawhide fell away. Slocum had not realized until that moment just how deeply the thong had been cutting into his throat. The relief was enormous.

The woman bent swiftly and cut the other bindings

as well. Slocum almost collapsed once their support was gone. He leaned gratefully against the post and began rubbing vigorously at his hands and wrists. He wanted to sink down to the ground to rest for a moment but was afraid if he did so he would not be able to get up again.

Still without speaking, the woman bent and picked up a bundle that she shoved against his belly for him to take. It turned out to be his clothing. His Colt was missing, of course, but his sheath and the big Bowie were, incredibly, still on his belt. He guessed that the Kiowa had enough knives even though they seemed to be in short supply when it came to guns.

He was still shaky and the woman had to help him into his clothing. She did not seem to know how to fasten buttons so he had to manage those himself. By the time he was done he was wondering why in the hell he had stood out there in plain sight beside that pole to do his dressing, but no harm seemed to have been done. There had been no cry raised.

The woman took him by the hand, painful now as the circulation returned to it, and pulled him away from the central part of the village.

They slipped among the lodges barefoot, Slocum carrying his boots in one hand and the heavy knife in the other. The camp was apparently in sound sleep, and like many Indian villages seemed to have posted no guards.

For a people so constantly at war, Slocum thought again as he had so often before, it seemed incredible that Indians so seldom mounted guards. But they did not and they frequently had to pay the penalty for their negligence. From a white point of view it seemed a foolish habit, but other Indians seemed to find it quite normal.

The Kiowa village, he noted, seemed to be short on dogs too, many fewer of them than he had seen in

Cheyenne and Sioux camps, but he was not complaining about the lack. It made things much easier for him now. And for all he knew, maybe the Kiowa as a rule did not keep dogs.

It took only minutes to reach the edge of the village and to leave the last of the skin lodges behind. Since the woman seemed to know what she was doing so far he asked no questions but followed her blindly—almost literally so, since it was so dark—and trusted her judgment. At this point anything she might choose to do with or to him would be a step up from where he had been a few minutes earlier.

Off to one side he could hear the shuffling of hooves that meant they were passing the Kiowa horse herd. The woman avoided that carefully, circling out of her way to go around the herd.

That made sense enough, Slocum decided. The horses were much more likely to have a guard than the camp itself, and she probably knew if there was danger there. Beside which, a man on foot can drop off the face of the earth, at least as far as a tracker is concerned, where a horse will leave deeper impressions that can be found and followed by a skilled pursuer.

A time or two in the past John Slocum had accompanied friendly Indians on horse-stealing raids and he knew that most of the time a thieving party will leave their home territory on foot with the intention of riding freshly stolen horses home. They were much less likely to be discovered, or once spotted, to be followed, if they were afoot.

Once they were well past the horses Slocum tugged at the woman's sleeve and signed for her to wait. He sat and pulled his boots on and for the first time since he had regained consciousness back in that smelly lodge felt that he had some reasonable measure of control over his own life and destiny. He stood again and returned the Bowie to its sheath.

"Lead on, little lady," he said softly.

He had no idea if she had understood him but she seemed to get the message. She nodded rapidly and said something, what he had no idea. Her voice at least was pleasant enough, and she sounded young. He would gladly have gone with the old hag who had been fondling him earlier, but it seemed that this was a different female.

Shortly before dawn she brought him to a pile of rocks in the middle of the rolling grass. How she could have found one particular spot on the limitless plains, afoot and in dead darkness, John Slocum could not pretend to understand. His own sense of direction was good but it was nothing compared to this woman's, if indeed she had brought him intentionally to this precise place.

By wriggling under a low overhang they were able to disappear inside a protected pocket covered with rock and protected on nearly all sides by other boulders the cap rock was lying on. It was an ideal hiding place, which made Slocum suspect all the stronger that she had planned to find it from the beginning. From any distance at all and certainly from horseback it would be impossible to spot them lying there.

They had no sooner reached the safety of the shelter than the woman reached for him and began to stroke his groin again.

She was too late, and John Slocum was too tired. He was already beginning to snore.

She said something to the sleeping man in a low voice, cradled her head against his shoulder, and settled herself for sleep.

Tall tales to the contrary, Indian women are generally about as attractive as your average hog wallow. This one was something more than a cut above that.

She was, Slocum decided when he finally awakened,

a damn fine-looking girl. She was small and was built on the slender side. Certainly a contrast with his still-lamented Anna. But this Kiowa was a fine-looking little squaw, and no doubt the Kiowa brave who had just lost her was mightily upset by this time.

Her hair was long and black and well tended. Her face was small, the features delicately formed. She seemed to be awfully thin—poorly fed, in fact—and very young. He could not tell about her figure, not quite yet, but under the scraps of rag that were serving her for a dress she seemed to be bed-slat slender and probably not too well built.

She was damn sure pretty enough, though, and from what he remembered from the night before was plenty old enough to comfort a man in a time of need. The brief, hazy memory of that period brought Slocum fully awake and fully erect again.

No time like the present for finding out what else there is to her, he decided, and she'd slept as long as he had probably and should have needed it less.

Slocum shook the girl gently awake; it took only a touch. She wakened with a smile, he was glad to see. She spoke to him softly in some Indian tongue that sounded vaguely unlike the harsh, guttural Kiowa language but he did not know what she was saying in any case. Nor at the moment did he really care. He rolled her against him where she could nestle close and began to kiss her.

Damn pleasant way to pay off a debt, he thought.

They lay like that for some time, tongues probing and hands beginning to move almost without direction, the girl's as much as Slocum's. After several minutes the touching became groping and the Indian girl pulled herself away. She sat up and swept her crude dress over her head and tossed it aside.

Slocum had thought her pretty when she was clothed. Naked she was lovely, absolutely lovely.

She was thin, as he had already guessed, but her breasts were firm and high and as classically shaped as any that could be found on a Greek statue. The dusky tint of her skin, lighter than the Kiowa he had seen in the camp so recently, gave her an exotic appeal although she was no darker than many Mexican girls Slocum had bedded in the years past. Her pubic hair was a jet triangle set against flesh that looked invitingly soft and warm. Slocum touched her belly and ran his fingers into the thatch of curly, soft hair and she opened herself to him eagerly.

He ran his fingers deep into her and found that she was wet and warm and obviously ready for him, but they were in no hurry. There was no need to move until sundown. In fact, it would be dangerous to do so.

The girl fumbled Slocum's buttons open while he enjoyed the feel of her slim body, and when she was done she moved down on him to take him again into the warmth of her mouth. She was as talented with her tongue as she was with her lips and he had to restrain himself firmly to keep from spending himself so soon.

"You didn't learn that from any red Indian," Slocum told her, knowing she would not understand him but wanting to speak to her anyway.

She disengaged herself for a moment and turned her head to smile at him. She said something in return, very softly, and bent to reapply herself to their mutual enjoyment.

"You could make a fortune in Kansas City that way, girl," Slocum murmured.

She brought him, apparently deliberately, to a swift surge of pleasure. She seemed to be able to feel the first throbbing pulses of approaching climax and quickly moved off of him, stroking his balls gently and licking him occasionally to let him down slowly.

"Mmmmm. An artist, no less," Slocum said.

The girl swung a leg over his chest and moved backward on him to present her own damp openings for him to tongue, and he did as she was asking. She smelled and tasted as fresh as mountain air. After only a few moments she shuddered and bucked against him in a powerful climax and grabbed the insides of his thighs in a painful clutch. She fell limp on top of him, her legs pressing against his ears and her belly warm on his chest, and after a moment more she talked to him, speaking at great length and with apparent delight.

"I wish I could make out some of that, sweet girl. I surely do," Slocum said when she quieted. "But that's enough talk for right now. Good as you are with your mouth I still don't know what the rest of you feels like."

He was sure she could not understand the words but she seemed able to catch the tone and the intent of his voice. Happily she lifted herself off of him and changed position to offer herself, legs apart and ready, for him to mount her.

Slocum lay atop the girl and eased himself deep into her, and he was pleased with the receptive, joyous look in her eyes as he did so. He began to move and felt her meet his every thrust with a convulsive, matching rise of her own hips. She reached down to take hold of his ass in her long-fingered, work-hardened hands and to pull him deeper and ever deeper inside her.

He wanted to wait and to make the pleasure last, but she was tight and delightful and there could be no waiting. He pumped faster and harder and still she met his every motion, and he felt himself being lifted in a sudden, spiraling flight toward distant, majestic peaks higher and faster until his climax was an explosion more powerful than a keg of giant powder being set off inside his balls and all of its force being channeled out in a great gout of hot sperm. He collapsed against her and for several long moments afterward continued to shudder in aftershocks.

"Lordy, girl, but you are *fine*."

She smiled and kissed him and shoved against his chest, telling him to move off of her now.

He did so, feeling spent and totally drained. There could be no more where all of that had come from.

Slocum was wrong. There was more, although where and how she managed to find it was beyond his knowledge.

She pressed him down flat on the sandy gravel that formed the floor of their hiding place and for a minute she stroked his chest and stomach. Soon she again bent over him and took his limp cock deep into her mouth, licking his come away patiently until he was clean again.

By then, incredibly, he was also erect again, and with another smile and a toss of her long hair she bent to begin the tryst all over again.

This was indeed the finest way possible to pay off a debt, Slocum decided.

CHAPTER 15

In addition to her other qualities Slocum found that
the girl was a fine guide. They started out from the pile
of rocks as soon as it was full dark, and a few minutes
later she brought them to a hidden seep of water that
Slocum could not have spotted in broad daylight with
a map to guide him, for as far as he could tell there
were no obvious landmarks anywhere around. The girl
had no trouble at all in finding the water, though, and
it was good to drink.

Slocum fell on his face beside the seep and dipped
his head into the refreshing liquid. He drank all he was
able to hold and forced himself to drink some more.
He had no idea how long they would have to go before
they reached the next water.

When he was satisfied, the girl drank and then motioned for Slocum to drink again. She waited patiently
until he was done and then, since there was water remaining in the small rock basin where the seep had
collected into a miniature pool, she pulled off her dress
and bathed herself a cupped handful of water at a time
until she was again as clean as when he had first seen
her.

"You're tidy as a cat," Slocum told her. "I kinda
like that in a woman. Come to think of it, out this far

from the Big River that kind of cleanliness is about as uncommon in women as it is in men. You should smell some of the whores I've poked my stick into. They'd gag a goat some of them if a man wasn't so drunk an' so horny he just didn't care anymore."

She returned his comments with a flow of her own talk, as liquid and as refreshing as the water. She kept it up even as she motioned him in a new direction and walked swiftly at his side to meet Slocum's long-legged, ground-covering strides. Whatever pace he set, though, she had not yet uttered a word of complaint.

She did not complain about hunger either, although Slocum knew she had to have been at least as hungry as he. And it had been too damned long a while since he had had anything to eat.

They walked through half the night, Slocum becoming increasingly worried about the lack of food. Soon his strength would be seriously affected if they did not find some nourishment. It probably already was less than it should be, although a weakness like that comes over a man so slowly it is hard for him to feel it until it is already too late.

The girl seemed to be looking for something in the scant moonlight. The previous night that darkness had been an ally and a blessing, but now it seemed to be a problem. If Slocum had known what she wanted he would have helped her search, but he did not know and she could not tell him although she frequently renewed her chatter as they walked and looked.

Finally she got down onto her hands and knees to examine the ground closely. She felt the cool soil with her fingertips and sat back on her haunches to talk to Slocum about whatever it was that she had found or thought she found.

She gave him a shrug that he interpreted to mean

maybe this was it and maybe it was not but they were going to give it a try. When they began walking again it was in a different direction.

Another hour's hike brought them in smelling distance of her goal, and Slocum thought he knew at last where she was taking him. The scent of death, ugly despite its sweetish odor, was strong and growing stronger as they walked.

A few minutes more and they reached a place John Slocum remembered all too well. It was what was left of the buffalo-hunting camp.

They entered the camp, and the girl dropped back while Slocum inspected the site of the slaughter. She stood silent at the edge of the scene so as not to intrude on his privacy at that moment.

Not that Slocum had been strongly attached to any of the men who died here, but still . . . .

Little remained of what had so recently been a well-organized hide camp. The wagons and running gear had been set afire by the Kiowa and now were charcoal skeletons. The Indians had tried too to burn the stacks of buffalo hides, although they had not burned well at all and were scarcely damaged.

The piles of fresh hides were about all that remained reasonably undamaged, though. The food and weapons, gunpowder and lead and mercury primers had all been carried away by the Kiowa. Anything the Indians could not use they had smashed. Their own arrows and lances had been recovered for use again in the future except for two broken lances, and on those the iron heads had been removed and taken away.

It was the bodies, though, that dominated the dead camp. They were not highly visible in the small amount of moonlight—and starlight of the night, and even had it been daylight they would barely have been recognizable as human remains. The Kiowa had hacked the dead men apart so thoroughly that Slocum was not now sure which body was whose or even which pieces of rotting meat were human and which might have been old chunks of buffalo meat left behind by the Indians as not worth salvaging from the mess they had created.

By now, after several days of sun heat and bloating gases, the bodies were so many lumps of stinking, collapsing offal. Slocum had to use all of his willpower to keep from gagging and bending into a fit of dry heaves while he poked in the rubble for a stray scrap of food or a weapon overlooked by the Kiowa. In the end he could find nothing.

As soon as his shoulders slumped in defeat the girl came to his side and took his hand. She pressed the back of his powerful hand against her lips silently. After a moment she led him away into the darkness.

It was not far to the stands where the now dead whites had so recently been killing buffalo and at last Slocum began to understand why she had brought him here.

They began to pass rotting buffalo carcasses in the night, but eventually he realized they would find some that had been killed freshly enough that their meat would still be good.

They found a freshly shot stand shortly before dawn, forty-some carcasses spread over little more than two acres. It had been a good stand, Slocum observed with professional interest. The buffs had been put down cleanly and without excitement. The hides were gone, of course, but the kills where less than twenty-four hours old, taken by some party that probably did not yet know about the Kiowa rampaging in the area. Both facts were good to know, because where there was a party of white men there was a chance for Slocum to get a gun and a horse and get the hell out of this country.

The Indian girl borrowed Slocum's big knife and used it to hack a hump from one buffalo. She went to another and stripped its back fat with her own, smaller knife. She collected the back fat and thin strips of loin meat from several of the carcasses and carried them all in a fold of her dress. The load must have been awkward to carry and heavy as well, but she gave no indication of discomfort. When she began walking again it was toward the north, toward the Canadian.

They found a buffalo wallow with water at the bottom of it, water fouled by trampled manure and buffalo piss but still water and they drank from it, although sparingly.

By dawn the girl had found another broken nest of rocks where they could hide. This one was not much of a hiding place, since anyone riding close enough could see them there, but it would conceal them from anyone passing at a distance and by now Slocum was willing to accept the idea that it would be the best possible place within reach before daylight found them. The girl seemed to know quite well what she was doing.

Only then did she begin to pound the meat and fat together into a thick, pulpy mixture that did not have to be cooked—they could not risk a fire of any sort—but that had a surprisingly delicate flavor.

To Slocum by then a piece of meat green and slimy with rot would have been a delicacy, and the heavy paste that the Indian girl gave him was a treat indeed. He gorged himself to the point that he was not at all sure he could stand the exertion of another round of screwing.

He found soon enough that he was not *that* full after all.

They spent the daylight hours napping, waking to frolic and fuck and talk to each other without knowing but half of what was being said and to gorge again. At nightfall the girl stood and took Slocum's hand. It was time to move on again.

CHAPTER 16

It was past midnight when the girl brought them to the hunters' camp. How she had managed to find it Slocum did not know. She seemed to have almost an instinctive ability to know where she wanted to go and how she could get there, but get them there she did.

Slocum could smell the dying fires before they arrived and the stink of garbage and uncovered shit and drying hides that always built around a camp within a few days after it was pitched.

They entered the camp warily, afraid someone might spot them in the darkness and decide to shoot before they said hello.

"Hello the camp," Slocum called when they were close enough. "Hello the camp. Strangers comin' in. Strangers comin' in."

From ahead and to his left he could hear the distinct click of a rifle hammer being drawn back into a cocked position.

"We ain't armed," Slocum called again. "Travelers in trouble here, boys. No need to fret."

This time it was Slocum who reached out to take the girl by the hand and do the leading. He took them in beside the nearest of the several fires and tossed some wood onto it so the occupants of the camp would be able to get a look at them. He could hear men beginning to stir in their bedrolls and undoubtedly to pick up their weapons as well.

"It's all right, boys. Don't get hasty." He stood in the rising glare of the firelight with his hands well out from his sides. "We got away from a Kiowa camp the other night, me and this girl here. We're needing some help here."

At Slocum's mention of the word "girl" the camp came alive, and men began crowding around them.

Several of the men Slocum recognized with a sinking sensation in his gut.

There's days when I can crawl out of my bedroll and begin picking nuggets of purest gold off the ground with a scoop shovel. And there's other days when I can't move without stepping in somebody else's shit. This one was turning out to be that last kind.

The men who were beginning to crowd around them included Hutchison and Big and that sorry bastard Mexican Cisco. Of all the camps to blunder into . . .

"John, my friend. Welcome," Hutch said with a broad smile. "And what a delightful present you have brought us."

Slocum glanced at the Indian girl and saw what Hutchison meant. In the firelight she looked particularly pretty anyway, and to men who had not been with a woman in who knows how long, well, it was not the very best of situations. Particularly with no Colt on Slocum's hip.

"What was this about the Kiowa?" Hutch asked. He, at least, seemed to have an orderly sense of priorities.

"You remember Charles Fortson?" Slocum asked.

"Of course. Come to think of it, we need to look him up and make a few collections. The man's credit is good and all that, but a friend only allows so much leeway or the friendship might be damaged, you know? Anyway, we've been away a few days resupplying and have fallen a bit behind. Where is the dear, limp-wristed fellow?"

"Buzzard meat out on the grass along with all the rest of his crew," Slocum told him. "And the limp-wrist, as you call him, died like one helluva man. It took two dozen Kiowa squaws near three hours to kill him, and most of that time he stood on his feet and didn't make a noise or a whimper. He might've been queer but he was one tough son-of-a-bitch too."

Hutchison's eyebrows went up. "Tell me about it, friend John."

Slocum did. Hutchison, he found, was more interested in details about Two Trees Walking and the Kiowa camp than he was about the loss of Fortson and all his men. That, though, was only reasonable. Even sincere sympathy will not bring back a dead man, but attention to detail can keep a living one alive.

"And this woman of yours?" Hutchison asked finally.

Slocum told him the story on her. Some of it anyway. There was no point in raising red flags and baiting them on when it came to the rest of Slocum's limited knowledge about her.

"A Kiowa? And she helped you that way? It sounds damn well unbelievable," Hutchison said. He turned and motioned one of his men forward. "Ask her about the story our friend John has been telling us, Baptiste."

Baptiste, who looked like an Indian himself in spite of his French name, broke into the growling, unpleasant Kiowa tongue.

The girl said nothing at first, just gave him a disdainful look and a scowl. She glanced at Slocum and seemed to change her mind about speaking, for she gave him a smile and then turned back to Baptiste to begin talking.

When she was done Baptiste was the one who was scowling. "I don' know wha' this talk is she is giving us, but it is not the Kiowa talk, no. This one I do na know, *ami*."

"I do." A gray-haired hunter who reminded Slocum of old Meriwether shuffled forward. "This'un ain't some pig of a Kiowa squaw. This here's a li'l Ute gal. Says her name's . . . well, the closest way to put it in English is Moon Silver on Quaking Aspen. Something like that anyhow. Call her Moonlight."

He moved closer to her and pointed a stubby finger over her heart. "Moonlight," he told her several times until she was able to repeat it. He turned to Slocum, pointed again, and said, "John." That one she was able to master more quickly. She seemed pleased to know what he would call her and what she could call him.

"Yeah," the interpreter said to no one in particular.

Now that the dam was broken the girl, looking at Slocum but pitching her voice to the gray-haired man, began to talk readily. She talked fast, pausing every so often for the interpreter to catch up with her.

"Her father is Talking Beaver. The whites call him John. She thinks that is a good sign. She is happy to know that her brave white stallion is also called John." That brought a flurry of smirks and grins from the rest of the men and from the interpreter a remark of his own, "She ain't even lyin' to make her old man out a chief. You really marked your stick with this'un, John."

Slocum grunted. He wished he could think of some way to get her and himself away from this outfit. Moonlight went on talking.

"She was stolen from her people about five years ago," the interpreter went on. "The Apaches took her. They sold her to some Mex Comancheros. Got a full cart of dried pumpkin for her. The Mexes kept her a while. A year, she thinks. She says they taught her much." He grinned and again added a sidelight. "I c'n guess what them bastards might've taught a pretty l'il thing like this."

That fitted in with what Slocum had been guessing already. No Indian had taught her those horizontal achievements Slocum had come to value so highly in the girl.

"A horny Comanche bought her off'n the Mexes. That was a couple of years ago, I think. She didn't like him worth a shit an' made him an' his regular wives pretty miserable an' after a while the Comanch' got tired of trying to beat her orneriness out of her. He sold her to a pox-faced Kiowa jus' to get rid of her. That wasn't so bad, she says. The Kiowa's got the most of his pecker whacked off in a fight one time so he wasn't no bother but she thinks the Kiowa are a dirty bunch an' she wants to go home. She sez John here c'n take her home."

He listened for a moment and broke into laughter. "Besides which, she says, she was gettin' awful horny an' when she seen how John is hung she knowed he could do her a lot of good over an' above takin' her home to her own people."

Most of Hutchison's men were getting a kick out of the translation, but Slocum noticed that Cisco was doing nothing but scowling as it went on.

"She sez she thanks each an' every one of us for the help we're fixing to give her an' her man John an' sez there'll always be a place for any of us in her father's lodge for helping her back home. She sez now that we've all talked some we should loan her an' John some ponies an' some guns an' a lodge so's they can hump on a buff'lo robe the way it oughta be done an' get rested before they start for the tall mountains tomorra."

Hutchison seemed to get the biggest laugh out of that.

"Is that what you intend to do, friend John?" he

asked. "You want me to hand over some horses and guns and anything else you need, do you?"

"I'll pay you for them," Slocum said. He said it much more calmly than he felt.

"You, uh, you're a rich man, are you?"

"You know better than that." Slocum stopped himself—barely—from adding that the only men who could get rich playing under Hutch's rules were Hutch himself and maybe one or two of his cronies. Slocum damn sure did not want to tell Hutchison that he still had his share of what Fortson had paid him for the hides he shot before the Kiowa attacked. The amount, though, was close to five hundred dollars. It was still in his pants pocket in a wad of bills that until now had not seemed very important.

"And what is it you and the little lady need, friend John?" Hutchison asked with an oily falseness that made Slocum want to drive a fist into his face.

"Oh, a couple horses. A carbine. I'll be quitting the hunting business, I reckon, so I won't need a big gun. A pistol if you've got a spare handy. Whatever kind of gear you can part with."

"And you will pay for all this?"

"Whatever is fair. I expect you'll want to make a reasonable profit on the deal. I got no quarrel with that. A man's entitled to some profit, I figure."

Hutchison smiled and nodded and turned to Cisco. "I seem to remember making you a promise, my friend."

"Sí."

"I think it is time that I kept that promise."

Cisco smiled. Slocum did not have to know what the promise was. He could guess it clearly enough.

Slocum's hand swept across his belly and raked back again with the big Bowie in his grip at the same time Cisco was leaping for him, but Big was quicker than either of them.

Slocum would not have believed that any man could be so fast, but Big had him by the wrist as the knife was pulling free. Big stood there with no expression at all on his face that Slocum could identify and squeezed —almost gently, it seemed—until the pain became too great to bear. Slocum had a clear choice: Drop the knife or let Big continue to apply pressure until the bones of his wrist gave under the steadily increasing pressure. The man certainly looked far from the end of his power. He did not look at the least bit strained, or even very much interested in what he was doing. Slocum dropped the knife.

"There," Big said. "You fight fair now, hear?"

Slocum heard all right.

Big stepped aside, leaving only a yard of dirt between Slocum and the waiting Cisco.

Slocum was in bad shape and he knew it. He had been through too much and had had too little to eat and drink in the past few days for him to be at his best in a hand-to-hand fight now. He dropped into a balanced crouch and waited for Cisco to come to him. If it was at all possible Slocum wanted to end the fight immediately. He would still have to deal with Hutchison, but with Cisco out of the way he at least might have a chance.

Cisco grinned and licked his lips. Unexpectedly then he let his fists relax and his hands fall to his sides. He grinned at Slocum. "I've got an idea, boss," he said.

"Yes, my friend?"

"I'm gonna kill this fella here, right?"

"I fully expect that, yes."

"Let's let this nice fella here watch us tear off some red pussy first. Let him watch us takin' some of his own tame red pussy first."

Hutchison shrugged. "If you prefer."

Hutchison and the others all turned their heads to admire the Ute girl standing uncomprehending nearby.

It was the best and perhaps the only chance Slocum expected to have. "Run, Moonlight!" he yelled and he leaped toward Cisco with his hands extended for the man's throat.

Slocum reached his target and hung on. Cisco elbowed him viciously in the ribs, but Slocum had the hold he wanted and he knew that the Mexican would not be able to break it in time to save himself from the strangulation he almost earned the first time around.

Someone else began to batter Slocum from behind, but he really did not care.

John Slocum was damned sick and tired of being on the receiving end of everybody else's crap and this was one time he could do something about it.

For days—hell, ever since he had come to this miserable, empty country—everybody and anybody he came across were trying to mix in on John Slocum's private business. Trying to rob him. Trying to kill him. Trying to use him any old way they pleased.

Well, John Slocum had had enough of that, thank you. And he just did not give a shit any longer what happened to him next, *this* time was his to do the howling and he fully intended to do it.

Slocum's fury was in his eyes, glazing them with green fire that was the purest hate for everything he could see and everything he could reach. The hate blinded him to all else, wiping caution aside, making him care not the slightest what might happen to him next. If only he could kill Cisco and anyone else he could reach.

He knew that someone was pummeling the back of his head, probably was using some hard object to hit him. Slocum did not care. He clung to his hold on Cisco's throat as tenaciously as a bulldog attached to a fighting bull's nose and *nothing* was going to knock him loose.

Nothing except possibly Big.

The Big man stepped in and brushed the others aside. He put one hand on Slocum's wrists and another —urgently—on Cisco's face, and he yanked the two men apart as effortlessly as if he had been plucking a dead fly from a piece of flypaper.

Slocum was aware again of what was going on. He reeled backward, knocking Hutchison or one of his men aside, and he looked up in time to see the Ute girl Moonlight flinging herself onto Big's back like a furious mouse attacking an elephant.

Damn, Slocum thought, she was supposed to have been running all this time.

It was too late to think about the girl now, though. He had reached the end of his rope in this camp of buffalo hunters and buffalo thieves and all he could hope for now was to do some damage to them before he went down for the final time.

Slocum threw himself back into the fray. Cisco was down on his knees again, his throat almost but not quite crushed before Big tore Slocum off of him. Now that Big was occupied with the girl, Slocum went for Cisco again.

But again Big reached the Mexican in time to save him, and this time the powerful extension of Hutchison's will took hold of Slocum and began methodically to break the smaller man's body, one crushing punch at a time.

Slocum could feel a rib go the first time Big hit him. He felt deep, interior agony and waves of blackness with the second blow. By the time the third landed on the already broken rib Slocum knew that he was probably a dead man already, and if he had any chance at all it was to pretend to be a dead man. He let himself sink into the twilight half world that was already beckoning him and he went completely limp, falling with no effort to avoid further injury or to soften the impact as his face struck solid ground.

Big and perhaps some of the others continued to kick him, and Slocum slipped even further away from his precarious hold on life. The punishment his body was taking was beyond anything he had ever known before, and John Slocum had been beaten by experts.

It was a rasping cough from Cisco that drew their attention away from him at last.

In some small recess of his mind where still a spark of life was kindled Slocum could hear the movement around him as the boots that had been slamming into his body now slammed against the earth.

"She slit Cisco's fuckin' throat," another said.

"Red nigger bitch!" someone shouted.

"Finished the job her man started."

"Yeah, Big. That's it. Hang onto her. Bring her back here where we can all have some."

There were sounds of heavy breathing. The labored panting of men who had been actively engaged in strenuous effort—as in kicking a man to death—and the quicker but equally heavy panting of men who are about to engage in violent sex.

There was the sound of a small body striking the earth and, immediately after, the sound of ripping cloth.

"Pretty li'l bitch, ain't she?"

"Too skinny. Not enough meat for my taste."

"Sweeter meat that way, I've heard."

"You'll find out soon enough."

There was the sound of men grunting out their pleasures against living, unwilling female flesh, although to listen to the sounds of their ecstasy it seemed more a matter of agony and of effort than of pleasure.

One man after another the sounds continued along with ribald suggestions and offers of comparisons for size and diameter and quickness in getting it off.

Throughout all of it there was no sound at all from the girl. There was no indication whether she was even alive. The men continued to use her regardless.

At length, and it could have been a matter of hours, the last of them tired of taking battered, bloody seconds or thirds or whatever they were on and the sounds began to diminish.

"I s'pose we'll have to bury Cisco," one of them said.

"Hell, no. We're moving camp anyhow come morning. With the Kiowa scratching the red ass around here it's time we moved south. Might be more buffalo down there anyhow. And more buff hunters. Leave him lay there. The other one too."

"Are we gonna kill the little bitch and leave her by her man?"

A pause. "I don't think so. She's still alive, I think. Yeah, see her move there? We'll pack her onto a pony." A laugh. "That's what she came here for, isn't it? The borrow of a horse? Well, she'll get just what she asked for. We'll pack her along with us. Keep her however long she lasts. I'm tired of a camp so far from women anyway. This is a good way to take care of that problem. If she decided to up an' die on us later, there's no harm done. In the meantime we might as well have all we want of that free stuff, right?"

"Right."

"So tie her up good. Don't let her fool you into thinking she's out neither. And for God's sake, don't let her get near a knife again. She damn near took ol' Cisco's head off his shoulders with that one swipe she got in. So don't take any chances with her. Knock her around some to let her know who's boss, and when she comes around again we'll have old Vetter explain to her that she'll be kept alive just as long as she plays along. Okay?"

"Sure."

"Good. Now get to bed. We want to get packed up and out of here at first light. I don't want those stinking

Kiowa finding us even if there are more of us than Fortson had. It don't pay to take chances with Indians."

Or with some white men. Slocum released his last hold on consciousness. But he kept firm what tiny hold he still had on life itself. He was *not* going to allow himself to die.

CHAPTER 17

Life is a sea of pain upon which a man floats until, inescapably, he drowns.

Jeez, but that sounds philosophical, Slocum thought. True, too. Or was it?

Either way he was not yet ready to trade the pain of living for whatever was to come afterward. Certainly not now. There were things he wanted to do before he quit.

He gave the matter a great deal of thought and decided that since he was alive anyway he might as well do some moving too. With enough effort and concentration he was able to open his eyes. It required a great deal of effort and concentration, though, for at first he was quite unable to remember how to control his own muscles. He knew he could do it but he could not remember how. He guessed that he had been beaten very close to death indeed.

The campsite Hutchison's men had vacated was not much to look at now, and Slocum had never seen it in daylight but it was certainly empty. There were several dark rings where fires once had been, and here and there some scraps of food and empty tins, most of these bearing the white and red labels of evaporated-milk cans. A camp cook's coffee traditionally had to be so heavily loaded with condensed milk and sweetening

166

that the flavor of the rank brew itself was disguised. Hot horse piss would probably taste good if it was laced with milk and sugar the way most cowhands took their coffee. The buffalo hunters seemed to have been no exception to that rule, judging from their litter.

Certainly, though, they had left neither weapons nor food for Slocum to use now.

He rolled his head a little and could see that the sun was slanting low in the sky, but whether it lay now in the east or in the west he did not have any idea. It could have been morning or evening, and any number of days might have passed since his last memory.

Slocum shifted his arms a little—he was much more in control of himself now—and received a sharp reminder that several of his ribs were broken.

A broken rib was nothing exactly new to John Slocum. He had received enough of them in the past, by one way or another, and there were times when he thought that a broken rib was more painful than a kick in the crotch. Certainly the pain hung on longer, even if it was not quite so exciting when it was received.

Pain was something he could live with when he had to, though, and now it seemed that he had to. But he did tell himself it was about time he quit being on the receiving end of so much of it. The scalp wound the Kiowa had given him still hurt, and he seemed bent on collecting more of the same.

The pain it was almost possible to ignore when there was so much of it. What he could not ignore was his need for water. It had been too long since he had had water, and healing, even when there is little loss of blood, seems to require water. Slocum damn sure wanted to get the healing under way.

There was no high ground anywhere around the camp where he might have gotten a good look at the country around him, and if he moved in any direction he might well be heading directly away from the nearest source of water. He lay pondering the problem for a while, but thinking was not going to make him less thirsty. Quite the contrary.

He lay idly watching the sun in its slow fall toward the horizon, and eventually—you're a slow-witted bastard when you're hurt, he told himself—he realized that if the sun was sinking, that direction was logically in the west. Which meant that just over that way was north. Which meant that the Canadian River was somewhere in exactly that northward direction, since he and Moonlight had not crossed the river before they reached Hutchison's camp.

He had no idea how far the river was but at least he knew where it was. He intended to get there.

Painfully, at the expense of his elbows and kneecaps, he began inching his way north toward the Canadian and the cool, wet succor it might be able to offer him.

Slocum had no idea how long it took him to reach the river, but he guessed afterward that it was only a matter of hours. He did not remember a sunrise and sunset between when he started out and when he found water, and while that was not proof positive it was a fair indication that the time had not been long.

He was not hurting a bit less when he got there, but he was hurting no more either and that could be taken as a good sign. He crawled out into the water and let it soak into his skin while he drank. The split in his scalp, he noticed, did not sting when he immersed it into the slow-flowing, silty water. That was good. It was beginning to heal. Any small signs of progress would be gratefully appreciated.

And, slowly, they were.

For three days Slocum lay in the sparse cover along the Canadian, drinking between long sleeps and occasionally trying to scrounge a fish or an egg or anything that might be considered remotely edible. For the most part he swallowed minnows he trapped in hand-dug weirs at the water's edge, and he counted himself lucky to be getting even that much nourishment, considering the physical condition he was in.

The fourth morning he could stand with some small degree of comfort and could walk without falling flat onto his face again. He began following the river upstream, watchful both for Kiowa and for wagon tracks crossing the shallow river.

He never did find any real fresh tracks, but on his second day of slow walking he found a pretty good substitute. He rounded a sweeping curve and found a pair of freight wagons in the water.

"Afternoon, boys," he said as he approached.

He must have made a hell of an impression on them to judge from their expressions when the freighters and their swampers, all busily concentrating on a mired wheel, looked up and first caught sight of him.

"I'm John Burton," Slocum announced calmly. "I seem to've been having a bit of trouble here lately."

He looked a total mess with a week's growth of dark beard smearing his jaw, his clothes in tatters, hatless under the harsh Plains sun and no weapons or horse for his own safety. It would have taken a complete fool to have failed to appreciate his problems, and few men in the buffalo trade were fools. The foolish ones just did not last that long in the harsh environment so far from the civilized comforts.

"I'm Horace Spivey," one of the freighters responded immediately. "You're welcome here and any help we can give you you'll get."

"I take that awful kindly, Mr. Spivey. I have to admit that I can use your help right now."

Slocum accepted assistance climbing into the tall wagon even before he met the other men. Later he sorted the names out to match the faces: Glenn Cordell, who was Spivey's swamper; Bert Spivey, Horace's brother and driver of the second wagon; and Bert's swamper, Elrod Pitkin.

They were a good crew and worked well together without argument or hesitation when there was hard labor to be done. Slocum liked them immediately and admired them as well. It was from the backbones of men like these, he knew, that the future prosperity of what was now a vast and empty land would be forged. John Slocum never expected to be like these men, industrious and honest, but he had had his own dreams along those lines at one time in the now-distant past, before the arrogant rule of postwar carpetbaggers had driven him onto the wrong side of the law.

Now it was too late for him to turn back, of course. But once he had held his own fond dreams that centered around the family's farmland acres and the hope of a wife to stand at his side and children to grow straight and tall behind him.

John Slocum had long since recognized that his dreams were shattered and gone forever. Oh, he had tried to bring them back. He had even tried a time or two to live them, hoping the joy would return with the opportunity. But he had found instead that he belonged now to the life of the fast horse, the fast gun, and the fast woman. The sweet, tempting lure of the gamble had seeped into his blood in those long, intervening years, and his gambles were table, his stakes were often for life itself instead of a few replaceable cents. And, no, he could not now go back to the old dreams. Those belonged to a former life. But he still had great respect for those who did have the dreams a younger John Slocum had been forced to abandon.

The Spivey brothers and their helpers hauled the stuck wheel free without having to go to the trouble of unhitching the teams on the second wagon and doubling up on the first.

"That's got it," Horace said. He climbed back into

his high, padded seat and picked up the four sets of lines that were his badge of office while he was in the box. "We'll pull onto solid ground over there, Mr. Burton, and see what it is we can do for you."

"A bite of the leavings from your last meal would be a good start," Slocum told him.

"Hungry, huh. Would you, uh, mind if I asked . . ."

"Nope. Under the circumstances I reckon you're entitled. I was with a hunting outfit. Charles Fortson's, if you know it."

"I do," Horace said. "Remember them, Glenn?"

"Of course. I got into a scrap with a fella from that crew. Beanass, I think they called him: In Tascosa that was. We got into a fight and then made up for it by getting drunk together and tearing up Longtooth Kate's whorehouse."

"You won't be doing it with Beanass again. He died hard, with a Kiowa arrow in his throat. Not as hard as Fortson, though. Him they took alive and gave to the squaws for them to kill him a quarter inch at a time. He took three hours to die."

"And you?" The suspicion in Horace Spivey's voice was plain enough.

"They took me along with Fortson," Slocum explained. "A little Ute gal wanting help to get back to her people turned me loose."

"Uh-huh." The unspoken part was still clear. If that was the truth, where the hell was the Ute girl now?

"We found another camp. Hutchison and his crowd. Hutchison left me for dead and took the girl with him."

"I know Hutchison too," Spivey said.

"Then you likely know he's a son-of-a-bitch," Slocum said. "And if you think I'm talking him down behind his back, don't. I figure to tell him that to his face the first chance I get."

Spivey nodded. "He is a son-of-a-bitch, I must agree."

Slocum had a rude thought just then. "I, uh, don't suppose you're hauling for Hutchison, are you?"

Horace laughed. "Hell, no." He swung his rig into the shade of a few straggly cottonwoods that were growing along the river there and whoaed his leaders. He crawled into the back of the wagon beside Slocum and began digging in one of the boxes for some food. "No, we're driving for a fellow name of Justin Perry. He has a pretty good-sized operation. Five shooters and a big crew of skinners and scrapers and us freighters and such. Big enough that he doesn't have to pay attention to petty thieves like Hutchison because he has guns enough and guts enough to tell the man to go to hell, which I have heard him do at least twice myself. So no, we aren't hauling for Hutchison. Say, though, I'd like to hear a little more about this Kiowa business. Where was it you ran up against them?"

Slocum described the country while he ate. Lord, but a few cold biscuits and tinned peaches had never tasted so good. Slocum would have given almost anything for some meat to add to that, but in buffalo country it would have been asinine for the men to pay for meat to be hauled out from a supply point when they were wallowing in wasted meat for miles in all directions day in and day out.

"We'll meet the rest of the outfit the day after tomorrow," Horace told him. "At least we'll be at the rendezvous point then. If they aren't there they soon will be."

"Unless the Kiowa found them too."

Horace shrugged. "It's a big outfit. They wouldn't go down easy."

"Fortson's crowd didn't go down easy, but they damn sure went down."

"Yeah, well, we'll talk that over with Justin first thing. That and what Hutchison done to you. I'm sure he can get you rigged out in some traveling gear or something. In the meantime we'll get you fattened up some. How's that?"

"Mr. Spivey, I could not have asked for more if a genie'd popped out of a bottle and offered me three wishes," Slocum said. He grinned. "Well, not for *much* more, anyhow." He finished the food Spivey had given him and leaned back against a pile of salt sacks. It was about time he started building up his strength, because he fully intended to have a good use for it in the near future.

CHAPTER 18

"Damned interesting story you tell, John. If it wasn't for that gash in your head and the bruises and broken ribs you undoubtedly have, I might find it hard to believe all of it." Which almost certainly meant that he *was* having trouble believing all of it, Slocum thought.

"I expect I'd lie if I had reason to, Justin," Slocum told him. "This time I just don't have a reason."

"Uh-huh. Well, that is beside the point, in any event. The question now is not where you came from but what to do with you now that we have you."

"I'm not a man to ask for nobody's charity," Slocum said firmly. "I had a good deal of money in my pocket, and I'll have that same amount again soon enough. Soon as I see Hutchison again and convince him I need it more than he thought I did. In the meantime I ain't afraid of work, and I'm not asking you for anything I'm not willing to pay for with whatever kind of sweat you need."

Justin Perry scratched himself and seemed to be doing some thinking. Perry was not exactly what Slocum had expected. Most buffalo hunters tended to be shaggy and unclean, most of them men of about Slocum's age who were still having trouble accepting a tame way of life after the uncertainties and excitement of warfare. Many of these men had put in their years and their countless miles on the old Santa Fe Trail as bullwhackers or meat hunters and already had reason to know the desolate Plains that Easterners still insisted on referring to as the Great American Desert.

Perry, though, was a young man barely into his twenties if he was that old. He was slightly built and clean-shaven, and Slocum got the impression that he was a sharp young businessman and merchant who was starting out with a stake toward his life's future and intended to use the booming hide market as his quickest way to a hoped-for financial empire.

It would not be a bad choice, Slocum reflected. Given a few thousand to start with—say, a bundle of seed money provided by a generous but not indulgent parent, or perhaps an inheritance of limited extent—the buffalo-robe trade could be a fine investment indeed. Buy the wagons and the gear, hire a crew of men, and gamble that the investment would pay off with returns large enough to make the next venture a major and a permanent one.

Slocum did not know if that was Justin Perry's story but it was the one Slocum would have placed his money behind if it had come to that.

Perry gave Slocum a close looking over and seemed quite undaunted by the lean, hard look of the older man. Even after taking so much physical punishment Slocum was a man to be reckoned with, and his pride and the toughness of spirit within him were untouched by all the Kiowa and Hutchison had been able to do to him.

"You look like a man who can handle himself," Justin said. "And one who can handle a gun too."

"I can," Slocum said without hint of arrogance. It was a simple statement of fact and there was no trace of boast in his voice when he answered the younger man.

"As it happens, I need another shooter at the moment. One of our hunters walked too close to the back end of a mule the other day. I think he might have had some harsh words to say about that animal, but his jaw is in several pieces right now and he isn't saying much anymore."

"A man shouldn't never argue with superior intelligence," Slocum said drily. He had small respect for a man who was not bright enough to keep himself out of reach of a mule's always-ready feet.

The remark drew a faint half smile from Perry. "Yes, well, his rifle has been sitting cold since then. That's a waste, and I am not fond of waste."

"Neither am I," Slocum said. It was not a lie.

John Slocum was a man who disapproved of wastefulness. Of course, he might cheerfully blow everything he had in his pockets in a hell-raising good time at his favorite Denver whorehouse, but he would not consider that to be a waste. If he gained a good time from it—a bottle or two of the best in the house and a tumble or three with the best whore, whores, or combination thereof in the house—then it was no waste but well worth the fun of doing it. Slocum kind of doubted that he and Justin Perry would interpret "waste" in quite the same way, but the sentiment was the same.

"Your ribs have to be hurting you," Justin said. "Do you think you can shoot comfortably?"

Slocum shrugged. The torso movement of just that was enough to be painful, but he could live with pain. None of it showed in his face. "Horace taped me up the other day so it ain't as bad as it was now. And I can still shoot accurate. I'll know about comfortable when I shoot."

Perry nodded. Accuracy was what he wanted. If that was unimpaired, the shooter's comfort was his own business.

"I'll give you a try, then," he said.

"I've been getting a dollar a hide from Fortson," Slocum ventured.

"That was a different situation altogether," Justin said. "Here you will get fifty cents. Or if you prefer I would hire you as a hide scraper at a dollar a day and found."

There was no point in arguing with that brisk, businesslike tone of voice. "I'll take the fifty cents."

"You supply your own powder, lead, and primers," Justin told him. "Those I supply at my cost. I take no profit from them."

Slocum nodded. Fair enough.

"The rifle is mine. There is no charge for its use, however."

"A Sharps?" Slocum asked. It almost had to be. There were competitors on the market but none good enough to be worth the few dollars of initial savings when compared with the needs of the buffalo trade. Those who tried to use only military Springfields or trapdoor conversions were amateurs who would not be seen on the Plains for long. Those who chose the Remingtons or, worse, the Winchesters, were cheapskates who might make a living but who would not do well where they could have prospered.

"Late-model Sharps. Have you shot them before?"

Slocum gave him an impatient glance. "I was making a Sharps talk in rhymes when you were still shooting slingshots at little birdies in a tree."

Perry took no apparent offense. "This one is the .45-100. Bottleneck case. Very flat shooting and hits nearly as hard as the heavier bullets. You can make your stands from much farther out when need be. If you can handle distance shooting."

"I'll want to get used to the gun before I use it."

"There's time enough for that this afternoon."

Justin rounded up the rifle and ammunition and enough bystanders from the camp to provide either a cheering or a jeering section, and they set some empty kegs out on the grass two hundred and four hundred yards from the wagons. Each of the casks was about the size of a buffalo's kill zone. Or a man's.

"If that's all you ask for, you're pretty easy to please," Slocum said. His tone carried more than a hint of brag in it.

"Dead center or don't bother shooting," Justin returned.

Shit, Slocum chided himself. Get cocky and outsmart yourself, why don't you. Thank you, I will. And do pretty damned often. "Give me a couple shots at each distance to get familiar with the gun then," he said aloud.

The rifle was fully as heavy as the .50-110-550 had been, even though it carried a smaller cartridge. The barrel was octagon-shaped and massive. The rifle must have weighed more than twenty pounds, Slocum judged. With the heavy barrel like that it would be slow to overheat but once hot it would hold the heat a long time. The front sight was a hooded post and the rear an adjustable vernier peep-mounted far back on the tang of the action. The stock was cherrywood, unbeautiful and utilitarian; cherry is not a tenth as pretty as walnut but will not warp under conditions that would send even stable walnut twisting into pretzel shapes. The rifle was as businesslike as the man who had chosen it.

"I like your taste in rifles," Slocum offered by way of apology for his smart-ass attitude a moment before.

Justin nodded but did not speak. He was waiting to be convinced.

Slocum grinned and sat cross-legged on the ground. He shifted his butt until he was as comfortable as he was going to get and mounted the heavy rifle on the cross-shooting sticks stand hunters used as a rest. In this kind of shooting, time was not a factor but accuracy certainly was.

Even so, Slocum was not one to linger over his sights. A Creedmoor shooter, used to firing over extremely long distances at inoffensive pieces of paper, might take two hours to satisfy himself that his paper patching, his sights, the wind, his heartbeat, his breathing, and perhaps the phase of the moon were precisely correct for making his shot. And no doubt under those conditions and with those objects in mind, the Creedmoor expert would outshoot John Slocum every day of the week.

Slocum, though, was raised as a short-pants boy with a light rifle and a heavy desire to bring game back for the table, and his targets then had been quick-darting squirrels and deceptively fast rabbits only an instant before they ducked out of view. And in recent years his life had depended time and time again on being the first to put his bullet into the other man's belly. Not the first to shoot necessarily but absolutely the first to strike flesh. And he had become good at it, good enough that he was still alive.

He bent over the sights of the Sharps as casually as another shooter might bend to check his barrel alignment before he got down to serious aiming, but Slocum's finger was already on the crisp trigger and his shot boomed out immediately.

"Trigger's lighter than you figured, is it?" Justin commented.

"Nope. The hole was dead center on the far keg. Signal your spotter to mark it for me."

Justin gave him a slightly disbelieving look but waved downrange to the hide scraper who had been asked to mark Slocum's hits so they could be seen over the distance. The man had been quite eager to have a break from the back-wrenching stoop labor of hide scraping.

"I'll be double-dip damned," Slocum said. "Four inches high. She does shoot flat. Better'n any gun I've ever handled before, I'd say."

"I told you it did," Justin said.

"Reckon you did."

"Personally, I'd say it was damn good shooting," Horace Spivey added. Slocum gave him a wink of thanks.

"Dead center, Mr. Burton," Justin prompted.

"Right." Slocum thumbed a fresh round into the Sharps and latched the thick breechblock back into place. He drew the hammer back and leaned forward. Again he appeared to give the sights only a superficial glance but again his finger squeezed and the big gun rocked back against him.

He was able to keep the pain of his broken ribs from reaching his face, but he was damned glad that the gun was not a pound lighter. He needed all the help he could get to absorb the recoil now.

Perry waved for the scraper to spot the shot without being asked. This time the marker was laid dead center.

"Do you want me to try the closer keg, Mr. Perry?" Slocum asked.

"That would be a waste of powder and lead, John. I thought I told you, I don't like waste."

"So you did, Justin."

Perry turned and extended a hand to Slocum. They shook and Justin helped Slocum back to his feet.

"Tomorrow morning," Justin said. "Take a skinning crew and get started. They know where the buffs are."

"Good enough. I, uh, I take it you weren't too impressed with my story about the Kiowa then."

"On the contrary," Justin said. "We'll drift south from here. We move our camp nearly every day anyway, and from now on we drive deeper into the herd and avoid the fringes. That's where the Indians will be expecting to find their targets. They won't be finding us there."

"It's your judgment."

"Yes," Justin acknowledged calmly.

Slocum might have chosen to do things differently, but then he had seen this bunch of Kiowa once. Perry had not. Slocum doubted that a man as sensible as Justin Perry obviously was would have held to a normal camp routine if he had been through a Kiowa attack like the one that wiped out Charles Fortson's outfit. But then very few people who had seen an attack like that were still alive to tell about it.

"Stop by my tent after dinner," Justin said, "and we will reach an agreement on how much to advance you against wages for your bedroll and other supplies, John. I think you will find me fair enough."

Slocum nodded. The time he would have to spend here in this camp galled him. He would have much preferred to be on his way at once. But what he wanted was long-term success and not an instant but futile attempt at revenge. He fully intended to have Hutchison's head for a plaything, and Slocum could be as patient as the seasons just so he could do it.

CHAPTER 19

At fifty cents a hide this was turning out to be damned slow work. Perry wanted twenty dollars for a Colt .45 with a holster and belt full of ammunition for it. He wanted fifty dollars for a scraggly horse and much-used saddle. He wanted ten dollars for a bedroll and coffee pot. He wanted twenty dollars for a Winchester saddle carbine. He wanted two dollars per box for extra ammunition.

The prices were, Slocum admitted, about what he would have had to pay for the same articles in any of the Plains towns. Perry could have chosen to charge almost anything he wanted. This was, after all, the only game in town.

Still the delay was maddening. John Slocum was a man who liked to pay his debts. Particularly blood debts.

By now there was little likelihood that Moon Silver on the Aspen was still alive. By now the men would have tired of having to watch her constantly, and they almost certainly would have killed her. Otherwise by this time she would either have run from them or killed at least one of them.

It was also just plain easier on Slocum if he simply assumed that the girl was dead. That removed not a jot of his debt to her, but it made it easier for him to wait until he could make the repayment. He knew good and well that he could pay the girl as fully by killing Hutchison as in any other way.

So day in and day out he made his stands and dropped the shaggy buffalo and turned them over to the attentions of Justin Perry's skinners while Slocum moved on in search of another stand. Each day, after deducting for the small initial debt imposed for gunpowder and lead and other supplies, Perry sat in the evening and computed how much Slocum had earned toward his outfit.

He bought out the Colt .45 first and some spare ammunition so he could familiarize himself with the gun, for each weapon off a common assembly line still has its own unique balance and shooting characteristics, and Slocum could ill afford to carry a revolver that was not as comfortable in his hand as one of his own fingernails.

He worked next—and after all the deductions, all legitimate, all understandable if annoying, it took him six days to do so—for the dun horse and cheap saddle that Perry had to offer him.

At least, Slocum knew, with a Colt and a horse he was his own man again and could fend for himself wherever and however might become necessary.

Next he got the bedroll and camp supplies and a heavy skinning knife that was not near the equal of his own fine Bowie but that at least would take a proper edge and seemed able to hold it once taken. That was important in a knife and all too rare.

He still needed the Winchester, because a man who expects to be living off wild game in the country he travels through—as Slocum expected he would have to do for some time to come—is at a serious and sometimes fatal handicap if he has only a short gun to provide his groceries.

There were men, Slocum knew, Hickok among them, who would make nine kinds of brags about their superhuman prowess with a six-gun, but there were not five men in the entire world who could have put two rounds out of six into an antelope's breadbasket at two hundred yards. Not with a handgun they couldn't. And of those few who were that good, a clear majority worked for Colt as factory demonstrators, and the others were showmen. All of them lived in the East and would never actually have to shoot an antelope for their dinner or have to go hungry if they missed.

Moreover, a revolver—any revolver, including the fine .45 Colt cartridge—is grossly underpowered and grossly overrated when it comes to long-range power. The same bullet that will do an admirable job of blowing a man off his feet at seven paces—the most common distance for gunfights, tall tales to the contrary— will be hard pressed to kill a coyote at a hundred paces and will do no more than annoy most animals at any distance greater than a hundred fifty paces. So Slocum needed that Winchester if he expected to pay his respects to Hutchison.

They were down south of the Yellow Horse country now, drifting steadily below the area where Slocum had seen the Kiowa and while there was no way to be certain they were safe because of the distance there was probably less danger here from Kiowa if more from Comanche than the country to the north.

Water was scarcer here and low-growing mesquite and yucca more abundant. The ground was altogether choppier and rougher than to the north.

That did make it easy to make stands because there was so much natural cover for concealment, but it also tended to make the great buffalo herds break up into smaller groups than were common to the north and so made John Slocum's income somewhat slower to bring in than he would have found on the wide-open grass of the already nearly extinct Northern Herd up in the Marias River country or even than would have still been possible closer to the Canadian.

"How many today, John?" Justin asked when Slocum came in bone-weary from a hunt.

"Too damn few, that's how many," Slocum told him. "They're scattered down here. Hard to find. I'm beginning to think I won't ever be able to get on the road again."

"How many was it, anyway?"

Slocum told him.

"A few more days and you should be clear, John. Though I must tell you I'd welcome you to stay a while longer. Cajun's jaw is slow to heal. I could use your help for another few weeks if you could see your way clear to give it."

"I appreciate that, Justin, but . . ."

"Oh, I understand, all right. No need to explain further. You seem pretty well healed anyway."

Slocum grinned. "Well healed, yes. Well heeled, no."

Perry chuckled. "Give me those two extra weeks and you might be. I could, uh, go seventy-five cents maybe."

"Justin, if you've gotten to the point where you're offering hard money then I know you're damn well deperate. But I still have to pass. Might be I could come back later for a while, but I have a burning in my belly to talk to Mr. Hutchison about something."

"Huh. I won't need you later. By the time you find Hutchison's camp, *if* you come out of it alive again, Cajun will be back to work. And while I couldn't say he's a better hunter than you are, he is one of my old crew. And I can count on him to be here making money for me long after you've gone off looking for another windmill to tilt at."

"Windmill?"

Justin shook his head. "Nothing. Just chattering."

"Whatever." Slocum was about to turn away but Justin stopped him.

"Have you seen Wallace today?"

Harrison Wallace was another of the shooters, an older man than most in the Perry camp and a veteran of the Santa Fe Trail trade who was an excellent shot if a silent companion around the camp at night.

"Not since late morning. He went one side of a ridgeline an' I went the other. I haven't seen him or his skinners since."

"That's odd. I haven't seen his wagon come in for a midday drop today either," Justin said.

The skinning crews traveled behind the shooters in light spring wagons that could be hauled over, under, or through most of the obstacles to be found in this kind of open country. They used the wagon teams to help pull the hides off downed buffalo, loaded the green hides into the small wagons, and carried them back to the base camp for fleshing and drying. The huge freight wagons were used only to get large masses of the hides out to market buying points. Because the small wagons could carry so little at any given time, the skinners usually had to make a noon trip back to the camp to dispose of the morning's take while their shooter was making his afternoon hunt. A failure to appear around noon or shortly thereafter normally meant the hunter was having a bad day, and with Wallace that would have been quite rare indeed. He was not a stand-out shooter but he was a steady hunter and a good one.

"You did say they were scattered down there, didn't you," Justin said as if to reassure himself instead of to verify Slocum's already given information.

"I said they were scattered, yes. I didn't say they weren't around. We're getting fewer at a stand, but there's a world of stands to be taken out there."

"Do you remember where you last saw him?"

"Of course."

"Take me there, would you?"

Slocum retrieved his dun and resaddled the animal while Perry was saddling a fine-looking sorrel that he used as a personal mount. The dun had been under saddle all day but little of a buffalo hunter's time was spent on horseback so the horse had been little used. Most of his days he spent with his girth hanging loose and hobbles or a picket line keeping him where his owner wanted him to be but with all the time he might ever want to graze and doze and live a contented life.

"It isn't but a couple hours from here. To the last place where I seen him, anyway. From there," he shrugged, "no tellin'."

"It will be dark in less than three hours," Justin said.

"Unless there's something awful wrong with the sun it will."

"Let's push it then. I'd like to know."

Slocum nodded and led the way at a high lope that covered the ground at a rapid pace. They had to slow the horses to a walk after the first hour. Slocum insisted on that. The animals were far from being overused, but in country where there was always the possibility of Indian trouble John Slocum was not about to fork an overtaxed horse. Not when he had no spare to switch to in a hurry.

"That's the ridgeline over there to the right," Slocum said finally. "His wagon tracks will be easy enough to follow."

Perry nodded and spurred ahead, perhaps fortunately not able to hear Slocum's cursing behind him.

Anybody who isn't willing to keep himself ready for the very worst that could happen has got no business separating from his mama's apron strings. Unless, of course, he has a death wish.

Slocum had no such death wish. He also had no control over Justin Perry. Slocum followed behind

Perry at the same gait the dun had been holding comfortably most of the time since they had left the base camp.

Wallace's wagon wheels had cut a clean track in the crumbly, gravel-pocked hardpan that served for soil here. The track was clear enough that a six-year-old girl from Brooklyn could have followed it with ease.

They passed a shot-out stand where the skinned carcasses of seven buffalo had been left, a missing hump indicating that the shooting had been done shortly before lunchtime.

"I was on a stand not three quarters of a mile over there," Slocum said, pointing. "I never heard a thing of Wallace's shooting, though."

"Wind and ground contours can do that sometimes. It works the other way too. Sometimes you can hear a man shooting five miles away if everything else is just right."

"I reckon."

A short distance farther they found the remains of a fire where Wallace and his party had stopped to eat. Logically the wagon should have turned back soon after that, but apparently they had elected to stay with their hunter for at least one more stand.

That decision had been a fatal one.

Perry, galloping ahead as before, was the first to spot them.

"Over here, John. Hurry!"

There really was no more need for Slocum to hurry, though. Wallace and his two skinners were sprawled face up in the middle of a mud-caked dry-pond bottom. The wagon and hides and their weapons were missing, and the men had been scalped.

When they got near enough Slocum and Justin could see that each of the men had had his belly ripped open, almost certainly by a lance.

"Those dirty red bastards," Justin said. He looked

somewhat shaken but he was not at all panicky, Slocum was glad to see. "You said those Kiowa had lances, didn't you? It certainly looks like they've come south too. Murdering red bastards."

"Murdering bastards," Slocum agreed, "but not red ones."

"What do you mean?"

Slocum stood in his stirrups and took a careful look at the country around them before he answered. He stepped off his dun and bent over the three dead men.

"Look at these smudges here. This one is over the blood so it happened after the fight. A mark like that ain't made by a moccasin. That was a boot. And there's no sign of a real fight. All these boys were gutted the same way, with careful strokes. They were stuck by somebody who was already right up near them when those lancetips came down or Wallace and them would have made more of a fight of it. That means white men to me."

Slocum pointed to the men's clothing. "Their pockets have been turned out too. Somebody robbing the corpses. That means white men, too, Justin. These boys was too savvy to let a bunch of Indians get that close without them being ready for a scrap.

"Yet they was gutted and scalped, the way an Indian will do. Or maybe a Comanchero. Now, if you want to talk about bastards, talk about Comancheros. They're about as bad as they come."

"I've heard of them," Justin said.

"Come to think of it, I've heard it said that the Comancheros use the Palo Duro for a sort of home away from home. They haul their stuff up in carts from Mexico and use the canyon as a headquarters up this way. The Palo Duro isn't too awful far from here if I remember it right."

Justin rubbed the back of his neck. "No, not far," he agreed.

Slocum shrugged and again took a careful look around. He was beginning to wish the country here was a great deal more open than was the case. A man can get awfully nervous about the things he cannot see.

"If I was to guess at it," Slocum said, "this was the work of Comancheros. They're white enough to be allowed close, 'specially if they were to wave a white rag and ask to talk, maybe ask for some meat or water. Once they were close enough . . ." Slocum made a thrusting motion with his right hand. "No complaints and a quick profit."

"I suppose we should do the decent thing and bury these men," Justin said, "but . . . Damnit, John, we can't take the time for that. We have to get back to the camp in case these Comancheros come paying a call on us there. The others have to know."

"You learn mighty well, Justin. You just may live long enough to make your mama proud if you keep on this way." He swung back onto the dun and reined it around the way they had come. He expected the horse to be damn well tired by the time they got back to the camp. "Let's go."

CHAPTER 20

They rode as hard as they dared push their tiring horses, but the Comancheros were there before them. Slocum and Justin could see the mounted men in the camp as they came near, the Mexicans' lancetips reflecting the firelight.

"They haven't been here long," Slocum said, "or they would've dismounted already."

"The question I'm wondering is not how long they've been here but how many of them there are."

"Too few to make an attack right now," Slocum said, "or I think they would have done it. Coming in out of the darkness against men blinded by firelight would be a fine advantage. I think this crowd must be checking to see how many of *us* there are and how well armed and prepared for trouble."

"What do you think then, John? Give them hell here and now so they know we're ready and will stay away? Or try to lull them in to where we can get the whole crowd by playing stupid?"

"That kinda depends, Justin."

"On what?"

"On whether you're more interested in the rest of the camp being safe or in getting back something for Wallace and those two skinners."

Justin gave him a thin, tight smile. "In that case, John, I guess we'd better be a bunch of fat old dummies ripe for some picking, hadn't we?"

"You know, Justin, if you ever live long enough to grow up, I think you're gonna do just fine."

"I'm not so sure I should thank you for saying that, but I think I do."

They held their pace nearly to the center of the camp before they reined to a halt and swung down from their sweating mounts.

"Sorry to be so late getting back, boys," Justin said. He sounded cheerful and completely at ease. No one but Slocum could have known that he would be seething whenever he looked at the Comancheros.

Justin looked up at the lance-wielding Mexicans with an open, boyish smile. "Hasn't anybody invited you to step down yet? Then I reckon it's about time. Get off and have some supper with us, boys."

The Comanchero leader looked startled at first but his surprise did not last long. He turned to his men with a sly grin and told them to dismount. As guests, he added.

The Comancheros relaxed visibly and swung lightly down from their broad-horned saddles.

Whatever else these men were, Slocum noted, they were riders. It takes a rider to be a lancer, and it takes a monumentally fine horseman to win the respect of the fierce Comanche Indians with whom the Mexicans traded and from whom they borrowed the name they were known by.

The Comancheros would have made dashing troopers in anyone's army. They were a lean, rugged lot, long on mustaches and long on devil-may-care good looks. They wore gaudy scarlet sashes and hats with enormously wide brims and spurs with rowels three and four inches across. There were only a dozen of them in this group, but they looked to be brave enough and young enough and reckless enough to have attacked the whole armed camp of Americans if their leader had but given the word.

Their leader also looked bright enough not to give that word until he was reasonably sure of success.

"Here, we need some coffee and some cups for these fellows," Justin said loudly. To the Mexican leader he said, "I'm Justin Perry. Kind of in charge here, though we run a pretty loose ship really, everybody trying to make a buck, you know? We've been out a while. Glad to have some fresh faces to look at. And say, you wouldn't have some extra powder you'd be willing to sell, would you? We've been away from fresh supplies a bit too long. Have to go find some soon or we'll be out of business."

"I am afraid I do not, *señor*. But I will surely mention you if I find anyone who does." Like hell, Slocum thought. But the Mexican could be counted on to mention it to his own chief.

"That's damned kind of you," Justin went on. "What did you say your name was again?"

The Mexican smiled. He had not said. "Manuel Vallejos. I am at your service." He bowed elegantly low and swept off his broad hat. Slocum decided that he would have been much more impressed by the performance if he had not known so much about the Comancheros.

As a group these Mexican traders were probably as vile a bunch of subhuman bastards as could be found anywhere on the face of the Plains. And nowhere were men allowed to reach the depths of their own wickedness as they were on the Plains, where law was an idle theory that had no practical application to everyday life anywhere nearer than a five-day ride.

The Comancheros *routinely* dealt in slaves, acting as

middlemen in the human traffic engaged in by the
Plains Indian tribes, supplying Mexican mines with
human labor for sale, supplying the Indians themselves
with girls to warm their beds, taking trade-ins of last
year's models for something fresher and younger if that
was what the buyer wanted.

They also happily supplied the Plains tribes with
guns and ammunition so that the Indians could murder
white settlers and travelers and resupply the Comancheros with new, young slaves for sale to the highest
bidder.

Anything a buyer wanted was or soon enough would
become available, so long as the buyer had the ability
to pay for his purchases. The Comancheros made no
moral judgments whatsoever; their sole question regarded payment. Profit was their only interest. If the
slaves they dealt in and the people who died under
their guns did not like it, that was their problem. The
Comancheros were happy so long as they turned their
profit.

As a result the Comancheros were free to roam the
Plains wherever and whenever they wished without
fear of being molested by any of the wild tribes. They
could enter any camp and find themselves welcomed,
just as the Indians of any tribe could enter the Palo
Duro safely. A white man, though, or an army of them,
might enter the great canyon but would never be per-
mitted to leave it again.

Slocum looked at the Comancheros who were now
sharing their coffee, and his eyes flashed like dark-
green obsidian. If these dashing lancers chose to have
themselves a little scrap and perhaps take themselves
some spoils it would not break John Slocum's heart to
have to drop a few of them into the dirt. Or more than
a few. He would be tickled to take on as many of

them as wanted to try him, one at a time or all in a rush. He did not give a fat crap.

The opportunity, at least a sampling of it, came soon enough.

One of the Comancheros, a broad-shouldered, beefy man with drooping mustache and thick arms, passed Slocum carrying a cup of steaming hot coffee. Slocum gave the Mexican a hard look and made no attempt at all to conceal his distaste for this bastard and for all Comancheros in general.

The Mexican must have seen the look. He made a thinly veiled pretense that he had tripped, and the just-off-the-fire contents of the cup were dumped down the front of Slocum's shirt.

"Cabron," Slocum told him. *"Maricon."*

"Gringo son-of-a-whore," the Mexican greeted him. "I have an accident an' you curse me, gringo dog-fucker. I am a guest here, no?"

"Not mine you ain't."

The Comanchero's hand darted toward the brace of pistols jammed into his sash, but years of familiarity and inborn reflexes made Slocum's hand the quicker by far. By the time the Mexican had taken hold of the gutta-percha grips of his revolver, Slocum's was cocked and leveled at the man's midsection.

"Go right ahead," Slocum invited. The Comanchero, Slocum noted, seemed far more angry than afraid, even looking down the muzzle of the big .45.

"Here now, John, no need for that," Justin said quickly. He and the Comanchero leader hurried over beside the two angry men.

Vallejos tumbled out a rapid flow of Spanish too fast and too heavily loaded with slang for Slocum to follow. The Comanchero released his grip on his pistol and put his hands stiffly down at his sides.

"Now what is this crap, John?" Justin asked. "Don't you know these people are our guests?"

"I just finished telling this greasy bastard here that he wasn't no guest of mine, by God. I don't figure to start treating him like one neither. He's an ugly son-of-a-pig and I don't like him, and that's the way she lies."

Vallejos had been in quiet conversation with his man. Vallejos turned to the two Americans and said, "My friend Obregon here has been telling me much the same about your tall gringo, Señor Perry. I am beginning to think perhaps these two do not like each other so very much."

"Still that's no reason to pull weapons and kill each other."

"There wouldn't't've been no 'each other' about it, Justin," Slocum insisted sullenly. "I was fixing to beef this son-of-a-bitch an' I wouldn't need any help to do it."

"With the gun or the knife or the bare hands I would take you, gringo," the Comanchero called Obregon threatened. He seemed intent on ignoring the obvious fact that in a gun duel he had already proven himself no match for Slocum.

"No, guns," Vallejos warned him. The Comanchero leader, at least, had his memory intact.

"There needn't be a fight at all," Justin offered. "I see no reason why you two can't just shake hands and be civilized. I don't like fighting. Don't approve of it at all, I don't."

Slocum thought he saw Vallejos giving Justin a sideways smirk when he heard that. Easy pickings, the Comanchero leader was no doubt thinking.

"No need at all," Vallejos parroted.

"I see the need," Obregon declared. "This gringo has insulted me. This he cannot do."

"Give me your guns, Obregon." Vallejos took the

twin Remington revolvers from his man but—pointedly, Slocum thought—left a long, slim-bladed knife sticking in the Comanchero's sash.

If it was going to turn out like that, Slocum thought, that was just fine by him. Those busted ribs were not healed well enough yet to withstand any serious rough-and-tumble, and John Slocum was no stranger to a knife either. If the Mex wanted to have it out with steel he wouldn't be getting any virgin here.

Justin turned away. "That's better. Much, much better," he said. He went smilingly away, but Slocum was quite sure that the young hunter was no more satisfied that peace had been restored than Slocum was. If Perry wanted to present himself as a weakling before the Comancheros this was a fine way to do it, and after having seen the look in Justin Perry's eyes when he stared down at Harrison Wallace's body there was no way the man could so quickly have forgotten or decided to forgive. He was playacting, and that was fine by Slocum too. Just as long as he was not required to take water from Obregon.

As soon as Justin had rejoined a group of Comancheros and camp members beside one of the wagons, Vallejos smiled indulgently at his man and said to Slocum, "Perhaps I could do your employer the courtesy of carrying your very rapid Colt to him, señor?"

"I reckon I got no objection to that, amigo. Long as you don't turn it on me."

"Please!" Vallejos looked to be mortally offended by such a suggestion.

"You can fool Justin pretty easy. He's a nice, easygoing young fella. But I'm an old bull-o'-the-woods myself. I just figure I can turn this greasy prick into chilled beef as easy with a knife as with a gun, that's all. What I want from you, Vallejos, is to know that it'll be me on him, or I keep the pistol and play with the both of you."

"But *señor,* I have no quarrel with you. No."

Slocum grinned at the Comanchero and unbuckled his gunbelt. He handed it to Vallejos and felt considerably lighter and more vulnerable as he did so. But Justin, he was sure, would be watching even if he did not appear to be, and there was a long-barreled Sharps leaning against the wagon where Justin was standing.

Vallejos accepted the gunbelt and turned saying, "I will take this to Señor Perry now. I suggest you two work out your problems however you wish."

No sooner had Vallejos spoken than Obregon's blade was flashing in the firelight. He was obviously expecting Slocum's attention to be on the other Comanchero and wanted to take advantage of that split-second's gain to lop Slocum's head off with a sweeping slash of his long knife.

The Mexican grunted with effort as he put his whole weight behind the sweep of his blade.

But Slocum was no longer there.

Slocum ducked away easily and came up with his own knife. He stood balanced lightly on the balls of his feet, the handle of his knife lying loosely against the palm of his hand, the bright tip of the blade upraised and slightly extended. His left hand was held forward and just above the waist-level height of his knife. He looked relaxed and perfectly at ease in the classic knife-fighter's crouch.

"So," Obregon whispered through bared teeth, "you know, eh?"

"I've been there a time or two before. And you're there for the last time, *amigo.*"

"I think not, gringo." Obregon had recovered now and had dropped too into the balanced stance from which he could parry or thrust. He would not, Slocum thought, make the mistake of a wild sweep again.

The two men circled each other warily with small, shuffling steps, feeling the ground beneath their boots carefully before they committed themselves to a placement of any weight, for a turning pebble could be enough to destroy a man in this slow game they played.

Perry and Vallejos and the others who were drawn into a silent circle around them might have compared their motions to an intricately constructed dance, for each movement by one was met and matched by a motion from the other.

With their knives held low and their total concentration centered on the other man, Slocum and Obregon shuffled and circled and waited, bobbing and weaving very slowly as they turned.

The tension of the game was belied by its slowness as they measured each other, yet each knew what he stood to lose and neither was willing to take any chances.

A fight with knives is a peculiar thing for, unlike a fistfight, once it is begun it is ended nearly as quickly as a gunfight. Those who have not seen a fight between two expert knife men tend to think of it as a sword duel with shorter weapons. Yet sword fighters may engage in a hacking, blocking, thrusting struggle for several minutes before one finds the opening he seeks and drives his steel home into the other. With knives there is practically no such thing as a completely parried blow, and once the fighters close the end will come in seconds or fractions of seconds.

Obregon, still testing his opponent, tensed the muscles of his left forearm and flicked the point of his long knife to the right. It was a feint, and Slocum did not bite. The man had not changed the position of his feet ready for a thrust and obviously was not yet ready to commit himself.

Slocum in his turn tried a feint, dropping deeper into his crouch and raising his knife hand a fraction of an inch.

Obregon grinned at him. "Not as easy as that, gringo."

"Easy enough. Soon enough."

They made another complete circle. Obregon got a faraway, almost bored look on him. Slocum did not believe it for a moment.

Without warning, without changing his expression or shifting the set of his feet, the Mexican lunged forward. His left hand flew up to distract and his right sent the long, sharp blade of his weapon lancing in a snake-quick upthrust toward Slocum's belly.

Slocum sucked his lean gut back enough, just barely enough, to let Obregon's blade pass, and while the Comanchero was off balance and extended Slocum flicked his own edge upward beneath the man's out-thrust arm. Obregon was already trying to withdraw, but he was too late. The keen, rising edge of Slocum's knife swept along the underside of Obregon's wrist.

The tendons there were severed and the knife fell from Obregon's suddenly nerveless fingers.

Obregon looked up with stark terror in his eyes this time as Slocum stepped in close to him and thrust the point of his knife against the hollow beneath the Mexican's jaw.

"That's twice now, *amigo*. I don't wanta have to tell you again," Slocum hissed.

Vallejos was yelling something in the background, but Slocum was not listening. With the green fire flashing in his eyes again he grinned into Obregon's fright-ened face and jabbed lightly upward another few inches with the shining steel of his blade.

Hot blood flooded Slocum's wrist, and the sight of

John Slocum's victorious combat grin was the last thing the Comanchero Obregon saw in this life.

Slocum stepped aside to let the body fall and turned to Vallejos and the other now-silent Comancheros. "Anybody want to say it wasn't a fair fight?"

CHAPTER 21

"They'll be back, you know," Slocum said.

Justin nodded glumly. "Don't I know it. Did you see that bastard Vallejos giving us the once-over? You would have thought he was wanting to make a cash offer the way he was inspecting everything so close. Damn him. Well, at least we're partway avenged for what they did to Wallace and those boys."

"Partway," Slocum agreed. "We'll get another chance tomorrow."

"I'll tell you what surprised me," Justin said. "That's the way they hung around and drank coffee with us after you killed their man. They didn't really seem very upset by that. I can't really imagine what men must be like who would see a comrade die and then have coffee with the man who killed him."

Slocum shrugged. "It was a fair fight. Hell, it was their setup, they thought. They figured they could whittle you down just that much more and have a little sport doing it. An' as for that Obregon fella, hell, they didn't care anything about him, nor any of those Comancheros care anything about any other one of them but themselves. Those are not nice people, Justin. Life don't mean much to them. You could flood these Plains six inches deep in blood and they wouldn't care as long as none of it was theirs personally. And if you'd give them a way to make a profit on it, they'd applaud you for your help. Then kill you for your share."

Justin sighed. "I suppose you're right, but it seems a terrible way to live."

"Terrible people live terrible lives, Justin."

Perry called the camp together. When the shooters and the skinners and the scrapers and the swampers and the cook and helper and nighthawk and all were in one spot they had a fair-sized group assembled. They should be more than enough to defend themselves, Slocum thought. The Comancheros were not riflemen the way Americans were. The Mexicans were much more adept with the lance and the knife than with the precision rifle, and that would weigh to the Perry party's advantage.

"We have reason to believe we are going to have a problem here," Perry told them. "With the men who just left here and a good many like them. They already killed Wallace and his skinners. Now they want to kill you and steal all we've worked to put together here. I don't want them to do that, boys. Now here is what we're going to do about it. . . ."

The men went to bed that night smiling.

The same small group of Comancheros who had visited the camp the night before rode in again late the next morning. They came openly, waving friendly hellos and keeping their long, deadly lances slung at their backs. They came as old friends.

Somewhere close behind them, Slocum knew, the others would be hidden and ready, like so many rattlers coiled and poised under the lip of a desert ledge, ready to strike swift fangs into the first unwary foot to come near.

The camp they rode into was typically slack for a buffalo camp at that time of day. The hunters were nowhere in sight; they would be expected to be out gunning, their light wagons and skinning crews with them.

The scrapers had not yet had time to begin receiving their day's work from the returning skin wagons. The scrapers clustered in the shade of an idle freight wagon with decks of cards.

Another freight wagon was parked near that one, and one of the light wagons was out of service, propped up on blocks with a wheel missing.

Perry was seated at a table erected beneath a tent fly. The camp boss had a file and set of screwdrivers laid out before him and was tinkering with a shotgun.

Only the cook and his helper seemed to be very busy, and they were hopping, juggling slabs of meat on an iron grid over the coals, dipping into one pot to stir and another to taste. Before long the crews would begin stopping for their dinners, and the food would have to be ready whenever the men were, for time lost to waiting was money lost to the wind.

Justin watched the Comancheros ride in. His expression was friendly enough. He called a greeting to them and waved Vallejos and his men toward the always-ready coffee pot.

Vallejos touched the brim of his broad hat and led his men to the spot indicated. The Mexicans helped themselves to the pile of tin cups lying there and to the steaming coffee.

The Comancheros squatted in the sun to drink the extraordinarily strong, black coffee. They sat balanced on the toes of their boots, their long, rakish spurs rising nearly far enough to make them goose themselves with their own rowels. If they had not been such a deadly group they might have been laughable.

Vallejos carried his cup into the shade and took the chair Justin offered him at the end of the table to Perry's left.

"Buenos días, amigo." Vallejos sounded genuinely friendly.

"And howdy to you too," Justin said. "Nice day for it, isn't it?"

"For what, *señor?"*

"For dying."

"You are making a joke, yes?"

"I am making a joke, no."

"I do not understand."

"I think you do." Justin was doing all the smiling now.

"But I assure you . . ."

"Save it." Justin laid down the screwdriver he had been fiddling with. "Speaking of saving things, though, you can still save yourself."

"¿Señor?"

"I said you can still save yourself."

"I heard you, but . . ."

"If there's any way you can call off the rest of your dogs, you're free to do so. It'd save all of us a lot of trouble."

"I do not know what you mean, Señor Perry."

"In that case, Mr. Vallejos, my friends and I are making a very great mistake. But I think we will insist on making it anyway."

Justin nudged the front trigger on the 12-gauge L. C. Smith that happened at that moment to be pointing toward Vallejos's chest at a distance of little more than a foot. The result at that range was a gaping pulpy mess where the Comanchero's heart used to beat and the loud, dull, booming report of coarse black powder exploding in a rather large tube.

The gunshot was all the signal that was needed to turn the sleepy camp into an interlocking series of small fortresses, each bristling with gun barrels.

From each of the seemingly empty wagons, from

the cook tent and the hide stacks suddenly appeared armed men, their rifles and shotguns belching fire.

The Comanchero lancers, caught sitting on their butts with coffee cups in their hands instead of revolvers, never had a chance to begin to draw before the fusillade of sudden gunfire smashed them flat onto the ground to become so many bloody piles of carrion.

The noise died as suddenly as it had begun. From the stillness and drifting powder smoke Slocum's voice sang out loud and clear. "Some son-of-a-bitch went an' put a hole through the coffee pot."

The remark brought a round of laughter, which was just what he had intended. As a cavalry commander with a captain's braid on his gray collar he had well learned the value of morale, especially in troops who might be green to the kind of gunfire that includes another man shooting back at you on the far end of your rifle sights. The first hurdle here had been cleared. These men knew now that they could kill Comancheros. If he could help keep them relaxed before the next and far more dangerous encounter they would have an even better chance.

"That gunfire was clear enough, boys," Justin called out to them. "Those Mex bastards will be coming now, so look sharp and don't worry. A man plays hell trying to shoot from horseback, and we all have plenty of time and proper rests to shoot from. So let 'em come in and bust 'em down, boys. We still have a score to settle on them."

"And *stay* where you been *told,*" Slocum hollered. "We got these firelanes figured out real nice. Don't you go messing them up with any bright ideas. Now look sharp 'cause I sure as hell see some dust rising over there west of us."

The main body of the Comancheros, the tables of surprise turned against them instead of their intended victims, came charging over a distant rise with their lances couched and hate on their faces.

It was not supposed to be this way, though, and they had begun their hard charge much too distant to allow them to reach the hunters' camp with their horses still fresh and agile. Stupid fuckers, Slocum thought as he watched them come. They can plan a slaughter real nice, but mix things up a little an' they don't know how to handle it. That's the difference between a fighting force and a bunch of plain old dog-ass murderers.

There were fewer of them than Slocum had guessed, too. Not more than forty in this group and eleven already lying dead on the ground.

The camp's buffalo shooters, Slocum among them, placed their shooting sticks when the Comancheros were within a half mile. At a third of a mile the heavy Sharps rifles began to speak. At a quarter of a mile the Mexicans began to fall, and the survivors among them began to spread apart from the close, racing knot they had been riding in.

"I think they're getting worried," Slocum yelled into the noise of the firing.

At four hundred yards the men with the Winchesters and Spencers and Kennedys and the one unlikely fellow who somehow had come into possession of an old Volcanic repeating carbine opened up with a sound like rolling thunder.

At three hundred yards the Comancheros began to waver.

"Back off. *Back off*, damnit!" Slocum yelled. "Let 'em close on us now."

"Listen to him," Justin hollered after him. "If we let them get away from us now they'll be laying for us later on. They think we're low on ammo anyhow. Let them think we've shot our wad."

Two hundred yards away the Comanchero charge became firm again, their leaders rallying and encouraging the men to press the attack now while they were so near.

The Americans' fire slackened even further and now they could hear the beating roll of horse hooves and the shrill yelps of the oncoming Comancheros.

This was the time to do any worrying that might be needed about the stoutness of Perry's defenders. Slocum looked around at the men who flanked him in the freight wagon where he waited.

The scene reminded him all too strongly of another wagon box where he and Charles Fortson and Hank and Beanass had stood and waited while the Kiowa came to overwhelm them. They had lost, those boys, but they had been stout, and Slocum would have been glad to have them at his side again.

At a hundred yards the Comancheros became silent and intent on their rush toward the hunting camp. At seventy-five their lancetips lowered ominously, and for a newcomer to combat, it would have been hard not to think about those polished steel tips ripping into warm flesh.

Slocum was more interested in thinking about hot lead ripping into Comanchero flesh. With his dark eyes flashing green in their depths he laid his Sharps aside and took up the Winchester that was leaning by his knee.

"Now, boys!" Justin called when he saw Slocum's change. "Pour it on them."

Again the camp erupted in a sheet of flame and smoke and flying lead, and the result was like pulling a chain across the path of the Comancheros' horses. Screaming horses and dying men began to fall all across the front of the charging Comanchero line.

Horses pressing close behind the leaders ran into the fallen animals ahead of them and began themselves to tumble in confused heaps, where it was impossible to determine which flesh was human and which was not. The Americans shot into all the flesh they could see, and the dirt turned red.

Slocum slammed a shot into the pile-up and levered a fresh round into the chamber. He picked out an approaching rider—a mistake of the young and the foolish was too often to shoot at the general mass of a charging enemy body instead of choosing one and downing him before moving on to another—and the Winchester pointed with his eye as handily as a custom-stocked fowling piece.

The horse carrying Slocum's target stumbled over another sprawling animal and went down, spilling its rider over its neck like a rudely dropped sack of cornmeal. The man's head struck the ground first, and the weight of his flying body twisted his neck to an impossible angle as Slocum's finger instinctively tightened just as sights and target and trigger let-off snapped together.

Shit, Slocum thought, I just shot a dead man.

If that was the worst mistake he made that day it would be just fine.

It was hard to tell in the smoke and the confusion, but there seemed to be very, very few Comancheros left now.

The Americans continued to pour their fire onto the few that were left.

The Comancheros were good, very good indeed, at what they did, but they were not good at dying to no purpose. The few who remained turned and fled, but there were only a handful who could do so. The rest they left dead behind them.

"Justin!" Slocum called.

"Yes, John."

"We got us a problem here, Justin."

"We do?"

"Uh-huh. The bastards've fixed it now so we gotta

go to the trouble of moving camp or get stunk out when they start to rot."

"John, I think we'd better move camp then. Danny, Louis, go fetch in the horses and other wagons. I think the man is right."

"Can't we at least eat first, boss?" someone called. They were all in a good mood after their victory.

"Aw, shit," the cook moaned loudly, "I went and burned our steaks." No one seemed to mind that at all.

CHAPTER 22

Justin Perry called Slocum into his tent that evening. They had moved the camp a dozen miles that afternoon, and while they had taken no buffalo that day nor added any hides to their stacks they did not consider the day wasted. Justin invited Slocum inside and motioned him to a seat on a folding cot.

"I have something here you might be interested in," Justin said. He rummaged in a wooden locker at the foot of his cot and pulled out a bottle. "I've been keeping this for some time. I think this might be a good time to try it."

"What is it?"

"Damned if I know. My father gave it to me when I left home. I'm not much of a drinker myself."

"I can make do for the both of us."

Justin poured a half inch of liquor into each of two cups, noticed Slocum's disappointment and added several fingers to one of them. He handed the heavier jot to Slocum. His own cup he raised toward Slocum in a salute. "To you, John. Without that plan of yours we probably wouldn't be here tonight."

"I think you'd have made out all right, Justin. You have the makings." He grinned. "But I won't refuse your liquor."

They downed the potion, and Slocum smiled. "Your daddy has good taste."

"I'll tell him you-said so. Another?"

"There's no saying no to one of those."

Justin poured again. "The reason I wanted to talk to you, John, is to tell you two things. One, fair is fair. You more than earned the rest of your outfit today and some walking-around money to go with it." He reached into a breast pocket and handed Slocum a fold of bills. "If you don't object to paper money . . ."

"Hell, Justin, I don't object to anything I can spend, swap, or sell off." Slocum accepted the bills. There were a hundred dollars in the wad. Slocum had no reluctance about counting it in front of Perry. "That's damn generous, Justin. Thanks."

"Like I said, you earned it."

Slocum shrugged. "No point in arguing with you. An' I can use the money if I ever get to someplace to spend it."

"You might not," Justin said.

"From the way you said that I'd guess you have a reason for your choice of words."

"I do." Justin looked uncomfortable. "In a way I'm reluctant to tell you this, John. I like you. I don't want to see you end up the way Wallace did. Death is a damned ugly thing."

"Inevitable, though. Leastways I've never heard of a way to avoid it."

Justin gave him a thin smile. "That's a strange attitude and one I'm afraid I can't share with you. But I suppose it can be useful. Anyway, Billy Jamison had a word with me earlier."

"I saw him." Jamison was the nighthawk who normally tended the camp's horses and mules overnight and slept during the day. This day he had had to take the livestock beyond reach of the Comancheros and keep them close-herded until the fight was ended. He was a quiet boy and a loner, a bit dull-witted, Slocum thought, but that was not a drawback for a kid who would have to spend nearly all of his waking time alone after dark in a wild country. A combination of youth and imagination could be most uncomfortable for a nighthawk.

"Yes, well, Billy ran into a shooting crew today. A couple boys teamed up and ready to make their fortunes with a pair of old needle guns."

Slocum made a face. Whoever they were they weren't going to get rich that way. They would be lucky to get home with their hair intact.

"They told Billy they had been having some trouble east of here, which was why they moved into this part of the country. They said there was a man over there—Bill didn't remember his name—who wanted to take one of every four hides these boys got."

"Now, don't that just sound familiar," Slocum commented.

"I thought so."

"Did Billy say just *where* my friend Hutchison is camping these days?"

"If the hunters mentioned it to him he didn't remember except that it was east of here somewhere."

"There's not a helluva lot of water out in that country. You wouldn't think there'd be much to choose from."

"Nor for the Indians to choose from. These boys told Billy they saw what they thought might have been the pony tracks and travois drag marks of a village on the move."

"They *thought?* Hell, Justin, a blind man could find that much trail."

Justin shrugged. "I'm just telling you what I was told."

"I reckon I'll know for myself soon enough anyway."

"You insist on going then?"

"I do figure to have a talk with Mr. Hutchison. You, uh, wouldn't have another snort left in that bottle, would you?"

Justin poured for Slocum but left himself out this time.

"You're free to take your gear and leave anytime you like, of course. I hope you know that you are welcome to stay and work with us as long as you want, though."

"You don't need me anymore, Justin. I appreciate the offer, but come morning I'll be in the saddle."

Justin sighed. "I can't say that I'm surprised."

"I do appreciate your help, Justin. An' your whiskey."

He nodded. "Take any supplies you need, then. We have plenty and the next wagon will be here in a few days. If they don't get drunk or highjacked."

Slocum stood and extended a hand to the young hunter. "Good luck to you, Justin."

"You'll be the one needing that."

It felt good to have a horse between his knees again and a seemingly limitless expanse of grass to cover. Slocum pulled his hatbrim low against the slanting early-morning sun and rode the dew off the grass before he stopped to fashion himself a cold breakfast. He could have waited and eaten with the camp crew before he left, but he was impatient.

The Ute girl was dead, of course. It had been weeks since Hutchison had taken her. But John Slocum had a debt to pay, and he was a man who did not like being beholden. He loosened his cinches and let the dun horse graze on a long line while he ate a leisurely meal. There was no real sense of urgency in him now. He was on his way and would do what he must, and that was enough for the moment.

He found water by the purest chance that afternoon and stopped at it while he had the chance to do so. If he rode farther he might be dry for some time to come, so he drank then and refilled the two canteens he had brought from Perry's camp and drank again after dark although he did not make his bed near the water. Before dawn he watered his horse and drank again before leaving the spot.

At midday he found the trail the two hunters had told Billy about. There was no question that it was the trail of an entire village on the move. The grass had been trampled by many hooves, and the hard earth was scored and gouged by the passage of travois poles dragging roughly across it with their burdens.

There was no way to tell if this was a Comanche village or Kiowa, but the probability was that it was one or the other. Few other tribes invaded this heartland of the southern Plains tribes.

Slocum had the germ of an idea and he would like to have known if this might be the same Kiowa village of Two Trees Walking. He was not entirely sure what he might do with that information, but he knew he was curious and he was not a man given to idle curiosity about such things.

He rode on away from the drag marks, continuing toward the east, but the question continued to nag at him for what remained of the morning. When he stopped for his noon meal he reached his decision. The hell with logic. He wanted to know whose village that was.

Sighing and mildly upset with himself when he returned to the saddle he reined the dun west, back the way he had come. Those marks were not but a few days old, and an Indian village moves slowly and not too far at any one time. If he wanted to know that badly he would damn well find out.

CHAPTER 23

It took Slocum a day and a half to find the Indian camp. The distance was not all that great, but John Slocum tried to be no more of a damn fool than was necessary and he rode with caution on the trail of the moving village. The last few hours in particular he made very little forward progress, spending most of his time studying the surrounding countryside for any hint of movement before he was willing to proceed another foot along the cold trail.

"I think we found something," he mumbled to his horse finally. Immediately he reined away from the thin stream of rising smoke in the air a few miles ahead. He was not about to approach that camp in daylight. It would be dangerous enough after dark.

He found a shallow coulee, dry but offering protection from prying dark eyes in dark faces, and there he waited, his horse saddled and the cinch pulled tight, until nightfall.

After dark he ate and took a scant swallow of precious water from one of his canteens. The horse would be all right until morning. He pulled his saddle and blanket and gave the animal a thorough rubdown under the cover of the night and rubbed its legs to help relax and soothe the animal before he resaddled. If he had hard need of the horse this night he wanted it to be in the best possible condition.

"I'm game if you are, fella," he told it.

You hear bad things about people who talk to themselves, he thought, but a man who don't talk to his own horse when he's alone in the middle of the big grass would worry me.

He mounted and checked his weapons carefully, even though he knew perfectly well that they were loaded and in good working order, before he nudged the horse ahead over the lip of the coulee.

John Slocum's sense of direction was strong and he had no trouble guiding himself across the unmarked grass to where the smoke had been rising. He saw the glow of numerous campfires against the night sky and crept in closer.

"Jesus Christ," he whispered to his horse bitterly.

There had been good reason for there to be smoke in the sky that afternoon. Apparently he had not been very far behind the Indians after all. Or perhaps they had made their fun last an unusually long time. Whatever the reason, in addition to a wide circle of lodges where fires now burned, in the center of the encampment there were the charred and still-smoking remains of two heavy wagons.

The wagons might have belonged to anyone. It was unlikely now that the names of whoever had been with them would ever be known, for the Indians would not care, and any white relatives or friends would never know what had become of the ones they lost.

There were two poles set into the ground near the burned-out wagons, poles that looked altogether too familiar to John Slocum.

Both poles bore the remains of what once had been men. From where Slocum watched the bodies looked like a pair of bright scarlet rags tied to wooden shafts. They might have been blood-red banners hanging limp from a pair of flagpoles expect that they did not stir in the night breeze, and it was no vat of dye that had given them their color.

Slocum looked at them and remembered Charles Fortson and remembered being himself tied to a similar pole—perhaps even one of those same poles, since such sturdy pieces of wood are not easily come by on the Plains—and his throat tightened at the thought.

It was too far and the light too poor for him to be able to distinguish individual Indians among the shadows he saw flitting between himself and the fires, but he was convinced that this was the camp of Two Trees Walking.

The poles, the extended torture, the layout of the lodges . . . all said that this was the Kiowa camp. Slocum was beginning to hope that it was.

The temptation was strong in him to leave the horse and belly in close. It was a good bet that he could get close enough undetected to find the tall Kiowa leader and bring him under the sights of the good Winchester. A .44-40 slug through Two Trees Walking's skull would do a great deal to improve Slocum's spirits, and the shades of Charles Fortson and the others in his party would probably approve too.

There was even a strong likelihood that he could get off the one good, well-placed shot and slip away into the night before the Kiowa could respond to the attack. The night was still young, barely a few hours old. He could make his shot and be gone quickly. By the time the rest of the Kiowa had daylight to track by he would have nearly a full night's travel behind him, too much of a lead for them to try to make up. They would quit the trail long before they would be able to catch up to him. He knew that quite well.

He sat on the patient horse and hooked a leg over his saddle horn while he debated with himself. He wanted a cigar badly, and Perry had given him a supply of the precious wraps of tobacco before he left. Lighting the thing would be just too dangerous, though. Instead he took one out of his pocket and smelled the biting-sharp scent of the weed and stuck it into a corner of his mouth unlit.

That was one of the advantages of a good cigar. If a man couldn't smoke the thing he could get almost as much satisfaction from chewing it. And there had been a good many times in the past when John Slocum had been unable to risk the light or the carrying smell of burning tobacco.

He thought about the camp that lay before him and about the ease with which he could move in on it. He even saw an unusually tall Indian moving in front of the larger fires, an Indian who might very well have been Two Trees Walking himself. From where Slocum sat, already mounted and ready to spur away into the darkness, he could have pulled the Winchester from its boot under his leg and dropped the Kiowa.

Slocum sighed. Not yet. He did not know why, but he did not want to provoke the camp yet.

Left alone they should be in this spot for some time. They probably would not move again until the surrounding ground was so littered with filth that even they could not stand it any longer. Smells and garbage that would gag a buzzard did not seem to bother these Kiowa, and this particular camp would be regarded as an auspicious one because of their success in taking and torturing to death the surviving whites who had been with those wagons.

No, Slocum speculated, it was unlikely that the Kiowa would be moving from this spot for several days, possibly for several weeks, unless something happened to make them move either to or away from something else.

And he did not yet want to lose track of this particular village.

With a sigh of uncertainty but a willingness to trust his own instincts, Slocum reined his horse away from the Kiowa village and began riding once more toward the east in search of Hutchison's hunting camp.

Come to think of it, Slocum thought, the two camps weren't all that different. The whites slept under canvas and the Kiowa under skins. The two peoples lived inside different-colored hides themselves. But the nature of one seemed to match the nature of the other. Both were viciously unnecessary killers. Both seemed to enjoy the anguish of others, without regard for what others might feel or want or dream. Both had earned John Slocum's anger and his desire for vengeance.

The question now was how he could accomplish his revenge on both counts.

And the more he thought about it, the more he began to feel that an answer to that problem might be at hand.

By dawn John Slocum was whistling happily to himself while he rode.

CHAPTER 24

He had thought the Plains here would be full of both buffalo and buffalo hunters. He was wrong on both counts. Whether it was the pressure of the hunting or the recent passage of the Kiowa or some other cause totally unimaginable to him, the land he traveled through was empty now, sterile except for the grass and the yucca and an occasional small herd of antelope or an isolated jackrabbit. Even the wolves and the coyotes seemed to have gone wherever the buffalo now were.

Slocum had already come more than twenty miles from the Kiowa village, and there was no sign yet of Hutchison or any of his men. Until he located the fringes of the Southern Herd and the hunters who would be with the shaggy beasts he could not expect to find Hutchison, he knew.

At least out here in daylight he could enjoy a cigar when he wanted one. That was something.

The dun horse he had gotten from Justin Perry was a good traveler. The animal moved with a pleasant gait and seemed not to tire badly although it was a far cry from the well-bred getaway horse he had had to abandon back at Salt Creek. That still pissed him off.

A man can't lap up much nourishment from spilled

*milk, though. Once it's gone, leave it be and move on
to something else.*

He began finding fresh buffalo kills late in the morning, skinless carcasses sprawled in pale lumps that were
hard to spot among the low-growing scrub that was so
prevalent this far south. Soon afterward he began picking up small groups of living buffalo although they
were badly scattered here and must have been shot
over a good bit to make them so. As a rule the buffalo
seemed to prefer a herd existence in great masses.

Just before noon Slocum spotted a wagon and single
team perched on a ridgetop several miles distant. He
kicked the dun horse into a quick lope and headed
that way.

There were three men with the wagon, he saw as he
came nearer. Likely there would be one shooter and
his pair of skinners working with him. The shooter, he
saw, picked up a long rifle as Slocum came into range,
but the man only stood ready, not threatening.

"Who the hell are you?" the shooter demanded when
Slocum was in hailing distance.

"Just a man passing by," Slocum returned. The
name Burton was on the tip of his tongue but he called
it back in time. Hutchison knew him by that name too.
"Tyler I am," he said instead. "John Tyler."

Slocum reached the wagon and pulled up beside it
but he made no move yet to dismount. It was up to the
shooter and his men to determine if he was welcome or
not, and if they chose that he was not, it was their
privilege; he would not contest it.

"Just riding by, you said?" the shooter asked.

"I did."

"You ain't working for any crew around here?"

Slocum shook his head. "I got tired of taking an-
other man's wages. Thought I'd head up through the
Nations and see if I can find some pussy." He grinned.
"It's been a powerful long time, I'll tell you true."

"Jeez! Ain't that the truth." The rifle, a Remington rolling block, dropped butt first to the ground. "Light down then, Mr. Tyler. We're about to have a bite of dinner. You're welcome to join us if you don't mind fresh buff'lo hump."

"I don't mind it at all in spite of all of it I've had the past few months."

The shooter grinned. "Good thing at that, ain't it. But I'm the same way. Just never seem to get tired of the stuff." He extended a hand. "I'm Kip Rumford. This's Barney Veight and Bill Wolz, my skinners. Partners too, for that matter."

Slocum tied the dun to a wheel of the light skin wagon and loosened the animal's cinches. "Is there water near? I could use some and so could he, I reckon."

Rumford gave him a dark, unhappy look. "Aye, goddamnit, there's water near enough."

"Now, I'd kinda have to say that that's a funny way of putting it."

"Huh!" the shooter snorted. "Not so funny when you know the whole story of it."

"I'm a pretty fair listener."

"Grab yourself a plate then, Tyler, an' we'll sing you a sad story."

They squatted in the dust with slabs of roast hump and hot, black coffee and nothing more to stretch out their meal. No beans or rice or panbread to add a change of flavor from one bite to the next. It could not have been a very prosperous camp, Slocum thought.

"What happened was this," Rumford said as if there had been no interruption. "We come out here on the free grass along with everybody else, thinking this here land belonged to nobody except maybe the government and prob'ly not even to them since they don't take no interest in it nor do nothing to protect folks as are out on it, right?"

Slocum nodded his agreement. That was about the way he saw it too. There was more than enough for any and all and no one really owned any of it, including the Indians, who crossed it with no more claim than he had himself or the fat-cat politicians half a world away who never would see it even if they occasionally talked about it.

" 'Course I'm right. Anyhow," Rumford rambled on, "we come out here trying to make a living for ourselves, and what do we find? I ask you, what do we find?"

Slocum shrugged. "Open grass, damn little water, and plenty of buffalo ready for the taking, I'd guess."

"No, sir. No damned indeed, sir. That is what we *expected* to find. It ain't at all what we did find." Rumford looked downright agitated. "There's all the grass in the world, it's true, and plenty of buffs here chewin' it. But the water. Now, that's the thing. The water. Man nor beast can't get along without it, right?"

A nod. There was no arguing with that, and the shooter knew it as well as Slocum did.

"Yeah," Rumford said. "You gotta have it. Well, by God, we get here an' set up and what do we find but a bunch of sons-of-bitches squatted on the only decent water for thirty miles, and they're saying it's their damn water an' if we want to use it we got to pay for the privilege. A quarter a day per man an' a dime per head of stock *plus* a flat 25 percent of our hides. Or we don't get any water. Pay or go thirsty, that's the way it is. And there's no other choice around here neither. We either pay or we leave the grass. An' we gotta be where the herd it, don't we? Well, don't we?"

"If you expect to shoot buffs I expect you do," Slocum agreed.

"Damn right we do. But I sure don't like it. They tell us they got water rights from the state of Texas so they got the right, but hell . . . I don't even know that this here patch of ground is *in* the state of Texas. Could be in the Nations, for all I know. Or even New Mexico. Hell, I don't know nothing about maps, an' there's no lines drawed out on the land. I don't know as those fellows know either. I think they're just bullshitting us so they can steal a quarter of what we kill," Rumford said.

"I'm sure they're shitting us," Wolz put in. "But there's nothing we can do about it. Nothing."

"Have you tried just standing up to them? Telling them you're going to get your water anyhow?" Slocum asked.

"Huh. Fat lot o' good that would do," Rumford said. "You haven't seen these bastards, Tyler. You don't know. Not yet you don't. There's a bunch of them, and they ain't shy about flashing artillery at a person. Truth to tell, I was hoping you was one of them. If I ever get aholt of one of them at a time I'll damn sure find some straight talk from him. That much I'll swear to be the truth."

"Any one of them except maybe the big guy," Veight said.

"Him!" Rumford's expression was one of disgust.

Slocum raised an eyebrow.

Wolz looked at the newcomer and grinned. "Kip ain't entirely fond of that one. Neither are Barney and me, for that matter. The big bastard lit into us when we set up a howl the second time we went to the water. You got to say one thing about him, though. He's a fighting knocker. He took on the three of us all at one time, an' when we was all done he was the only one standing. I wouldn't've thought I would have to tell that on myself about any one human person, but it's the truth. That son-of-a-bitch they call Big naturally whupped the three of us."

Slocum's ears might well have turned pointy he became so interested. There could not possibly be two men called Big in the same corner of the Plains. That *had* to be Hutchison's crowd doing the water hogging. They had not changed their operation, just expanded it by adding an extra inducement that probably was better than threats could ever have been. They still wanted a quarter of everybody's hides and they still had a crew large enough to keep them safe from retaliation by the unhappy buffalo hunters they preyed upon.

"Tell me about this camp," Slocum asked.

"Aye, if you like, though you'll have to be seeing it yourself soon enough," Rumford said.

They told him about the camp itself and the directions to reach it, but that was not what John Slocum was interested in hearing.

"What about the people?" he asked when they ran down. "Tell me about them, if you don't mind."

Bitching about Hutchison and his crowd was one of the Rumford camp's favorite topics of discussion, it seemed, so it took no more prompting.

They did not know Hutchison by name but they did by description, and of course there was Big. Slocum did not recognize any of the others from the descriptions Rumford and his friends gave, but they said there must have been twenty-odd men in Hutchison's camp still, all of them rough customers and all of them heavily armed.

But there was—predictably—no mention of a woman in the camp.

And if any of the three of them had had any hint that there was a woman in the camp, they damn sure would have mentioned it. Half the men in the buffalo trade would have risked their lives for a quickie with that Ute girl or any other warm female with all the appropriate openings. Or with any one of them.

Slocum had known already that the girl Moonlight was dead. She had to be dead. But still he had been hoping. He owed her. He also wanted her. A couple days of screwing was just not enough with one that good. Just thinking about her was enough to give him a hard-on. He could practically *feel* the way she took him into her mouth and tongued him.

Damn. He shivered and brought himself reluctantly back to the real world with Rumford and Veight and Wolz. Damn and double damn, he thought. But she *had* been fine.

"I wonder," he said, swinging the subject away from his own thoughts, "if you'd be kind enough to sell me some water for me an' my horse. I think it might be better if I don't run into those boys, and I'd sure be willing to pay you more than it would cost to replace whatever I take."

Rumford looked first at his companions. When they offered no objections he said, "Nothin' wrong with that, I don't suppose. What do you think would be fair?"

"I'd give you a dollar," Slocum said.

"You got yourself a deal, neighbor."

CHAPTER 25

Rumford's directions had been good, and even in the dark Slocum was able to find Hutchison's camp easily. The lay of the ground helped. There was a natural basin here, with the well-guarded water collected at the bottom of it, according to Rumford. From the west lip of the basin Slocum could see the glow of half a dozen fires. That fitted in, too, with the number of men Rumford said Hutchison had with him now.

John Slocum eased as close as he dared with the dun, then ground-tied it and left it standing in a direct line between the Hutchison camp and an upthrust spear of rock that he should be able to see skylighted against the stars from down below. He might have to hit that animal at a dead run with bullets at his heels, and he wanted to take no chances about wandering around in the dark while Big footed it after him.

He left the horse fully a quarter mile out from the fires. He did not know the animal well enough to know if it might nicker or get into a snorting match with some of the camp horses. He left the cinches tight and began catfooting closer, the Colt loose in his holster and his Winchester lying lightly in one hand. Whatever happened he was as ready as he expected to be.

Slocum moved in within fifty yards of the camp and

began a slow circle, belly to the ground and making no sound at all. That was one of the things he had learned from growing up in a patch of squirrel woods. He could move as silently as any sly Indian even in brush and heavy timber. This open grass was a snap for him.

He continued that way with all the patience of a cougar stalking a mountain-goat kid until he had made a complete circle around Hutchison's camp. This was no batch of Kiowa but they seemed to be just as lazy when it came to posting guards at night. That suited Slocum just fine.

Only when he was satisfied that the way in was safe did he turn the line of his crawling progress and begin edging closer to the fires.

It was not yet late but already most of the men seemed to be asleep. At least there were enough bed-rolls spread out with man-shaped lumps in them to indicate that that was the case.

Slocum crept in among the sleepers farthest from the fires and lay with his head propped on one hand and the Winchester in the other while he studied the camp before him.

There was little movement, but a clutch of men sat on piled boxes near one of the six fires, and one of those men was Big. Another was Mr. Hutchison himself.

The temptation was just plain damned strong to raise the Winchester and pop Hutchison one between the horns. With just the least amount of luck Slocum would have time, too, to put a .44-40 slug into Big's broad chest before any of the sleeping men near him could react.

He thought each motion out in his mind while he considered it. Line the sights carefully in the poor light to drop Hutch with a head shot. Come up to one knee while the hands did the automatic work of cranking a fresh cartridge into the chamber. By then Big would be in motion. Bring the barrel in line with Big and the rifle butt to the shoulder with one motion and squeeze it off with, at this distance, just a tiny amount of lead. Take the big man in the body. And run like hell.

It was that part, the run-like-hell part, that bothered Slocum. He would be leaving close behind him—hell, all around him—a swarm of very angry, very tough, very plainswise men. The first part seemed a grand notion, but being chased so closely by a group like this crowd did not. There had to be a better way.

A few feet to Slocum's left one of the sleepers moaned slightly. Low though it was, the noise was enough to startle Slocum and grab his attention immediately.

The sound was followed soon afterward by a rhythmic slapping sound, very faint, that started slowly and increased in its speed until it was a frenzy of soft slapada-slapada-slapada.

Slocum grinned into the darkness. One of Hutchison's men was whacking off in the privacy of his lonely bedroll.

I've had to take that road often enough myself, Slocum thought. Why not?

The man groaned through slightly parted lips and arched his back.

Messy, messy, Slocum thought. Shouldn't oughta get your own gear all sticky, he silently advised the man. Go jack off in somebody else's blankets instead. He started to chuckle and barely caught himself in time to avoid making a noise doing it. Dumb shit, he told himself.

More carefully than ever now, Slocum crawled deeper into the camp and moved around outside the faint light of the buffalo-chip fires until he was near the boxes where Hutchison and Big and two other men sat.

One of the two men Slocum did not know seemed to have taken Cisco's place as second in command of the group. At least he was the only one bold enough to try to tell Hutchison anything.

"I think you're wrong as hell, Hutch," this man said. "I think with this water scam we don't need to be feeding so many of these lazy fuckers. We got practically no fighting to do anymore. Pay them off and let them go rustle their own groceries. They're costing us a fucking fortune in coffee, never mind their wages. We could all get bigger cuts for damn sure if you paid off at least half of them."

Judging from the weariness in Hutchison's answering tone this was an argument they had had before. "Goddamnit, Luther, I'm the boss here, an' my hair means aplenty to me even if you don't care about your own. There's Injuns out here. Bad bastards, every one o' them. And if any of those copper-colored cocksuckers come around here bothering us we got to have enough guns to keep our hair. Think of it as payin' insurance if you like. Hell, that there is a business that's made a lot of round-hat Easterners rich. Well, just figure that it's what is keeping you alive so you can enjoy bein' rich yourself one day."

"I don't think . . ."

"Luther, I really don't much give a fat crap what you think. You know that? I really don't."

"I worked that out by myself, Hutch," Luther said dourly.

"Don't mind him, Hutch," the fourth man said. "He's just greedy."

"Sensible," Luther corrected. "And a whole lot poorer than I ought to be."

"You consider yourself sensible," Hutchison said. "I consider myself prudent. I also consider the subject closed."

Luther grunted and grumbled but a moment later he and the other man stood and headed for their bedrolls.

Hutchison turned to Big. "The camp's quiet enough, I think, Big. And no one's coming in this late. Go fetch me the cook's helper now."

Big nodded. He stood, and it was like seeing a giant sequoia pick itself up out of the logging woods and stand upright again. Slocum had forgotten just how *big* Big was. From where Slocum lay with his chin in the dirt Big looked even bigger still.

Big walked out of the firelight toward one of the wagons parked around the camp area. A moment later he returned with a bedraggled youngster. The boy was still beardless and judging from his complexion must have been a Mexican kid. He was short and very thin. His tattered old overalls hung about his body like a horse blanket hung on a Great Dane. He did not look at all frightened of either Big or Hutchison but he damn sure looked resentful of them.

Hutchison took the kid by the hand and impatiently waved Big away. The big man picked up a still-rolled cylinder of bedding and disappeared into the darkness.

Hutchison looked at the boy and grunted. He pulled the kid closer and undid the buttons at his fly. Hutchison reached inside the kid's pants and began fondling him.

Well, I will be a dipshit son-of-a-bitch, Slocum thought. The woods is full of them, and there ain't even any trees here.

Hutchison pulled the kid down beside him and kissed him deeply. The boy sat with his hands limp in his lap, offering neither to resist nor participate in the indignity. Slocum, watching, thought he might puke.

The rough, tough gang leader—who seemed to like little boys—stood and led the kid away from the firelight. They headed almost directly toward the spot where Slocum lay.

If the queer son-of-a-bitch steps on me I'm gonna break his balls before I cut his throat, Slocum thought.

Hutchison stopped less than fifteen feet from where Slocum lay. If Hutchison had not so recently been staring into the fire, Slocum knew, Hutchison could have seen the intruder in his camp easily.

They lay on the ground between Slocum and the fire. It was the best seat in the house to get a look at the way fags operate, if Slocum had wanted to get such a look. As it was, there was no way he could avoid it, want to or not.

Hutchison began to peel clothes from the cook's helper. Hutchison pulled the overall suspenders down to the kid's waist and lifted the kid's shirt to chin level.

He began squeezing the firm, pointed little mounds there.

Jesus Christ!

Slocum's heart began thumping against his shirt. That wasn't any damn boy. That was Moon Silver on the Aspen or he was those brass monkey balls that were all the time freezing.

It seemed utterly imposible that she should still be alive. She had no right to be alive. But she was alive. Definitely alive and warm and with both her hair and her pussy intact. No, correct that, he thought. With her scalp intact but not her hair. That long, glorious fall of jet-black hair was not likely to tickle his balls again. It had been cropped short so she would pass as a boy when there were strangers in the camp. But she was still alive, being kept on a long leash obviously as Hutchison's private piece.

Slocum could not imagine how she had been able to keep herself whole so long, although of course she had managed to survive several years of captivity by the Comancheros and the Comanches and the Kiowa before John Slocum wandered into her life. But still. It was a damned incredible thing he was seeing, but it was true.

Hutchison pulled her overalls down around her ankles and spread her knees apart, ready to force himself roughly into that tender flesh Slocum remembered so well.

Stupid bastard, Slocum thought. If he had treated her decent she would have given him the best he ever hoped to have and quite a bit more. Instead he had been too greedy, and now all he would ever get from her would be a warm place to stick it, a pink bag to pump sperm into and nothing more.

And as it happened, ol' Hutch was fresh out of opportunities to learn what he had been missing all this time. He was fresh out of new experiences of nearly every sort.

Now there was only one left. Pete Hutchison was about to learn how to die.

Slowly, carefully, a tight grin of impending combat pulling his face into a caricature of pleasure, John Slocum shifted his Winchester into his left hand and with his right silently withdrew his heavy skinning knife from its sheath.

Like a wisp of summer mist he ghosted up from the ground and glided forward. Moonlight, ignoring Hutchison pumping against her slim body and preferring to look at the stars instead, saw Slocum coming. Smiling and quite unabashed by the posture he had found her in, she lifted a hand to wave at him.

Slocum slid into position behind and above the straining, ass-humping Hutchison. He took a moment to blow a silent kiss to Moonlight and leaned down to offer his knife for her to use.

She took the weapon. She used it most effectively.

CHAPTER 26

Slocum took a moment to kiss her and did not regret the time as being lost. It was far from that.

Oh, she had not forgotten him. Not the least little bit.

She rose lightly, stooped again to wipe the blood from her hands onto Hutchison's shirt, and turned into Slocum's arms.

Yes indeed. That was very nice.

There was only so much time to lose, though, and none to be wasted. Slocum made the Plains sign for horse and cocked an eyebrow at her. She got his question and took him by the hand. Together they slipped through the sleeping camp.

Slocum picked out a proud-looking dark horse—he could not tell its color in the night but he liked its shape, and it is what is on the inside of a horse's hide that counts—and the girl nodded her agreement with his choice.

He moved to another, a bay he thought it was, with one white forefoot and a blaze on its face, and again the girl nodded.

He touched the rope of a long-legged Appaloosa, but this time she shook her head no emphatically. All right, he decided, maybe she knew something he did not. He moved on to an overo paint with white on its chest and underbelly and this time she was pleased, so he cut it free too.

The girl reached for his knife and he let her take it. She moved toward the picket line again where the camp's saddle horses were tied, but when she went to begin cutting tie ropes to free all the horses he stopped her.

Slocum shook his head. He was grinning when he did so. She seemed ready enough to accept his judgment. She reversed the knife and handed it to him handle first.

Leading the three horses they had stolen but leaving the others where the men in the camp could easily find them in the morning, they slipped out of the camp and circled back toward where Slocum's dun stood waiting.

With the four horses and the girl, Slocum rode out of the basin to the rock-rimmed lip three quarters of a mile away. There he stopped.

The girl gave him an odd look but she did not protest when he dismounted and motioned for her to join him. He loosened the cinches on his horse and on hers and staked all four animals on short ropes.

When he was satisfied that the animals were the way he wanted them he lay on the grass and signaled Moonlight to join him there.

She did but when he took her into his arms there was a stiffness in her slim body that he had not remembered finding there before.

She pulled away from him and stood, and he thought that perhaps she did not want to come to him so soon after Hutchison was inside her body or that she might never again want voluntarily to lie with a man.

But she did not leave him. Not for long. She went to the dun horse and from his saddle took down one of the canteens that hung there.

Moonlight removed her clothing, every stitch of it, and stood for a moment like a warm, perfect statue in the dim starlight. She uncorked the canteen and carefully, a scant handful of water at a time, began to wash herself, scrubbing briskly at her sofness until the last taint and smell of Hutchison would be gone.

The water was all they had and all they might be able to find for some time to come, but she would know that even better than he did. He understood her need to come to him clean again and so he waited while she washed herself, and this time when she came to him it was fully and openly, the way he remembered her from before, and their lovemaking was a joy that could have gone on forever, for there was nothing about her that was not his, more totally than he had ever known with any woman of any race or age or depth of commitment.

He was exhausted when she had sucked the last drop of pleasure from him, but it was a pleasant exhaustion.

Slocum did not believe there was any possibility that he might oversleep but still he signed to her to waken him when the morning star began to fade, and he was content to go to sleep knowing that she understood and would be there in the morning.

On the rim of the basin, with Moon Silver on the Aspen in his arms, he drifted into the deepest sleep he had known in more than a month.

The horses were saddled and their cinches tight. The spare mounts were fitted with improvised war bridles and lead ropes tied to the saddlehorns of the other horses. Slocum and Moonlight sat on the rocks rimming the deep basin and watched the camp still in darkness below them come slowly to life.

The cook was the first to stir, building his fire and no doubt wondering where his helper had gotten to during the night. That first predawn work had probably been Moonlight's, Slocum reflected. The cook would just have to get along on his own.

Others began to move around soon enough. Men stumbling and sleep-drunk, fuzzy-brained in the cold, pale light of the dawn.

Slocum grinned and sat with an arm tugging Moonlight close to him. He was not yet ready to let her go, but he would have to soon enough.

Below them the camp seemed to be fully awake now. Men finished pissing last night's coffee away and walked, more briskly now, toward the breakfast fire.

It was too far away to hear, but someone must have shouted, for all of a sudden the routine of the wakening was changed and men began to trot and then to run toward a small speck on the ground that Slocum and the girl had left there.

"Reckon they found our dearly departed friend," Slocum said.

The girl said something back to him in the Ute tongue. He could not understand the words but the meaning was clear enough. And she was not at all unhappy about Pete Hutchison being cold beef down there.

"We'd best get mounted, girl," he said. He motioned toward the horses and she scrambled to her feet before him.

Taking his time about it, Slocum checked her cinches and his own and spent an unnecessary moment straightening her reins so they would lie comfortable in her hands.

"There now. That oughta be all right. I sure do wish those bastards'd done something useful, though, like teaching you English while they had you there. I think I'd have thanked them for that if they had." He was smiling while he spoke to her. She would not know the words but his purpose was to reassure and not to inform, and that much he could do despite the lack of a common language between them. Since he could not explain what he wanted to do she was bound to be wondering and maybe worrying. It was one hell of a compliment that she was so trusting with him as to go along with his desire to stay right on top of the camp when they could have been miles away by now.

Slocum swung lightly into his saddle. The thing was finally becoming comfortable to him.

There is damn little on the face of this earth as personal to a man as a good saddle, Slocum thought. Thank goodness this one was finally beginning to feel like it belonged under his butt.

Slocum reined his dun parallel to the basin rim. He knew perfectly good and well that he was skylighted in hard silhouette there. If any of the former Mr. Hutchison's men should happen to look up to the west they would be unable to miss seeing him there.

To make damn sure they did look up he pulled his Winchester from its boot and held it at an angle of about thirty degrees above the horizon.

The distance was half a mile too long for any kind of accuracy from a saddle gun and he had no hope of hitting anything smaller than the Plains, but he did not much mind. He figured if he made a little noise and put a bullet within a quarter mile of them he was doing all right.

He smiled and blew a kiss toward Moonlight and began cranking shots out of the Winchester as rapidly as a Gatling gun crew could have ground off their first half-dozen rounds.

The girl's mouth dropped open in wonder, but Slocum was no longer paying attention to her. He was watching the men down below in the camp by the waterhole.

Yeah, they had spotted him all right.

And he must have come closer than he expected to. The group that was bunched tightly around Hutchison's body scattered like a flower bud popping into a split-second blossom.

"Honey girl, I think those boys down there are kinda pissed at us. Lookit them run for that picket line, grabbing guns an' dropping saddles and getting in each other's way something fierce. Oh, jeez, did you see that one take a header? Maybe he's got a faceful of cactus spines, the shithead. I hope. Oh, they ain't lazy now, honey. Lookit them haul ass. Uh-huh. The first ones are up and comin'."

He turned to her with a wink and a grin. "Moonlight, li'l gal, let's take off now before they get close enough to be a bother. But not *too* fast, hear? We wouldn't want to lose them, would we? No," he answered his own question, "that wouldn't do at all. We just wouldn't want those good ol' boys down there to lose track of us after all the bother we've gone to here. C'mon now. Yah!"

With a crack of his rein ends and a sharp dig with his spurs he sent his dun plunging off toward the west and a little bit south. Forty-five miles, he figured. Three hours if the pursuers' horses were up to it. Maybe less.

My God, but a man feels good when he has a horny little gal at his side and he's rolling the big dice with his own life pledged against the revenge that is making his heart sing and the wind feel fine on his face. Nothing could be better than that.

He glanced at Moonlight on the white-faced bay at his side. Well, almost nothing.

CHAPTER 27

With a lead of three fourths of a mile and the best horses they could steal from the pursuers' camp, Slocum figured they should be all right. Otherwise he would not have risked the run. Not with Moonlight along. By himself he might have tried to regardless, but he wanted to bring no more grief to this pert and sexy little Ute girl.

Behind them several dozen men were bellowing and snorting in a rather unhappy manner. A few of them were foolish enough to waste powder and lead trying to bring the two mounted figures down from such an extreme range, but even if they had been using their buffalo rifles from a solid rest Slocum knew there could not be a shooter within a thousand miles who was both good enough and lucky enough to come within fifty yards of them. Shooting saddle carbines from the backs of running horses, those boys back there were not even nuisances. If anything they were jokes.

Moonlight seemed to have caught the spirit of the chase, for she was grinning as happily as Slocum was.

She rode lightly in her saddle, leaning forward over the neck of her running horse, and her hair, even cropped as it had been, was streaming in the wind of their passage. She looked young and very much alive that way, and her oversized coveralls did nothing to take away from her femininity.

Slocum was amazed now that he could have failed to recognize her the night before, overalls and poor light or no.

And Hutchison, that colossal prick, was where he belonged now, stretched out on the grass with his blood spilled out into the soil and his carcass left to the scavengers. For surely a crew like his would not care enough to bury the bastard once he was dead. Slocum found it quite fitting that buzzards and coyotes would end up with the final victory over Pete Hutchison. The man had been a first-class bastard.

And Slocum had Moon Silver on the Aspen too. That was the really incredible part of it. He still had that lovely, slim girl to warm his bed and drain his balls. He looked at her again and then behind them and he laughed his pleasure into the wind.

The hunters had not been able to gain an inch on them in the first mile of the run and might indeed have been dropping a little farther behind in an effort to save their horses for a long chase.

Hell, Slocum thought, that would make it even better. If they were easing their pace in anticipation of an all-day run, he and the girl had it made. He knew almost exactly how long the chase would be—if nothing went wrong—and could arrive there with the spare horses in fine shape for the second run.

Slocum checked his dun slightly to match the falling pace of the hunters, and the girl reined back to stay even with him.

She called something in her own language.

He had no idea what she might have said, but he yelled to her over the thunder of their horses' hooves, "We're doin' just fine, girl. Just fine. Stay beside me there an' let me bring them in where I want them. Then you an' me, girl, will go find us a hidey hole to crawl into and we won't come out until one of us is wore plumb raw."

Her response was laughter even if she did not know what he was saying to her. They were enough in tune in other ways that they really did not need speech too. That had it all, with or without the prop of language.

Slocum looked at the girl again and smiled. This way there were no lies, no secrets hidden or memories excluded. This way whatever they did with and to and for each other was its own truth, with nothing before and nothing after that might take away from what they had at the moment. Damnation, but this girl was a joy.

They raced across the short grass and flashed over the low scrub, and Slocum kept a constant watch on the men who were intent on trying to catch them and to kill them.

Knowing their fate if something should go wrong did nothing to take away from the pleasure of the run.

Gambling it all, including his life, on the turn of a card or the sure-footedness of a fast horse was Slocum's way of living, and when he did it his blood bubbled like fine champagne and he felt more alive than he ever could have in a Sunday suit and boiled shirt. At moments like this he did not regret his way of life in the slightest, for here was the thrill that made it all worthwhile.

Not for him the petty pleasures and the petty worries of an orderly life. This was far, far better.

They topped one of the undulating rises in the vast Plains grass and dipped swiftly toward the bottom. For a moment they were out of sight of the men who were chasing them, and Slocum used that time to check his horse so the hunters could get closer without realizing that Slocum was baiting them in. He wanted to encourage them, to add incentive to their run so they would be sure to continue the chase. For them to drop away now would not be what Slocum wanted at all.

By the time the hunters cleared the rise they were within a half mile of Slocum and the girl, but their quarry was running and there was no indication that they had paused deliberately in their flight. Several of the hunters were so enthused by their gain that they again opened a sporadic fire on the two people who fled before them.

Their bullets had no effect, of course, but perhaps it made them feel better to make the attempt.

Moonlight was obviously puzzled but she was unable to question Slocum's judgment. He doubted that she would have even if she had been able to. Once she had given her trust she seemed to have given it totally. That was just one of the things Slocum liked about her.

They ran for an hour like that and for another. Their horses were heavily lathered now, but the animals' breathing still came easily and they were in no danger.

The pace had slowed to a fast lope after so long, but still the hunters clung to their dust, and once every five minutes or so one of the men would loose a futile shot in their direction. Only once did a bullet come near enough to be heard, and that was only a whining ricochet that sizzled through the brush near ground level some yards to their right.

Slocum ducked violently to the side in his saddle when that slug passed, play-acting that it was close so he would encourage the men to fire again and again. The lower they got on ammunition now the better, and they would not have brought any great quantity with them in their haste to catch Hutchison's killers.

Come on, you dirty bastards, Slocum called to them within his thoughts. Come and see the same wondrous sights and feel the same hellfire that Hutch has seen and felt these hours past. Ride hard, boys, and die.

The third hour passed slowly, and Slocum wished his sturdy dun had been better watered before the start of the run. The chase was telling on him more than on the girl's horse or either of the two led animals. That was only to be expected, since it was the dun that was asked to carry the greatest load, but still . . . it was a shame, but if the run killed the horse, so be it. Slocum would regret it but not as much as if he allowed concern for the horse to kill him. He made the tiring animal hold to the pace he wanted from it.

The hunters were a little closer now, perhaps a third of a mile away, and their firing was more intense now than it had been in several hours.

Continually, stupidly, they sat back there and wasted their ammunition on targets they could not possibly expect to reach.

There was damn little reserve left in the dun now, though, and Slocum began to worry. If he had miscalculated somehow, if he was not where he thought he was after this cross-country run following a dead-reckoning course that he had not traveled in a direct line before, they would not now have time to switch his saddle to a fresh horse when the dun became exhausted.

He could go it bareback if he had to, even attempt to jump to the led horse at full gallop the way the rough-riding Mexican *vaqueros* were so fond of doing as a challenge to prove a newcomer's manhood. But that was one hell of a dangerous stunt and was better used as a test of courage or a show-off trick for a pretty little brown-eyed gal than it was a useful tool. Somebody friendly really ought to be there to pick up the pieces afterward in case the jumper missed.

And bareback a man, at least one who was not raised wearing a breechclout, had just too damn little purchase if his horse should stumble on the uneven footing. A misplaced hoof that would hardly be noticed from the security of a saddle could spell disaster for a man running bareback for his life.

And the girl, damn her, would stop to help him if

he had any trouble. He was sure that she would, but if she did it would probably only mean the loss of both of them instead of just one.

Slocum listened to his own thoughts and had to laugh at himself. He was being as worrisome as a spinster at a pimps' convention. The hell with all that, he told himself forcefully. If you ain't gambling you ain't living. They loped past a jagged outcrop of white and yellow stone, and Slocum's heart took a great, joyous leap. He had seen that formation before. He was sure of it. And he was right where he wanted to be.

Yelling to Moonlight to get her attention, he reined the dun a little to the left of the course they had been running.

Behind them the pursuers saw the change and set up a howl. They were close enough now for their shouting voices to be heard, and their carbines banged almost continuously as the riders veered to cut the distance still farther across that new direction.

"Let's go, girl," Slocum hollered, forgetting for the moment that she could not understand him. "Spur that son-of-a-bitch an' gain us some ground now."

The tiring dun had heart left if he had nothing else. Slocum had no need to rake the horse. A touch of his spurs was enough to summon the last of the dun's strength into a lunging gallop.

Behind them the hunters spurred their horses on as well and kept up their fire.

"That's good," Slocum called to the girl. "Lots of noise. That's what we want now. Half a mile now," he told the dun horse. "Half a mile farther an' you get your rest."

They burst around the end of a low, mesalike mound and Slocum grinned. He was right on target.

The girl's eyes widened, and she gave Slocum a frightened stare but he kneed the dun closer to her and leaned out to touch her hand in reassurance. He gave her a quick smile and hooked his thumb over his shoulder toward the pursuing men, now and again out of view for a moment.

Moon Silver on the Aspen understood. She smiled back at him and returned her attention to what lay before them.

A hundred Kiowa lodges were spread in a broad circle immediately in front of their charging horses.

Indian women looked up in sudden fear from the buffalo robes they were tanning. Old men stood on spindly legs and tried to make out through the haze of dimming vision what it was that was sweeping into their camp. Old women tending the cooking fires scuttled away from their stewpots into the safety of their teepees. The few warriors who were in the camp at that moment leaped to their feet in a flurry of scattering ashes as their pipes were forgotten and their boasts left hanging unfinished in the air. They scrambled for their bows and lances and few rifles.

"Eeeiii-i-i-i-i-*hah!*" The Rebel yell ripped from Slocum's throat as automatically as if he was still fighting for that hopeless cause, and for that brief moment he yearned for the feel of a saber in his strong right hand.

Their four horses raced through the camp, flashing hooves scattering ashes and destroying a meticulously detailed sand painting that must have taken its maker many days to complete.

Beyond the village lay a stream, flanked with a dense growth of willows and wild plums and a very few stately cottonwoods. Slocum headed the flagging dun toward that growth, veering to the right behind a screen of Kiowa lodges as Hutchison's hunters rounded the tiny mesa and found themselves plunging into a hornet's nest already stirred to swift anger by Slocum and the girl.

They raced for the protection of the trees, and behind them they could hear an outbreak of gunfire—too much gunfire for it to have been the Kiowa doing the shooting —and Slocum laughed loudly in his pleasure.

If Big and those other idiot bastards had been smart enough to lay down some elevens with their horses' hind feet, yank them down, turn them around, and get them the hell gone before they ever allowed themselves to be swept into that village behind the fleeing man and the girl, they might—just might—have had a chance to get away.

There was even the possibility that then the Kiowa would have chosen to pick up the chase where Hutchison's boys left off and would have left the stronger party of hunters alone in favor of easier game. That was part of the gamble Slocum had been playing out.

But they had torn it now. Once they got in among the lodges and opened fire on those Indians they were as good as gone. It would have been easier all around if those boys had just put their muzzles to their own heads and blown their own skulls open like so many overripe watermelons, for the Kiowa were not about to overlook an attack on their own village. And any of those whites who might manage to fight their way free of the circle of lodges would still face the prospect of a forty-five-mile run on jaded horses against fresh and fully rested Kiowa ponies.

"Hot damn, Moonlight, I think we're home free," Slocum called exuberantly as they reached the thin, green line of growth along the stream and crashed in among the dense plums.

He hauled the dun down to a well-earned halt and spilled his saddle from the tired animal's back. The dun stood spraddle-legged, running sweat and its sides heaving, but it was still as game as when it started and Slocum began to hope that it might be able to keep up with them still if there was no immediate pursuit by the Kiowa. He wanted to keep that horse as much as he had ever wanted any nonhuman, nonfemale animal.

The girl had made her saddle switch by the time Slocum was done with his, and on fresh horses they quickly left the thin, visual protection of the tree line and headed west across the big grass at a trot.

If luck was with them now. . . .

CHAPTER 28

High in the heart of the Rockies, in the wide basin that the old mountain men had once known as the Bayou Salado, John Slocum stretched his arms and yawned.

He lay back against the sweet, lush, thick grass that grew here in abundance. From where he lay he could see a herd of several hundred fat ponies and at least three smaller herds of antelope. Another light patch seen against the distant grass was probably a fourth herd of the fast little pronghorns.

The mountain buffalo were gone from this place, killed off for meat to feed the miners who burrowed underground at the north end of the basin, but the Utes still came here and knew they could find food for their long, snowy winter nights. On the mountain slopes rising above the village were countless mule deer and elk, and there was grass and water aplenty for the herds of fine horses the high-country Utes bred here.

Slocum smiled and reached beneath his head to the lap that cradled him more pleasantly than any down-filled pillow could have done.

He reached a hand gently beneath the doeskin skirt of the girl who had been watching him while he slept the afternoon away. She shifted her legs slightly to accommodate his searching fingers, and he fondled the soft, scant growth of hair that covered her pubic mound.

He heard her sigh happily as his fingers probed deeper, and he knew that in another moment she would not be able to stand it any longer without plunging into the enjoyment of it with him. In a moment she would be fumbling—much less awkwardly now after so much practice—with the buttons at his fly and would be bending to bring the sweet, moist heat of her mouth down onto him.

She did as he had expected, and John Slocum smiled happily.

This night he would sit as an honored guest at the right side of her father when they formed the eating circle within the lodge, and later there would be the dark closeness of their sleeping robes with the girl lying naked and clean against his body.

Tomorrow there would be more of the same.

On some tomorrow—but not this one—he would leave this place, he knew, because even the sweetest of pleasures begins to cloy after a time, but that tomorrow was not now and Slocum's wandering nature was taking its rest along with him and Moon Silver on the Aspen.

Slocum closed his eyes in contentment and began to pump his hips in time with the dip and pull of the girl's lips. He sighed.

It hadn't hardly been any trouble at all when you considered what the reward was at the end.

J.D. HARDIN

"THE MOST EXCITING
WESTERN WRITER SINCE
LOUIS L'AMOUR"
—JAKE LOGAN

___16844 THE GOOD, THE BAD, AND
THE DEADLY $1.95

___16840 BLOOD, SWEAT AND GOLD $1.95

___16591 BULLETS, BUZZARDS, BOXES
OF PINE $1.75

___16555 THE SLICK AND THE DEAD $1.50

___16657 THE MAN WHO BIT SNAKES $1.75

___16843 FACE DOWN IN A COFFIN $1.95

___16869 THE SPIRIT AND THE FLESH $1.95

___16842 BLOODY SANDS $1.95

___16761 RAIDER'S REVENGE $1.95